PRAISE FOR SASSER HILL
AND FULL MORTALITY

"Hill, herself a Maryland horse breeder, is a genuine find, writing smooth and vivid descriptive prose about racetrack characters and backstretch ambience that reek authenticity."
— Jon L. Breen, *Ellery Queen's Mystery Magazine*

"The gritty, exciting *Full Mortality* by Sasscer Hill [is] a thrilling, eye-opening read written by a former steeplechase jockey who now breeds racehorses. Hill knows what she's writing about."
— Betty Webb, *Mystery Scene*

"Nikki is one of the most appealing fictional characters I've ever met. You are rooting for her every inch of the way. The descriptions of backstretch life are enchanting."
— Lucy Acton, Editor of *Mid-Atlantic Thoroughbred*

"I thoroughly enjoyed *Full Mortality* — the pages fly by, the characters are vivid, and Hill captures life on the backstretch perfectly."
— Charlsie Cantey, racing analyst for ESPN, ABC, CBS and NBC.

"If you like the work of Dick Francis or Sue Grafton, you will like Sasscer Hill. With a true insider's knowledge of horse racing, Hill brings us Nikki Latrelle, a young jockey placed in harm's way who finds the courage to fight the odds and the heart to race for her dreams."
— Mike Battaglia, NBC racing analyst and TV host,

PRAISE FOR RACING FROM DEATH

"When Nikki Latrelle swings into the saddle and takes the reins, all we can do is sit back and enjoy the ride. Hill [is] is a major new talent and the comparisons to Dick Francis are not hyperbole."
— Margaret Maron, *New York Times* Best selling author

"Great characters, great action, and as for the setting, Hill could be the next Dick Francis. It's that authentic."
— Ju'· S ·th   ·   · · · ·   Award

D0878264

Racing from
Death

A Nikki Latrelle Racing Mystery

Sasscer Hill

WILDSIDE PRESS

For Donelson Christmas, Jr.

RACING FROM DEATH
A Nikki Latrelle Racing Mystery

Copyright © 2012 by Sasscer Hill.
All rights reserved.

Published by
Wildside Press, LLC
www.wildsidebooks.com

1

It was the worst ride I'd ever seen.

A length ahead of me on the Laurel Park homestretch, eighteen-year-old Paco Martinez lurched wildly in the saddle every time he tried to whip his horse. He looked barely able to stay on, let alone achieve the explosive pump-and-drive essential to a strong finish.

I wasn't doing so well myself. I plodded behind in last place — hardly a surprise, as my longshot mount had earned the nickname Chokey Pokey. I waved my whip and pumped my arms, but mostly for show. Hitting Chokey was pointless, but a female jockey can't afford the label, "weak finisher."

Paco, an apprentice rider on the two-to-one favorite, could afford it even less. As we closed in on the wire a good eight lengths behind the rest of the field, Paco swayed hard in the saddle. His left foot flew from the stirrup, and his arms clutched desperately at his horse's neck. I was afraid he'd fall, and Chokey would run him down. Somehow, he held on until he crossed the finish line, and the horse made it safely back to the groom waiting for Paco's horse near the paddock.

After dismounting, I got my saddle, stood in line behind Paco, and weighed in with the clerk of scales. Heading toward the building that housed the jockeys' rooms, I winced when a group of irate bettors gathered on the concrete apron and shouted verbal insults at Paco. Once inside, he stumbled in the hall ahead of me.

"Paco, are you all right?" What was wrong with him?

Without answering me, he shuffled away.

Sometimes, people don't want you to help them. I shook my head and took an abrupt right into the cramped rectangular area reserved for women.

I didn't feel that bad for Paco. He'd lost a race, but he'd bounce back. And unlike me, he had the more spacious guys' section farther down the main hall. With a large professional sweatbox. We ladies had a tiny glassed-in booth with floor-mounted steam jets that burned our feet. The guys enjoyed an expert masseuse. We had to settle for Ben Gay.

I stripped off my riding clothes and stepped into a shower, groaning when a stream of hot water hit my tight shoulder muscles. Paco's bizarre ride had scared me. I didn't want to see him hurt. I liked him.

In a strange country, struggling with the language barrier, the kid had always been polite and friendly. After I was thrown from a horse one morning, he'd come by my barn to see if I was okay. He'd pulled a small silver-colored religious medal from his pocket and pressed it into my hand.

"Is San Raphael," he'd said, his smile shy. "Patron of healing. Is for you."

I couldn't forget a kindness like that.

While pulling on my street clothes, I heard a thump from the hall. A dull thud followed. What were the guys up to now? Curious, I buttoned my shirt, fluffed my short hair, and opened the door.

Outside, Paco lay on his back, the fingers of one hand splayed against the baseboard as if he'd grabbed at the wall before falling.

"*Paco?*" I knelt, staring at his flushed face, hearing his ragged breathing. A faint chemical smell drifted from his skin. His eyes fluttered open, then closed. I grabbed his wrist, felt a weak, uneven pulse, and scrambled to my feet.

"*Help!*" I yelled, as I ran down the hall toward the men's locker room, slowing before busting into the domain of half-naked men. Screw it, Paco needed help.

"Hey!" I called and rushed inside, almost colliding with one of the Belgado brothers running toward me from the side with a towel around his skinny hips.

I heard pounding footsteps from the back of the room. Mike Jones, the ex-jockey who managed the racing silks, ran toward me.

"What's the matter, Nikki?" he said.

"It's Paco, he's *hurt*."

I took off, and the guys followed. Then Mike saw Paco.

"Oh, man." He squatted next to Paco and cursed softly. "I told the boy to stop that diet crap. They won't listen, none of 'em."

Standing, he pulled his cell and tapped in numbers. "Is Doc there? Tell him to come to the jocks' room quick. We got a boy passed out."

I sank to my knees next to Paco. His flush had faded to a gray pallor. Who should we call? Did he have family in the States, or was he on his own? I knew what that was like.

Mike closed his phone and shot a look at Belgado who stood open-mouthed, staring at Paco.

"Put some clothes on," Mike said.

Muttering, Belgado trotted back toward the guys' locker.

"I watched him ride the ninth," Mike said. "Looked like he had one foot in the grave, way he rode. That boy had the favorite, he should have won! Bettors was cursing 'n throwing their tickets on the pavement."

"I know," I said, glancing away. "I heard them."

Motion near the entrance caught my attention. Doc Johnson hurried toward us with a large medical bag in his big, capable hands. He set it down next to Paco, his dark face tightening as he examined the jockey.

"Mike," Doc said, "You'd better call an ambulance." His voice was low and steady, but his eyes held an edge of fear.

Nervously, I twisted the horseshoe ring on my finger, remembering Mike's reference to "that diet crap." Paco had passed his weight check after our race; I'd seen the scales' needle settling at 108 pounds. But the kid had stumbled and almost fallen when he stepped off the rubber plate.

As an apprentice jockey, he was allowed a lower weight. This gave his horse an advantage and racehorse trainers a reason to hire him. At twenty-three, and blessed with a fast metabolism, I didn't obsess about calories. But Paco's sturdy build resembled a fireplug. How had he made 108 pounds?

"Nikki, you need to move." Doc's words startled me.

Rising, I scrambled back as Belgado and some other jockeys came up the hallway. Their faces were quiet and worried. We all stared at Paco.

Will Marshall separated from the group and stood next to me.

"You okay?" he asked, touching my shoulder.

I nodded. Will had ridden against me a few times. He tended to be straightforward and fair, and I liked his green eyes. I found his closeness comforting.

Doc removed his stethoscope from Paco's chest and unzipped a canvas bag. He whipped out small disks and wires connected to a machine with a monitor.

Will leaned forward. "I used to work as an EMT...."

"In that case, here." Doc shoved a blue bottle with a tube and plastic mask into Will's hands, then pressed the disks against Paco's chest. His dark eyes focused on the monitor. With a sharp intake of breath, he pumped his hands frantically on Paco's chest.

Will slipped the mask over Paco's face as a siren wailed in the distance.

Doc's words to Will were almost a whisper. "No heartbeat."

Paco couldn't die. I glanced at the faces of the other jockeys. Worry. Fear. We were the only athletes routinely followed by a moving ambulance whenever we competed. Racing was so dangerous, it could be any of us lying there. It could be *me.*

Lights from the ambulance reflected off the floor by the entry door.

Paramedics burst in with a stretcher, their heavy work shoes loud on the tile floor.

Doc called to them, "We need a defibrillator."

A muscular, female medic gave the doctor a dismissive nod. "We'll take over," she said, and all but pushed Doc and Will aside before going to work on Paco with a piece of equipment that must have been the defibrillator. Another medic slid an IV needle into Paco's arm

Doc scooped up his stuff, and he and Will moved out of the way.

I felt like an intruder and walked closer to the entry door. By the time I glanced back, they were maneuvering the stretcher next to Paco. Then, they loaded him up and strapped him down.

The glass door opened, and a tall figure blocked the autumn light. Damn — Maryland Racing Commission's chief investigator, Offenbach. He walked toward us, frowning when he saw Paco's limp form on the stretcher.

Everyone watched as the medics hoisted Paco up and rushed him out the glass doors to the ambulance.

Offenbach stepped past me to Doc, leaving me to stare at the back of his buzz-cut head. No surprise he'd shown up, since his office was next door, but I was shaky enough and didn't need the investigator on my case again. He always seemed to have it in for me.

I'd been falsely implicated in a crime a while back, and Offenbach had ruled me off the track. Though cleared, I was still uncomfortable around him. Maybe I could ease out of the building. I took a few slow steps sideways, but Offenbach turned, nailing me with those cop-eyes.

"Latrelle," he said, "Don't leave. I want you in my office when I'm done here."

Oh boy. I was too nervous to stand still, so I got a Diet Coke from the machine, then paced the hall. One word from Offenbach, and the stewards could pull my license, stripping me of job and income.

Get a grip, Nikki, you haven't done anything wrong.

I should get over to the backstretch where I worked a second job as exercise rider for trainer Jim Ravinsky. No doubt my racehorse, Hellish, was getting indignant that I was late with her evening feed. Jim didn't like her raising a ruckus, disturbing the other horses.

Instead, I read some notices on the bulletin board, not absorbing the words. Damn. What had happened to Paco?

2

Unreadable as a brick wall, the chief investigator made me want to squirm as I sat facing him in his corner office. Three desks and some filing cabinets crowded the small room. One wall had a cell-like window, and outside, the night was settling in. I felt Paco's presence, as if he were nearby.

Palms flat on his desk, silent, he just stared at me. I almost confessed, except I hadn't done anything.

"What do you know about jockeys using weight loss drugs?" Offenbach asked.

My face usually gives me away, so I tried for expressionless. "I don't know anything about it."

Offenbach's manner shifted. He placed his elbows on the desk slouching his tall frame forward. "But you've heard something?"

No way a one-time diet drug would make Paco so sick. More likely it was abuse over a period of time. I'd heard of jockeys who "flipped" their meals like a bulimic. I didn't want to get involved in any of this.

Offenbach had the patience of a barn cat at a mouse hole. I fidgeted on my wooden seat.

"I don't know anything." I hadn't heard anything, and wouldn't snitch on my buddies if I had.

"You're better than that, Latrelle."

Was that a compliment? From Offenbach?

The desk phone rang, and Offenbach's face never altered as he answered and listened to a man's voice I could hear faintly through the receiver. He set the phone down.

"Martinez is dead. DOA at Laurel Hospital." Offenbach's flat eyes assessed my reaction.

A small, "Oh," escaped me. I swallowed. "Do they know what killed him?"

"Not till the autopsy comes in. I suspect something to keep the weight off. You sure you don't know anything about that?"

"I told you, I don't."

"You might want to rethink your allegiance. Stopping substance abuse will only benefit you people as a group."

"I don't know anything about *substances*." I abandoned my attempt at a poker-face and glared at him. "Maybe a few get carried away with diuretics or the hotbox, but mostly, we're the fittest people in the world." How else could we whip, pump, push, steer and stay balanced on thousand-pound animals for distances that stretched as far as a mile and a quarter? "Can I go now?"

Offenbach nodded. I marched out his door through the empty lobby of the racing secretary's office. Outside, a little breeze scattered discarded bet-tickets, and a rising full moon reflected sharply on the small white papers. I hugged my denim jacket tighter against the night's increasing chill. I'd told Offenbach the truth. Didn't know anything about substance abuse. Didn't want to know.

But someone once told me ignorance is the devil's best friend.

3

Eight in the morning, the day after Paco died. The track was closed for the half-hour morning break while three tractors dragged equipment around re-smoothing the dirt surface. I'd already galloped five horses and had a few more to get out between eight-thirty and the track's final closing time at ten A.M.

Lying low in Jim's office, I avoided my fellow backstretch workers. They reminded me of paparazzi, hounding me for the story of Paco's death.

A headline caught my attention from the scattered sheets of the *Daily Racing Form* covering most of Jim's desk: NEW JERSEY JOCKEYS QUESTIONED IN DRUG USE SCANDAL.

I grabbed the article, sank into a chair, and braced for the barn's fat tabby cat to pounce on my lap. He did, and once he'd curled in a heap, I studied the paper. Authorities had questioned two jockeys at Monmouth Park about drug abuse. A paragraph of speculation, careful avoidance of the jocks' names. Not enough information to warrant the big headline.

I wadded the page into a ball and tossed it to the floor of Jim's office. The cat was after it in a flash. The paper bounced off a gallon jug of Bigeloil liniment like a ping-pong ball, rolled over a few leather lead shanks, and landed in an empty doughnut box.

Jim stepped into the room as the tabby smacked the newspaper ball into the barn aisle. The cat disappeared after it in a blur of grey and brown fur. My boss didn't say anything, but something that might have been a smile tweaked the corners of his mouth. He sat behind his desk, shoulders stooped beneath his grey hair and blue MYERS MEED cap.

"Hope you didn't need the front page of the *Form*," I said.

"Nah, looks like you made good use of it." Jim's attention settled on me. "Nikki, something I've been wanting to talk to you about."

What had I done now?

Jim waved a hand. "Stop looking like a nervous filly. They're having a late fall meet at Colonial this year. Need you to take our Virginia-breds down for about six weeks. Stay there, act as my assistant trainer."

"Me? Run the whole barn?"

"You got your license, didn't you?"

"Yes, but…" Could I do it? How many Virginia-breds were there? Six? Eight? I'd gotten my assistant's license, but only so I could saddle one if Jim couldn't make a race, since only licensed trainers are allowed to saddle a horse in the paddock.

"Wait a minute," I said. "You want me to act as trainer, morning exercise rider *and* jockey?"

"Yep."

What if I let him down? This man had taken me off the streets of Baltimore, given me a job, acted like the father I'd never had.

I stood. "You think I can do all this?"

Jim knuckled his shaggy eyebrows. "We've only got five or six Virginia horses. You can take Ramon and Lorna to help out."

He *was* serious. Not that Jim ever joked. Sure, this was a great opportunity, and Colonial Downs was a beautiful track in rural Virginia. But what about my cat, Slippers, and my horse, Hellish? My *apartment*.

"Why the special meet?" I asked, surprised I'd heard no gossip.

"Sprinkler system's messed up. Laurel's closing the turf course 'til next spring."

"The Maryland horsemen will *love* that," I said.

Jeez, they'd just put in the new turf course. Wider, with excellent drainage, horses traveled on it like on a springboard. Except lately it'd been dry, the surface more like concrete than grass.

Jim moved on. "They pay fifty percent on top of purse money for Virginia-breds running at Colonial. Owners are hot to go."

I nodded. It made sense. A racehorse registered with the state thoroughbred association as being bred, or more accurately *born*, in Virginia received a big dividend. I did the math. If a horse won a race with a purse of $30,000, his share would be about half, or $15,000. Then the state-bred fund would kick in an additional $7,500 bonus. I'd heard Virginia paid extra money down through third or fourth place. Who could ignore such a lucrative payoff?

Jim gathered the newspapers on his desk. "And the horses will run better if they're stabled at Colonial and not shipped."

I nodded. The track lay halfway between Richmond and Williamsburg. The meet usually took place in the summer when tourist and beach traffic choked I-95 and Route 64, causing accidents and hot tempers. In the fall, the drive would be easier. Still, a long van ride could take a lot out of a racehorse. Runners stabled at Colonial would definitely enjoy a home-track advantage.

Ramon passed by the office door, leading a grey filly down the barn's dirt aisle. The light caught the glitter of the groom's gold earring and the glow of oil on his dark, slicked-back hair. He was a good groom, and I'd be lucky to have him in Virginia. Lorna might need a little watching.

A familiar whinny shrilled from a nearby stall.

"Can I take Hellish?"

"Don't want you leaving her here. She'd tear the barn down."

Jim glanced at the battered Purina wall clock. I'd just been dismissed.

4

Spitting rain and a lead-colored sky echoed my mood as I stood across the street from Saint Mary's Catholic church in Laurel, where the track had arranged a memorial service for Paco Martinez.

Appropriately, the event was being held on a "dark day" — a Monday when Laurel's wide turf and dirt tracks were closed to live racing. This allowed jockeys, trainers and backstretch workers time to attend the afternoon service.

Nineteen-year-old exercise rider Lorna Doone caught up with me on the sidewalk. Though shorter and rounder than she'd like to be, muscles from galloping race horses made up a healthy percent of her deceptively curvaceous figure. I'd learned the hard way not to tease her about her name. She'd get hot and sharply remind me her name came from the famous British romance novel, *not* the Nabisco shortbread cookie.

When I held up a side to make a wing for her, Lorna scooted beneath my rain poncho. We huddled together, waiting for a break in traffic before splashing across the avenue.

A flotilla of black umbrellas and raincoats floated along a flooded walk, bobbled up stone steps and through a set of double doors into the church. We followed in their wake, entering the foyer, where I stuffed the wet poncho into a tote, fluffed my short hair, and inspected the crowd. Several pews near the front of the church had room, and Lorna and I navigated through the dawdlers and secured two seats on the right-hand side.

When we settled, I turned to Lorna. She seemed subdued, almost a slow motion version of herself. Her eyes appeared dilated. Was she on something again? She'd been clean, out of rehab for three years. In the two years I'd known her, she'd made me feel I'd found a younger sister, someone precious, someone I'd fight to protect.

I followed Lorna's intent gaze to the front of the church. Three rows ahead, a small group of dark-haired mourners crowded together in the first pew. The respectful empty space on either side suggested they might be Martinez family members. Men in black jackets faced straight ahead. Two women with thick braids down their backs sat to their right.

A third woman wore her hair loose, a black mass spilling on her shoulders. She turned sideways, partially revealing a young face, a dark brow, and an eye laced with thick lashes. She leaned over, her attention drawn to something I couldn't see. A small child?

To her right, water beaded and slid down the outside of a stained-glass window, causing the uplifted eyes of a martyred saint to appear to run with tears. Above the altar, Christ on a cross. Brought up Presbyterian, I was unfamiliar with the Catholic Church. I found the warm glow of candles and light scent of incense far more appealing than the religious agony depicted on walls and windows.

Somber organ music rolled to a crescendo, and I realized the priest in white robes stood next to a dark casket. *Paco.* I looked away, only half listening as the priest spoke about Paco. I tuned in only when the solemn voice described Paco as, "showing great faith and courage as he strove to succeed in a foreign land."

Remembering the little silver San Raphael medal Paco had given me, I didn't doubt his faith.

The priest's gaze rested on the dark-haired mourners in the first row. "His young wife and child must now share this faith."

Lorna's breath hissed in, and her body stiffened, making our wooden pew creak.

In the first row, the raven-haired girl collapsed forward into sobs. A smaller wail rose from the seat beside her. One of the older women leaned over and gathered a small boy into her arms. A murmur flowed through the congregation. A woman seated ahead of us dug in her pocketbook for a tissue and dabbed at her eyes. Someone behind me whispered, "Tragic."

Lorna shifted again, and ignoring our pew's creaks and groans, she sighed and leaned into me. She whispered in my ear.

"I didn't *know*. He didn't *tell* me." She looked lost, and ridiculously young.

"Didn't tell you what?" I hissed.

"He was married. And we…" She didn't finish the half-whispered sentence.

I stiffened, and the priest continued, but I wasn't listening. Lorna had a thing with Paco?

The rain ceased streaming down the leaded windows, and feeble sunlight glimmered through the stained glass. As the priest droned, I wondered if the woman behind me had used an entire bottle of perfume.

By the end of the service, the scent of incense, flowers, and perfume choked me almost as much as the dark, oppressive grief inside Saint Mary's. Pushing through those double doors into the freshly washed sunlight was like escaping a dungeon. Lorna and I gulped in the cool air.

"Can we leave, or do we have to stand around and talk?" Lorna asked.

"Give it a minute. See what happens." Like I knew about funeral etiquette. The only one I could remember was my Mom's, and I didn't want to go there.

We stepped onto the wet grass in our waterproof paddock boots, both of us curious, staring at the Martinez family where they crowded together on the sidewalk.

"She's pretty," Lorna said.

I didn't have to ask who.

Lorna pulled off her jacket, revealing a blue tattoo of Pegasus on her left forearm, and flipped a tangle of red curls away from her right eye. Now anyone could see the gold ring piercing her auburn brow. She'd raised up her tough wall, the one that said, "Don't mess with me."

A tall, slender figure wrapped in an expensive-looking brown raincoat hurried along the glistening walk. A hood covered much of the face, even though the rain had stopped. But the form was obviously female. A bright ring of yellow crowned her brown vinyl boot-tops, flashing unexpected color. Maybe a Panamanian mourner a rung or two up the financial ladder.

The majority of the crowd appeared to be Latino backstretch workers, many of them young, like Paco. A lot of dark athletic clothes and a few cheap suits.

"Uh-oh," Lorna said.

Bearing down on us, her hair flying back and her face dark with an emotion I couldn't quite read, was Paco's young wife.

5

Without thinking, I moved a half step and partially blocked the widow's path toward Lorna.

Her dark hair settled back on her shoulders as she slowed. Her gaze fixed on Lorna.

"I am Teresa Marie Martinez," she said in a surprisingly soft voice.

Close up, the expression I'd been afraid was anger looked more like despair and pain. Teresa Marie was about Lorna's height, only smaller boned and thinner, her dress hanging too loosely on her frame.

"I'm Nikki, and this is Lorna." I said, clasping Teresa's slender hand. "We are very sorry for your loss."

"*Gracias,*" She turned to Lorna. "Paco, he tell me about you."

Lorna's eyes widened, and I waited for a bomb to explode.

"You in picture he send me," Teresa said, fingering a gold cross on her neck.

Oh boy. My gaze slid to Lorna, who looked ready to bolt.

"He say you *muy simpatica amiga*, you…how do you say, *encourage* him?"

"Um, yeah, I thought he needed a friend to…I just wanted to make him happy." Lorna looked like she'd swallowed a wasp.

"We all did," I said quickly. That hadn't sounded right, either. "Paco was a great guy."

For the first time, I was grateful for the language barrier. Made it easy to smile, nod, and say almost nothing else.

One of the male family members made a come-here motion to Teresa, and the small child, still in the arms of one of the dark-haired women, began to wail. The man motioned at Teresa again, impatience on his face.

Teresa mumbled something quickly in Spanish that ended with *gracias* and hurried toward her child.

"You think we could just cut across the lawn and get out of here?" Lorna's gaze cut to the Martinez family surrounded by well-wishers on the sidewalk between us and the street.

"Good idea." I strode into the wet grass, once again grateful for those rubber paddock boots. The sunlight reflected off beads of moisture in the grass, and a light steam carrying the scent of damp grass and moist earth rose as we made a bee line towards my Toyota parked across the street.

While Lorna and I waited for traffic to pass, I noticed a man standing on the sidewalk next to my car. A broad-shouldered man with close-cropped sandy hair, he moved to the edge of the curb and stared at us.

"You know that dude?" Lorna asked as we skirted a puddle while crossing the street.

"No, but he looks like he's waiting for us."

"He looks like a cop," Lorna said, putting a hand on my arm as if to slow me down.

"You think everyone is a cop. Lorna, there are *cars* coming.*"*

We beat it to the sidewalk, and I searched for the keys in my tote, but they were buried somewhere under the still-wet poncho.

"Excuse me, are you Nikki Latrelle?" The man had a slight southern drawl, putting the accent on the "trelle."

Abandoning the key search, I turned to face him.

"Yes, I'm Nikki."

He had a nice enough face, but I noticed his legs seemed too short for his body size. His black shoes were dry and polished perfectly.

He stuck a neat, manicured hand out. "Jay Cormack. Operations and Enforcement, Virginia Racing Commission."

Enforcement?

"I *told* you," Lorna whispered, taking a step back and folding her arms across her chest.

The law had busted her for cocaine as a juvenile, sent her to rehab. Her Maryland exercise rider's license, until recently, had been "provisional." She had it provided she stayed clean.

Cormack's steady gaze gave her a quick, speculative once over. "Ms. Doone?"

Lorna responded with a short, defensive nod.

"Your Inspector Offenbach tells me you two will be in Virginia for the meet." He directed his next words to me. "Seems to think you're a stand-up gal, Ms. Latrelle. Quick on your feet." His voice grew softer, the Virginia accent more pronounced. "Y'all heard about this jockey problem? I'd like you to be my eyes and ears. On the inside."

He hadn't wasted any time, so I didn't either. "Rat out my buddies? I don't think so."

"No way," Lorna said. Fired with indignation, she suddenly appeared taller and almost menacing.

"Easy, ladies." Cormack's smile was gentle, like his voice. "Just a matter of lettin' me know if you see something about to go down. I wouldn't necessarily need names, just a heads up." He shrugged as if to say it was no big deal. "I've known Offenbach a long time. He thinks you can be trusted. Just thought you might like to help."

I glanced back at the people across the street. A number of jockeys and exercise riders still mingled over there, and that hooded woman's shadowed face appeared to be watching us. They probably didn't know this guy headed up security for Colonial. But I didn't need to be seen talking to him.

"Mr. Cormack, I can't afford enemies. Riding races is already dangerous. I don't want jockeys thinking I'm some kind of snitch."

"She could get hurt," Lorna added.

Cormack's breath whistled a little between his teeth as he pulled a slim leather wallet from his suit jacket and withdrew a card. "Keep this. Think about it."

I took the card and, stuffing it into my tote bag, I found my keys. When I unlocked the doors and we started to scramble inside the Toyota, he spoke again.

"Be real nice if you helped us out, Miss Latrelle."

His words sounded almost like a warning, and I didn't answer.

6

"Scared the hell out of me," Lorna said. "At first I thought she was gonna stab me with a knife or something."

Lorna sat beside me as we barreled down Interstate 95 south of the Washington beltway, the day after Paco's funeral. I stared straight ahead, concentrating on the traffic and the 18-wheeler crowding us from the lane to our right.

I drove Jim's 350 Ford pickup, a stretch-cab that pulled a trailer loaded with six Thoroughbreds. On the seat behind me, stuffed between suitcases and carryalls full of our personal belongings, Slippers, my Heinz-57 part-Persian cat, glowered in his cat carrier. In the rearview mirror, the tip of his tail twitched in indignation. At least he wasn't howling.

On the road behind us, Ramon steered an older Dodge 150 with another groom named Manuel. We only had Manuel for the day, but I got to keep the better man with Ramon. His Dodge pulled a two-horse trailer packed with stuff we'd need — stall gates, rubber mats, buckets, feed tubs, rakes, pitchforks, a wheelbarrow, and trunks filled with tack. Our little convoy headed for Colonial Downs.

Since the memorial service, we'd talked about everything but Paco, until a minute earlier when Lorna finally dipped her toe in. One step later, strong emotional currents seemed likely to rip out the whole story.

"I was, like, amazed she was so nice to me."

"Why shouldn't she be nice to you?" There it was, the big question.

Ahead, tail lights flashed red. Though I'd left a long space between me and the car in front, I eased off the gas and pumped my brake, my gut tightening. Didn't want to think about a six-horse-trailer wreck on a crowded interstate. Especially when I held the wheel.

"I didn't know he was married." Lorna twisted in her seat and faced me.

My attention stayed glued to the road. Ahead of us, traffic came to an abrupt halt, one car jerking onto the shoulder to avoid slamming the rear of the vehicle in front. I kept pumping the brake, flashing the rig's lights in case the guy behind me wasn't paying attention.

Lorna, apparently oblivious to the near crashes around us, plowed ahead. "If I'd known, I never woulda...you know."

"*Slept* with him?"

"Yeah, that."

The traffic reached a standstill. Lorna studied a tear in the blue denim covering her right knee. "We went out a few times, for beer and pizza. It was, you know, platonic. Until the night we went to that Karaoke bar and danced. I had, like, two beers. But I was cool. Then he sang one of those Latino love songs. The dude could sing." Her voice caught at the memory. "He sounded so lonely."

She met my gaze, her eyes wet with unshed tears. "I just sort of melted. But he wasn't even lonely for me, was he? He was missing *her*."

Engines whined, wheels inched forward, and I pressed on the gas as the traffic rolled south. "You didn't do anything wrong, Lorna. You didn't know."

As the traffic sped up, I glanced quickly at Lorna. "Let it go. You didn't mean to hurt anyone."

"But what if she finds out? I keep thinking about her, the baby, marriage in a church. Vows. All that stuff."

"Paco is the one who should have thought about that," I said. Seemed the guy had liked to tell women what they wanted to hear, and Lorna had bought the whole line. She seemed fragile. How much would it take to push her back to cocaine? My grip on the steering wheel hurt my fingers.

I'd had trouble with a gang of thugs, and the police, a while back at Laurel. Lorna had been a true friend, standing by me when others turned away. I wanted to make it up to her, or at least keep her safe.

* * * *

We found the entrance into the track grounds at dusk, driving slowly along Colonial Downs Parkway, a four-lane road with wide grassy shoulders. About a mile in, we reached an entrance to the grandstand. I slowed, but a small sign indicated the stables still lay ahead.

I almost blew by the turn at Horsemen's Road, an abrupt left with no advance warning. A chainlink fence crowned with four or five strands of barbed-wire surrounded the grounds. A sign announced we were entering the jurisdiction of the Virginia Racing Commission. It felt like a warning.

I was surprised to see the commission and racing secretary's offices in a long cinder block building just outside the gate to the backstretch. Usually these structures were inconveniently located at the grandstand on the far side of the track, instead of here, where the horsemen spent their time. I turned the Ford to the right, toward the stable gate with the inevitable guard house.

I eased to a stop, grabbed a folder with the horses' papers, and hopped from the truck. Lorna unfolded herself from the cab, and we made little groaning noises stretching out the road kinks.

A young blond guy, wearing a big cap with SECURITY printed on it, hustled out of the guard house. He gave us a narrow-eyed stare.

"What have you got in there?"

"Six for Jim Ravinsky." I handed him the folder. He marched back to the trailer, opened a small human-sized door and stepped into the rig. He compared the descriptions on the Jockey Club papers to the markings on the horses, then studied the attached health certificates, verifying the lab results were current. Probably disappointed that everything was in order. He strolled back to Ramon's trailer, looking inside to make sure it was filled with equipment like I'd said and not contraband.

The guard returned and handed back the paperwork, then unfolded a typed sheet and studied it a moment. "You're in barn 23, stalls 50-60. Use only your assigned stalls." Another hard stare. "Follow this road to the very last barn."

We cranked our engines and rumbled past the guard house into the Colonial Downs backstretch.

The sun had set a while back, and the few pink clouds riding the western horizon dimmed to a purplish blue. I thought I'd reached our stable, but it was only number 21. I kept going, not happy when the trees closed in around us, tall pines crowding against the edge of the paved road. The path curved, and I was relieved to see space open up, even if only two barns remained before the asphalt dead-ended at a dark expanse of forest.

No lights. No cars. Nobody.

"This place gives me the creeps." Lorna's fingers fussed with the rip in her jeans.

"Meet hasn't started," I said. "Most people haven't shipped in yet."

"I don't see why we had to get here so early."

"Jim likes the horses to get acclimated." When the truck headlights picked up the number 23 painted on the end-wall just below the roof, I rolled to a stop beside the last barn.

We got out, groping our way through the dark since the truck lights lit the darkness ahead, not the building to its side. Like most racing stables, the rectangular barn held about 60 stalls, 30 per side, backed up, with doors facing out. Wood posts supported a roof overhang that sheltered a dirt aisle outside the rows of stalls. The short ends of the rectangular building had rooms for tack, storage or a cot for a groom. The dirt path continued here, circling before these rooms, too.

The barn, or section of barn that housed a particular trainer's horses and supplies, was commonly called a "shedrow," possibly a shortened version of row-of-sheds. Maybe not found in most dictionaries, but the name's been around forever.

I stepped carefully into this one, my fingers scrabbling along the wall outside the nearest stall for light switches. I found one and flipped it. A single bulb cast a dim light onto the dirt path outside the nearby stalls. The second switch flooded the first two stalls with light. Now we were in business. I soon had our stalls located, with lights blazing all over the place.

Still, Ramon gestured at the woods. "Why they put us here? I don't like. Is so far away."

"Hey, they bedded us down." Lorna stared with relief inside the first stall.

Jim had arranged for supplies with a local feed company. They'd agreed to bed our stalls with straw before we arrived, but you never knew. We had enough work to do without having to shake out sixteen bales of straw.

"They put the hay here." Ramon held a wooden door open, peering into a stall about halfway along our shedrow. He disappeared inside, emerging with a handful of green hay. He sniffed it for mold, then shoved some in his mouth, tasting the quality of the dried grasses. His white teeth flashed. "Is good."

I could almost hear a collective sigh of relief. It was one thing we wouldn't have to worry about.

Manuel and Ramon set buckets, wire-and-metal gates, and rubber-covered chain ties outside each stall. We got a system going where I wound screw eyes into the inside walls, Lorna snapped buckets on them, and Manuel set up a hose and filled the buckets with water. Ramon worked on hanging the gates across the stall entryways.

Forty-five minutes later, we unloaded the six horses and led them into their stalls. Lorna and I unwound their shipping bandages, feeling through the hair on their legs for scrapes or unexpected heat. Ramon and Manuel loaded feed pails with late dinners. The horses picked up its scent, sweet and fragrant with molasses. They pawed and nickered, impatient for their grain.

Hellish prowled about her new lodgings, inspecting her fresh water, snatching hay from the rack filled with timothy and alfalfa. She shoved her head over her stall gate and stared briefly into the night, finally relaxed and got serious about her feed tub. Her contentment soothed me as few things can.

A moaning cry rode the pine scented air. It came again, soft, pitiful, and far away. I heard a rustling noise, as if something moved through the trees in our direction. A clank sounded just inside the pines, like metal striking a stone. The mournful wail echoed again deep in the woods, stirring the hairs on my neck.

Horse heads emerged over stall doors, their eyes boring into the woods, nostrils flared.

"What the hell was that?" Lorna stepped closer to me. Manuel picked up a metal pitchfork. Ramon whipped out a knife from his jacket pocket, and I grabbed the long metal bar I'd used to turn the screw eyes.

Armed and scared. Welcome to Virginia.

7

"*Madre de Dios,*" Manuel said, clutching the pitchfork with both hands.

Movement in the pines, the snapping of a branch. Our visitor moved closer. The pine needled forest floor muffled the person's footsteps. A dark image emerged from the woods to my left, a human form taking shape as it approached the stable lights.

Adrenalin sent my heart pumping overtime as a tall, thin man with hollow eyes walked toward us. Long scraggly hair grazed his shoulders. One hand dragged a shovel behind him. He stopped and I saw bits of soil clinging to his pants legs. Dirt smeared his shovel blade.

"What do you want?" My voice cracked.

The man stood still, his eyes wandering and unfocused. Ramon stepped forward, the blade of his knife catching a sliver of light from the crescent moon just rising over the trees. The man's attention fixed on the knife, as if his mind finally escaped the forest and caught up with his body. He gazed at us, his face etched with an anguish I didn't want to know about.

"Do you need help?" I took a half step forward.

He shook his head, muttered unintelligible words.

"Look, man. You scare the horses. Maybe you should go." Ramon punctuated his words by stabbing the long serrated knife into the air.

The man pulled his shovel forward, appeared to examine it, then raised haunted eyes. "You know. Don't pretend you don't."

"What are you talking about?" Irritation rose in me. The guy was obviously crazy, and we'd had a *really* long day.

"Everybody knows, but they won't tell." Anger and frustration edged his voice. His arm repeatedly jabbed the pointed end of his shovel into the earth.

My fingers tightened around the cold metal bar, but the man walked away from us along the grassy area outside the barn, his shovel trailing behind. He turned the corner and disappeared, the dark patch of sliced and disturbed earth the only evidence he existed.

"What was *that*?" Lorna asked.

I had no idea, but was grateful when the next half hour remained uneventful. The horses quieted, their interest returning to feed buckets. Ramon hosed down the horse trailer, while Lorna and I ran damp sponges over bridles and martingales, making sure they were ready for morning exercise. But I'd learned things could always get worse and kept the metal pipe close by.

Manuel sprayed a fine mist along the shedrow to dampen it down, then raked the aisle, the long metal tines leaving smooth patterns in the dirt. I watched from the grass as he locked the rake in the tack room. Out of habit he kept close to the wall so he wouldn't disturb his work. If anyone ventured into the aisle that night, we'd see the footprints in the morning.

Ramon and Manuel drove over to the small grooms' apartments closer to the backstretch entrance. Lorna and I pulled the big horse trailer into a gravel lot and unhooked it, leaving it next to a couple of empty horse vans. The grooms would return the rigs to Laurel the next day. Ramon would then drive back to Colonial in my Toyota.

On the way out, I stopped the Ford outside the stable gate and slid the electric window down. The security guard adjusted his cap and strolled over. I told him about the weirdo with the shovel. He looked at me in disbelief.

"Never heard of anything like that around here." His lips curled into an insolent smile. "You girls been drinking?"

"Asshole." Lorna's voice, low enough he didn't hear.

"Never mind," I shoved the truck into gear, sketched a brief wave at the guard and pulled out. I glanced at Lorna. "See if you can find directions in the glove box." Jim had rented us a cottage on a farm owned by a couple named Chuck and Bunny Cheswick. Lorna wrestled the paper from the glove box as I swung the Ford onto Colonial Downs Parkway.

Flashing lights bounced off the trees ahead, and curving around a bend, I eased off the gas, not sure what lay ahead. Police cars and an ambulance came into view. Beyond them a fire engine idled in the middle of the road, its shiny grille reflecting the red, blue, and yellow lights spinning from the emergency vehicles.

Looked like there might be room to slide past the fire truck, but curiosity and a memory of that cry in the woods slowed me down. I stopped in front of the fire truck and opened my window again. The smell of engine heat and oil drifted on the evening air.

On the left side of the road, a few firemen and cops stood motionless, staring at a lifeless form on a stretcher being lifted through the back doors of the ambulance. One of the paramedics shifted as he set down his end of the stretcher and the interior light revealed the victim's face.

"Oh, my God. Don't look," Lorna said.

Too late for that. I'd seen a face that looked like melted cheese. The image stunned me and, though my eyelids snapped shut, I could still see it.

"Excuse me, miss." A police officer had moved up to the Ford's window. "You should drive on through. There's room on the shoulder."

"Right," I said. "But officer, we heard some strange sort of wailing noise—"

"I can't discuss this." His hand motioned toward the ambulance. "Police business. We've got an investigation going on."

"Okay." I took a breath and swallowed my questions. "I'll see if I can get this truck past." I raised the window and steered slowly alongside the massive hook-and-ladder. *What had I gotten myself into?* Would Colonial's track investigator, Cormack, know anything about the wailing sounds and Shovel-man? Except, I didn't want to talk to him.

We remained silent as we spun down the dark parkway, the strobe lights diminishing behind us. Lorna picked at the ripped fabric in her jeans, and I tried but failed to push the horrific face from my mind.

The exit appeared ahead and Lorna held the directions near the dash light. "Go left when you come out of here." She paused a few beats. "That had to be the most disgusting thing I've ever seen. It's like somebody threw acid on his face."

"Or burned it." I felt a little sick and rolled down the window to drink in the cool night air. What had happened back there? I kept breathing until my stomach settled. "Let's find this farm."

I drove south and passed through a tiny town called Providence Forge, making note of a Food Lion grocery and a small drug store next door. Might be our best bet for household supplies.

A mile later I made a right onto a narrow road called Hemlock Lane. The directions said three miles, but with no streetlights or paint lines for guidance, the unfamiliar, twisting road seemed endless.

"There." Lorna pointed to where the headlights revealed a sagging wooden sign with the name "Cheswick." A rooster painted with an abundance of feathers glared at us from one corner. Across the bottom faded letters read, "Prize Cochins."

Apparently we were staying at a chicken farm. We bumped down a long and abusive gravel drive before stopping in front of the main house. A huge Victorian. Lorna followed me up a broken brick walk where dead summer weeds sprouted through the brick-joints. A big porch wrapped around the front of the house. A low-wattage overhead bulb revealed cracked and peeling paint on the gingerbread woodwork. A half-moon window sat above the door and I could see a light on inside.

My fingers had just touched the cold brass of an antique knocker when the door swung open. A woman in her late forties hesitated in the doorway. She wore a long pink-and-green flowered skirt that looked about twenty years old, and a shapeless brown sweater that had a loose button hanging from a thread. Behind her stacks of magazines, cardboard boxes, newspapers and a pile of clothes cluttered the hallway. A musty smell floated out the door.

"Nikki Latrelle," I said. "And this is Lorna."

"Bunny." She shook my hand. She glanced over her shoulder into the house, then stepped onto the porch and pulled the door closed behind her. "I expected you earlier."

I explained about the traffic and she nodded. "You must be tired. Let me show you the cottage. You can follow me in your truck if you want."

The drive wound to the right of the house, past a garage, a structure that looked like a workshop, and a long low building with chicken wire pens on the side. I had time to see all this because the woman moved with the speed of a tortoise. A slow motion tour that made me want to scream.

Lorna hid a smile. "You could honk."

Then, on a small rise behind some cedar trees our rental came into view.

"Wow. Way nicer than I thought it'd be." Lorna leaned forward, staring.

The place looked like a picture-book English cottage. Smooth white stucco covered a solid foundation of maybe brick or stone. The walls were thick, the windows recessed, the roof a simple gable. Ivy covered the walls.

We collected the essentials we'd need for the night, I grabbed Slippers in his cat carrier, and we headed for the cottage door. Bunny pulled a key from her skirt pocket and let us in.

I breathed a sigh of relief as I stepped into a simple and tidy interior. A long rectangular living room stretched across most of the front of the cottage, with a small kitchen at the left end. In the back were two bedrooms, a bath in between.

Bunny wandered around the place touching the couch fabric and the back of a side chair. She plodded into the kitchen, pulled out a couple of drawers and fingered the contents.

"We'll let you know if we need anything." I moved to the open front door, hoping it might encourage her to leave.

The woman leaned over and opened a cabinet. With a low cry she pulled out a softball. "My boys used to stay here." She cuddled the ball against her chest. "I don't come here much anymore."

A part of me felt like I should help this woman. Something in her voice when she mentioned her boys. But we had to get up at five and the horses came first. In the distance, I saw lights flash, then heard the sound of a motor.

Bunny's soft shoulders tightened, her breath sucked in, and an edge of terror showed briefly in her eyes before she clamped down her agitation. She moved with surprising speed from the cottage and rushed away into the dark, still clutching the softball.

Lorna's fingers worried a lock of red hair. "That woman's afraid of something."

I shut the door and fidgeted with a brass box lock until I drove the bottom bolt home.

What *had* happened to Bunny's boys?

8

At six A.M., a thin and chilly light slanted across the Colonial Downs backstretch. The sunrise was so pale Ramon's gold earring appeared flat and lusterless against his olive-brown skin.

He gave me a leg-up onto my chestnut filly. She promptly skittered, then bucked beneath me, reminding me why I'd nicknamed her Hellish. Ramon led us along the aisle, whistling a soft tune to instill calm, while I adjusted my stirrups and gathered the rubber-covered reins before Lorna and I rode out to gallop the Colonial dirt course.

So far, this highly regarded track gave me the creeps — weird noises in the nighttime woods, a disturbed man with a shovel, and that horrible disfigured face. I had questions about the place Jim had found for Lorna and me to stay, too. I needed to shrug it off, get to work.

Lorna, astride a bay gelding named Impostor, fell in step next to us as we left the barn. Scanning the grounds, I found the openness of Colonial appealing. The barns weren't crowded together, shoulder to shoulder with manure sheds like at Laurel. A stretch of woods separated the backstretch stables from the track, and we followed a wide dirt path that wound through pine trees like a painting before reaching a gap in the rail.

Hellish spotted the distant grandstand and planted her feet, refusing to move forward.

Ahead of us Lorna stopped her horse, then turned back to me. "What's with her?"

"Who knows?" I booted Hellish. Her front legs came off the ground enough to send a small wave of fear through me, then replanted themselves firmly in the dirt. *Bitch.*

Refusing to waste time, I slid off her, intending to lead her through the gap in the track rail. She wasn't having it. If I turned around and glared at her when she balked, it would only make matters worse, so I kept walking in place in the sand pretending I was going somewhere. I felt like a fool with a beached whale on a leash.

The lead shank went slack in my hands; now that *she'd* decided, the filly hurried through the opening like a shark on the scent of blood.

Lorna rolled her eyes. "Showed you."

Didn't she always? I'd hoped she'd behave at Colonial without the presence of her favorite groom, the old black man, Mello Pinkney. The two had some bond I couldn't get a handle on, but I hadn't wanted to uproot Mello from Maryland, and still hoped Hellish might be manageable without his help.

An outrider cantered over after a minute or two, reined in his track pony, hopped off, and gave me a lift onto my recalcitrant filly. His gaze slid over us. "Nice looking filly."

"Thanks," I said, stroking her neck. "But pretty is as pretty does."

Two weeks earlier Hellish had clocked a blazing work, going head-to-head with a stakes-winning older mare at Laurel Park. After a few days off, I'd been dismayed to see her come up gimpy in the right front. I cold hosed the leg, had the vets check it, and prayed. X-rays turned up nothing, she came sound, and this was her first morning back.

Lorna eased her bay into a slow gallop and, not one to be left behind, Hellish took off in pursuit. I almost sang when I felt her fluid motion. We were back in business. Had to watch her though, that big easy stride extended so smoothly she'd be rocketing before I realized she'd ignited. I stood in the stirrups, leaning back, letting my body weight pull on her mouth, reins long, a signal we weren't doing anything serious. She behaved. To my right, the Pegasus tattoo on Lorna's bare forearm moved in sync with her horse's rhythmic stride.

* * * *

Two hours and six horses later, Lorna and I walked up the gravel road to Colonial's backstretch eatery. At most every U.S. track these cafeterias were called the "kitchen." In this one the scent of steaming coffee, bacon, fresh eggs and fried potatoes almost made me whimper.

We got in line at the counter and ordered ham and egg sandwiches. Poured ourselves coffee, paid, then headed to the seating area. A number of people had come down from Maryland for the meet, and we sat at a Formica-topped table with Will Marshall and Sable, an exercise rider from Pimlico. I hadn't seen Will since that day in the Laurel jocks' room, the day Paco died.

Race riding and dieting had honed Will's face into well-defined planes. Though quiet and a bit introverted, he had an appealing sense of humor that popped up at odd moments. He peeled an orange over a plate of dry toast and two lonely pieces of bacon.

Sable had café latte skin and heavy-lidded eyes. She wore a tight, racer-back top that displayed her muscular arms. She worked on pancakes. "You guys hear the autopsy came in on Paco Martinez?"

My head snapped up and Will's fingers stilled on the orange rind.

"Said he was loaded with methamphetamine and some other stuff."

Lorna and I exchanged a glance. The weight. Always fighting the scales, chasing after unnatural thinness. For some it led to multiple health problems, and for Paco it led to death.

The woman behind the counter yelled, "Ham and egg sandwiches," and slammed her hand on a round buzzer bell. I trudged over to retrieve the order, my appetite shriveled by Sable's words. What had Paco been thinking? Even if he thought so little of himself, why hadn't he cared about his wife and young son?

The kitchen's swinging door pushed in, and a drop-dead handsome male stepped into the noisy room. Brown eyes that could melt you like candle wax and hair that flowed dark and glossy halfway to his shoulders. A narrow waist, and...

"Hey, you wanna these ham and eggs?" The Latina woman held a paper bag over the counter, one brow arched, a knowing look in her eyes. Watching me stare like a prepubescent schoolgirl who'd stumbled over a rock star.

Jeez, what was wrong with me? The guy was real young anyway, probably not 20. Warmth flushed across my cheeks. I grabbed the bag, sidestepped the apparition and retreated to our table.

They were still talking about Paco. "Couldn't believe he had a wife. And a kid," Lorna said, then glanced expectantly at my sack of food.

I sat next to Will, opened the bag, and pulled out a hot sandwich. Its wax-paper covering was translucent with grease as I passed it over to Lorna. She sat with her back to the guy who'd just come in, but I faced him.

He stood there like he owned the place. Trying to ignore him, I sipped some coffee and pondered being about the only mid-twenties female who still hadn't had sex. I was doomed to be a late bloomer, probably due to some unpleasant stuff that had happened years ago. Stuff I rarely thought about. Still, there seemed to be some desire simmering on a back burner, and this young man was stirring it up.

He walked past our table wearing fringed leather chaps molding long legs and probably the best butt in Virginia. Hadn't meant to gawk. Serious eye candy, but he struck me as a party boy. His eyes didn't focus right, like he was spaced out.

"You see that guy? Is he gorgeous or what?" Lorna practically shivered, her eyes bright, feeding on the boy's dancer-like body.

He moved to a table with some people I didn't recognize, spun a wooden chair around and straddled it like a horse. He crossed his arms, rested them on the chair back and glanced in our direction.

"Bobby Duvayne," Will muttered.

"You know him?" I asked.

"Rich boy. Father owns racehorses down here. Bobby gallops them in the morning. *If* he feels like it."

"He can gallop with me anytime," Lorna said, her breakfast forgotten, cooling on the wax paper. "Those eyes. They're, like, incredibly beautiful."

"You mean the incredibly dilated brown ones?" Will asked, shaking his head. "Guy's on dope, Lorna. He's a mess."

"Maybe," she said. "But look at him. He's beautiful."

I almost said, "Remember what happened with Paco?" but we weren't alone and it wasn't anybody's business. Not really my business either. Relenting, I said, "He's gorgeous all right. But maybe a little wild and unruly."

"Like a feral colt," said Will. "Probably gallop all over you, Lorna."

"I wish he *would*." Lorna's eyes held a dangerous gleam.

Sable forked a last bite of pancake, drained her orange juice and pushed up from the table, the muscles in her forearms popping. "Watch yourself, that boy keeps bad company."

Lorna raised a pierced auburn brow, the gold ring winking. "I'm not afraid of him."

Bobby stood up, circled toward us from the side, his attention fixed on Lorna's curves, red hair, and Fair Isle skin. He closed in, pulled out a chair and settled next to her. His long tapered fingers brushed the wings on Lorna's tattoo.

She hadn't seen him coming.

"Hey," he said. "I'm Bobby. Saw you out on the track this morning."

The way they stared at each other, I could almost hear the electricity arcing and crackling between them. *Oh boy*.

I looked away. Lorna was special and something about this guy gave me a bad feeling.

9

A light breeze blew down our shedrow carrying the distant sound of sharply raised voices. Earlier, I'd sent Ramon and Manuel back to Laurel with the trucks and trailers, leaving Lorna and me to do double duty. We'd cleaned stalls, filled water and grain buckets, and stuffed hay nets with timothy and alfalfa.

Now, Lorna trundled past me with the last wheelbarrow load of soiled straw for the manure Dumpster. In the distance, the angry voices grew more strident and stirred my curiosity.

I raked away a remaining wisp of straw in the dirt outside our stalls, set the rake down and headed to the right, toward the center of the barn. Like most track stables, this one had a break where the dirt path ran through the center, allowing quicker access to the other side and a shorter-turn option for grooms walking horses around the barn's perimeter. I passed through the middle and reached the opposite side.

An outfit had arrived earlier that morning, their shedrow set up neatly with a dozen or so horses contentedly munching hay. The trainer and grooms had finished their work and left before noon. The voices came from the next barn over.

Grass and clover rooted in red Virginia clay stretched across the ninety yards or so separating us from barn 22. Bobby Duvayne, at least it looked like his hair and body, stood with arms folded across chest, chin tilted in a defiant angle. An older man, his tone harsh with anger, jabbed a finger near Bobby's face.

As I moved closer, the younger man threw his hands up in a "whatever" gesture and stalked toward the end of the barn and two parked cars. He climbed into a red one. Looked like some kind of Mustang. The older man stared after him, shaking his head. In profile, his body was stocky, his loose green stable jacket partially hiding the beginnings of a beer belly. He muttered something and disappeared through an open stall door.

I headed back to my side, hearing the roar of a muscle-car engine. Lorna pushed the now empty wheelbarrow into the hay-storage stall, then stepped back into the aisle as the sounds of gasoline combustion, torque and driving pistons grew louder.

We were at the end of the backstretch, on the far side of the last barn, but here came the white-striped red hood nosing around the corner.

"Whoa!" Lorna trotted forward and leaned over the perimeter wood rail. "Man, look at that. Ford Shelby GT 500. That's a Cobra, dude!"

Why did people younger than me always know this stuff?

The car eased along the dirt and gravel drive running past our barn. The engine, at idle speed, reminded me of the heavy tha-dump of a big Harley in neutral. The tinted driver's window rolled down. Bobby. Knowing he looked sharp.

I could hear Lorna's intake of breath when his hot eyes found her. He winked, the window closed up, and the Cobra crept down the dirt side road. When it hit the main backstretch road, the car roared away.

"Dust on the horizon," I said.

Lorna seemed to come back from far away. "Huh?"

"That Bobby. He's the kind of guy, when you need him, he'll be dust on the horizon."

Lorna frowned. She didn't want to hear it. But then, if I'd received that wink, I wouldn't want anyone trying to pull the reins in on me either.

* * * *

Ramon showed up around four in my beat-up Celica. He unfolded himself from the car, yawning, his eyes droopy. "Jim say you got two more come in tomorrow."

"Two more horses?" I'd been hoping we'd stop at six — a nice round number. Eight felt a bit top heavy.

"Yeah, some lady. Her name is Chaquette? She got two Virginia-breds."

"He tell you anything else about this woman?"

A spark of interest lit Ramon's eyes. "He say she used to be, how you say…" He paused, suppressing another yawn, "fashion model."

I hoped that wasn't synonymous with prima donna. Ramon sagged against the side of my car. Must be all that driving.

"Why don't you get some rest, Ramon. We'll finish up."

He flashed a grateful smile and trudged off toward the grooms' quarters. Lorna and I fed the horses, tidied up, and headed for the grocery store.

When we got to the cottage, I wandered around looking for Slippers. I'd let him out that morning, placing his food and water dishes on the stone step outside the front door. I'd put his favorite mouse toy out, too. He wasn't a strayer, but I wanted to find him. I circled the cottage, calling, then headed down the drive past the stand of cedars that sheltered the cottage from the outbuildings and main house.

A sharply cooling October afternoon, the sky shifting to pink in the western horizon. The sun still warmed my back as I leaned over and picked up a piece of rose quartz from the gravel road. I fingered the cool stone, admiring a translucent white stripe blazing through the center. I headed toward the chicken coop. The old wire fence sagged to the ground in places and ragged holes darkened a few of the building's baseboards. It appeared the Cheswicks were out of the poultry business.

I stopped. An indistinct form lay in a shallow depression near the coop. I couldn't make out where it started or stopped. Fur? Feathers? Nerves tightening, I drew closer. Was it dead?

A fluffy black-and-white rooster hopped up, clucking in alarm. One beady yellow eye glared at me. He ruffled his feathers, drew in some air, and crowed. The fur object rose, stretched, and began washing his paws. Slippers.

I peered closer. Had he been pecked? Spurred? I couldn't see any spurs on the rooster's feet. A downy blanket of feathers covered his legs down to his toenails. My eyes cut back to Slippers. Being part Persian, his legs were draped in smoke-gray fur pantaloons. The cat matched the rooster perfectly.

I moved in, scooped Slippers into my arms, and headed back to the cottage. The rooster followed. Was everyone partnering up but me?

Lorna stood in the doorway. "What's with the chicken?"

I set Slippers down and he padded to his food dish. The rooster cackled and made a bee line for the Iams pellets. The cat crunched, the rooster pecked.

Lorna grimaced. "Isn't that chicken he's eating?"

"I don't want to think about it." I went inside.

I sauteed hamburger with stewed tomatoes, onions and Worcestershire, then boiled two potatoes and mashed them with butter. A comfort food dinner. We ate off mismatched crockery, seated at an oak plank table in rickety wooden chairs. Lorna got first call on the bath, and I stepped outside to continue my exploration of the Cheswick farm.

Slippers' dish lay empty on the stone doorstep. The cat, rooster and mouse toy had all disappeared. Dew moistened the grass and a pleasant cedar tang saturated the evening air. Above, shreds of dark clouds drifted across a pale semi-circle of moon.

Down the gravel road, past the wood frame chicken coop, something scurried in the brush. I drew in some air, exhaling slowly. Just ahead lay the building resembling a workshop, covered with buckling prefabricated siding. Four windows, maybe two-foot square, marched across the front of the rectangular structure.

As I edged over to the closest window, the moon dimmed. The glass was dirty and hard to see through in the dark. I pulled a wadded dinner napkin from my jeans pocket and rubbed it on the window pane. The moon brightened. My hand froze.

A pallid face with wide, unseeing eyes loomed behind the glass.

I stifled a shriek as my brain sought an explanation. *A doll.* A china-faced boy doll. My body sagged against the siding in relief.

The large toy stood on a shelf below the window. Someone had arranged the doll so it appeared to stare through the glass. Inhaling a steadying breath, I stood on tiptoes to get a better view inside. Dozens of dolls in various sizes lined shelves built against the interior walls. Doll parts littered a long rectangular table. Headless bodies, disconnected arms, wigs and outfits I realized were Colonial. A sewing table stood near the far wall, and on the shelf next to the doll that had scared me half to death was a box of little tricorn hats.

"What are you doing?"

I jumped about two feet. Bunny. Where had she come from? "Just… looking at these dolls. Do you make them?"

The woman stared at me, her expression guarded. A long, faded paisley skirt wrapped her plump hips, and another worn sweater hung on her shoulders. She sighed, her tension dissipating as if too difficult to maintain. "I do. They're my little men." A key appeared from her skirt pocket and she shuffled up two steps and unlocked the workshop's door.

Inside she turned on overhead fluorescents, highlighting the downward lines of discontent etching her face. Her short blond hair became gray-white in the glare. "I started making these after I lost my boys. They said it would be good therapy, don't you know?"

I didn't. "Ah, I like the colonial theme."

"Yes." She picked up a loose leg, setting it next to a single arm. "They sell well in Williamsburg." Her fingers kept rearranging the lifeless body parts.

Something brushed my leg, something normal. I leaned over and grabbed my cat, cradled him in my arms. A gray feather clung to his forehead. "So, you don't raise chickens anymore?"

"No, they're all gone. Except for one old rooster. Don't want any pets." She stared past me into the dark outside. "Pets are bad."

"Bad?" I asked.

"They could die."

Mentally, I searched about for something to say and came up empty.

Crunching gravel signaled someone's approach. Bunny's face took on a deer-in-the-headlights expression, her body tightening. A man's form emerged from the darkness. Well over six feet, but trim, with a head of thick silver-gray hair, he hurried toward us. Heavy black-rimmed glasses formed rectangles around his eyes, the thick lenses making it hard to read his expression.

"She all right?" he asked me.

I felt an immediate dislike for this man. "You're okay, aren't you, Bunny?" Why would he talk about her as if she wasn't there? But she wasn't. Her eyes had taken on a vague uncertainty, and she appeared almost feeble.

Exasperation and a look of long suffering washed over the face of the man I assumed was my landlord. He startled me by dousing the lights.

"Are you Chuck Cheswick?" I asked.

"Yes. Glad you gals could rent the cottage." His words were clipped and he made a motion to look at his watch, only it was too dark. "Come on, Bunny. Let's go to the house." He put a hand on his wife's arm, ignoring her flinch I could see in the moonlight.

Bunny allowed herself to be led away down the gravel drive. The darkness swallowed them up, leaving me alone, the night closing in.

10

The rooster's crow awakened me at 4:35 A.M. Rolling over, I squinted at the clock's red numerals, then grabbed my pillow and shoved it over my head, hoping to blot out the sound, entice Mr. Sandman back before he dissolved completely. My bedroom door creaked open, and I sat up fast, remembering the man with the shovel, the body on the road, those dolls.

Lorna stood in the doorway wearing rumpled pajamas with the words NATURAL BORN PLAYER written across the chest. She rolled her eyes as the rooster, apparently on our front doorstep, burst into another round of crowing.

"God damned chicken." Turning, she stomped across the wood floor, jerked a pillow off the green upholstered couch, drew back the bolt and flung open the door. "Get lost, McNugget!"

The pillow sailed out the door, the rooster's shrieks diminishing as he rushed away from the cottage. Slippers streaked out the open door after the chicken, and I burrowed into the bed, pulling the pillow back over my head.

But as I lay there, the lifeless, porcelain doll's face played across my eyelids, then the melted, burnt face on the roadside. Time to make coffee. Think about getting the barn shipshape for Ms. Chaquette and her two incoming horses.

* * * *

A few hours later we'd galloped and cooled out the six horses. The morning had been the type I prefer — uneventful. My filly had acted as agreeable as an old school horse, but such pleasant behavior left me suspicious.

I rubbed her with a clean rag, thinking how the reins had felt like telegraph lines that morning, my fingers receiving subterranean messages. I'd had a feeling she was like a can of gasoline about to take a walk with a match. As I polished her rich coat and massaged her muscles, I hoped she'd keep a lid on it.

"You gotta see this, Nikki," Lorna said, from outside the stall.

I stuck my head out. A metallic yellow Cadillac with a brown vinyl top was parked in the dirt-and-gravel path beside our shedrow. A tall, slender woman stood next to the car, rapid-firing what sounded like

Spanish at Ramon.

The groom, his back to me, nodded quickly and shifted his weight from one leg to the other. He whipped his head around, spotted me and made an anxious get-over-here motion with his hand.

Must be the Chaquette woman. Peculiar hair style. A series of dark brown and platinum blond streaks were slicked back on her skull. The rhinestones encrusting her large aviator sunglasses reminded me of an insect's compound eyes.

Long slender legs with coppery skin stretched from beneath a short, hot-yellow skirt. A matching yellow jacket with formidable shoulder-pads displayed wing-like epaulets.

Her attention landed on me, her mouth an angry scowl. "Who are you?"

I couldn't see her eyes, but fancied I felt them inventorying the dirt and horse hair on my clothes, smudges on my face. I probably didn't smell so good either.

"Ravinsky's assistant, Nikki Latrelle." I held out a hand. She ignored it, whipping off her dark glasses. Big deep eyes, no doubt pretty when not darkened by anger and disdain.

"Where are my horses?" Her accent was Hispanic, but whether Spanish, Mexican or South American, I had no idea.

Ramon threw me a helpless look. "I tell her —"

"*Silencio!*" The word shot from her mouth, a stream of venom.

Ramon took a half-step back. This woman was like a God damned wasp. No. A yellow jacket.

"Look," I said. "I don't know where you come from, but we don't treat our employees like that."

"You," she said, "will tell me where my horses are. *Now.*"

I folded my arms across my chest and glared at her. She threw her hands up and muttered something in a different language, maybe French.

"Are you the new owner?" I asked.

"Amarilla Chaquette." She gave me a curt nod.

That was probably as close to a handshake as I'd get from her. A small breeze stirred up a dust devil near our feet, bringing an exquisite scent of perfume to my nostrils. I wondered if it was French and how many hundreds of dollars an ounce the yellow jacket paid for it.

"Listen, all I know is Mr. Ravinsky said you were shipping in two horses today. I wasn't given any further information." As if on cue my cell rang — security at the stable gate letting me know a driver was try-ing to bring two horses in.

"Is there a problem?" I hunched over the phone, turning away from

Amarilla's probing antenna.

"Yeah, there's a problem." The guard's voice was contentious. "Horses don't have any papers."

Of course they didn't. "Uh, Ms. Chaquette, you have any papers on your horses?"

She threw me a disgusted look. "Certainly. I have their documentation. Why you ask?"

"Your horses are at the gate. Can't get in without papers."

In about three strides, her long, toned legs had her at the car. Without a backward glance she peeled off toward the stable gate.

"Who's on duty up there?" asked Lorna.

"From the sound of his voice, I'd say it was that obnoxious guard from the night we arrived."

The three of us broke into smiles.

We finished up stable chores, making sure the two new stalls were ready. Almost half an hour went by before a big commercial horse van rolled up to our barn.

Amarilla pulled up behind the van, her big sunglasses aimed at Lorna and Ramon as they led the two new horses down a ramp. A scrawny bay gelding resembling an overtrained whippet, and a tall, long-bodied filly with so much blond in her chestnut coat, she almost looked palomino. Amarilla shoved the Jockey Club papers at me, and I put them in the tack room, planning to file them with the track ID man later. I noticed the gelding's registered name was Stinger, the filly's Daffodil.

Amarilla waited outside the gelding's stall. "Stinger, he run on opening day. You are prepared?"

I blinked. Opening day was Sunday, entry day for Sunday races had been two days earlier. Who had entered the horse? Not Jim, I would have known. "Are you sure?"

"Am I sure?" Her scornful eyes slid over me. "Of course. I entered the horse."

Without asking the trainer? Oh boy, a runaway owner. "Did you draw in?"

"What you mean?"

An ignorant runaway owner. "Look, just because you entered doesn't mean the horse got in. There's only 14 slots in a race. Suppose 19 or 20 horses entered? He might not draw in at all, or wind up 'also eligible.'"

I hated being also eligible. You had to wait another two or three days for "scratch time," then if someone else withdrew their horse you might draw in late.

Armarilla made an irritated gesture with her hand, sending a waft of delicate perfume over. "So, Miss-know-everything, he get in?"

How the hell would I know? I held up my finger in a "just-a-minute" sign and marched down the shedrow, through the middle and over to the far side of our barn looking for trainer Lilly Best who I'd met that morning.

An attractive, substantial blonde, she hefted a last bale of hay onto a stack against the wall. She still had a copy of the old "overnight." Racing offices print these sheets soon after they finish drawing entries for a given race day. I ran my finger down the page, ignoring the turf and filly races and found the dirt-race with Stinger's name listed, the fifth race.

He'd drawn the four hole in a field of nine. Amarilla hadn't named a jockey. I'd look the horse over. If he appeared sound and ready to run, I'd name myself on as jockey, otherwise I'd scratch him. I almost shuddered at the thought. She'd be so mad she'd probably sting me to death.

I went back, told her the horse was in, asked for her phone number, then got busy with the rake. Fortunately, she didn't like the dust it stirred up and got in her Caddy and left.

What with Bunny and her dolls the night before, not to mention the dead body on the road, I had a hankering for my favorite toddy — bourbon, with hot tea and honey. After meeting our waspish new owner, I considered a bottle of medicinal booze in the cottage pantry a necessity, only I hadn't seen a liquor store since arriving. Being a Maryland girl, this fact seemed odd. In Laurel, just about every other street corner flaunted a liquor store. Usually had those machines for purchasing tickets from the state-run lottery too.

Seemed odd the activists and state legislators so against slot machines at the Maryland racetracks didn't complain bitterly about the practice of selling lottery tickets in the booze shops. Friday afternoons, the places were crowded with men sitting in cars drinking out of brown paper bags, lines from the lottery machines almost out the door, paychecks vanishing...

A bright blue Mini Cooper bumped along our side road, interrupting my thoughts. A nifty painting of the British flag decorated the top of this tiny car. Will Marshall eased the Cooper to a stop near where I stood outside Stinger's stall. Short, wiry and fit, he sprang from the car like a jack-in-the-box.

We exchanged hellos and I took him on a brief tour of our shedrow, telling him about Amarilla and asking where I could find some whiskey.

"Don't you know Virginia doesn't have liquor stores?" His green eyes glowed with amusement.

"That's ridiculous, of course they have liquor stores."

"They have state run ABC stores — alcoholic beverage control. But you can get beer and wine at the grocery store."

"Bourbon," I said.

"Go for it. But good luck, cause I've never seen a package store around here, and it'll cost you a lot more in Virginia, too."

I decided New Kent County was not my favorite place. And why was Will staring at me?

"You doing anything later?" His words were quick, like someone diving into cold water.

"Yes," I said. "Looking for booze." Was he asking me out? I'd never thought of Will that way. He felt more like a distant relative. Besides, I was taller than he was. But he did have that nice face, honed, handsome, almost ascetic.

"Okay, see ya." He climbed into the Cooper and left before I got another word out.

An odd feeling washed over me, like I'd lost something. Hellish pushed her head over her stall door and I automatically moved close, stroking her face, breathing in her rich horse smell. Will Marshall? Nah.

I found Lorna to see if she wanted to join me in my booze quest, but she said she'd hang at the track. I drove to the Kitchen, found an area directory and located a package store at a place called West Point. I climbed back into the Celica, stopping at a gas and food mart, where I bought a map and a chocolate bar.

I sat in the car eating chocolate and figuring a route to the package store, almost 20 miles away. As the chocolate's caffeine and sugar rush hit me, I gave myself a mental admonishment. Entirely too enjoyable, and here I was on the way to buy liquor.

I finished the candy, licking the last traces from my fingers, and suddenly wondered about people who get hooked into darker cravings.

What would it be like to have a need so strong it possessed you? Maybe even consumed your life?

11

Forty minutes and a couple of wrong turns later, I left New Kent County and crossed over the Pamunkey River on Route 30. The town of West Point sat on a peninsula between the Pamunkey and Mattaponi rivers. My map showed the two small rivers flowed together beyond West Point and formed the York River. A cell phone call had confirmed the town's ABC store lay in a strip mall near the bridge.

The area should have been beautiful, but an immense container-board mill squatted on either side of Route 30 as I came down off the bridge. To my left, tall buildings sprouted half-a-dozen stacks pumping gray smoke into the air, the unpleasant odor working its way through my closed car windows. On the right, a gigantic dumping ground of logs, boards and pulp.

With all my sightseeing I almost missed the strip mall entrance. My sharp pull on the steering wheel caused my shoulder bag to slide across the passenger seat and tip its contents onto the floor. My wallet disappeared below the seat.

I refrained from cursing at the inherent perversity of inanimate objects and parked the Celica at the lot's far end, closed in by thick evergreen bushes. Beyond the foliage, a broken-down fence failed to guard the large overgrown backyard of a dilapidated Victorian. Apparently the new strip mall had been plopped down on the edge of an historic neighborhood.

I climbed from the Toyota, wondering how the townspeople could stand the malodorous paper mill. Major job source, no doubt. Moving around to the passenger side, I leaned in and poked around for my wallet, hairbrush and other stuff strewn across the carpeted floor.

Rustling sounds and a disturbance in the brush rushed toward me. I straightened, clutching my wallet. Something jerked me away from the car door and slammed me onto the hood.

"Give me the fucking wallet." Eyes rimmed in red, sweaty face marked with sores and blackened scabs.

I was so scared, lying on the hood under his nightmarish stare, I couldn't move.

"Give it, bitch." He smiled, exposing browning, misaligned teeth that were dying in a bed of corroded and disfigured gums. I gagged at his breath, a chemical, rotten-egg stench. Tried to roll away.

He made a fist, clubbed the side of my face. I rolled with the blow, let go of my wallet and ended up on my palms and knees in front of my car. He stepped around the Toyota and kicked my side. Heavy boot. I went over. *Hurt like hell.*

A car pulled into the lot. I could hear the wheels. I struggled back onto my knees. The creep had my wallet, ripping the cash out as he scrambled away and disappeared through the green bushes. I knelt there a moment, taking inventory. Didn't think anything was broken. My neck hurt. The side of my face where he'd smacked me felt hot and sore. His boot had smashed my right hip and the pain was heating up.

"Jesus, lady, are you all right?" A man, eyes wide, with one of those little manicured beards on the end of his chin, stared at me.

"I think so. Guy mugged me." I rubbed at my neck, the oily scent of tar rising where the afternoon sun had warmed the asphalt. "You see him?"

"Saw something running through that fence, into that yard there. He have a blue jacket?"

"Yeah" The word came out a slow sigh. "That was him. Think he dropped my wallet after he took the cash. Could you —"

"I'm on it." The guy moved quickly, finding my wallet, then the keys, locking the car. He helped me into the store, where a double-wide, dark-skinned ABC clerk worked her way from behind the counter and fussed over me. She sent a younger woman into a back room for a chair and some ice wrapped in a towel. I sat on the chair pressing the cold towel against my face. Around me, the store was immaculately clean, spacious and well lit.

The clerk clutched the phone as she explained about the mugging to the 911 dispatchers.

"I've been telling you people we have some rough types been hanging around here." She was almost yelling into the phone. "This poor girl looks half beat to death."

I realized she was talking about me.

She listened a minute, then said, "All right. Just get an officer over here." She slammed the phone down. "Those paper-mill dope heads been hanging around here for months. I've called the police and —"

My rescuer with the little beard slid some bottles of Scotch on the counter, then cut his eyes to me. "You want a mini bottle of something? Gin? Maybe some liqueur?"

I shook my head and everything hurt. Maybe I should ask about a bathroom, find a mirror, clean up my face. I had some burns on my palms where I'd landed so hard on the pavement. Bits of asphalt peppered the flesh.

"You got a mini bottle of Wild Turkey 101?" I asked.

"Sure do," the big woman said. "But I can't let you drink it in the store." She paused a moment, then held up a paper coffee cup. "But if you was to take this cup and this little bottle and go into our ladies' room back there, don't suppose anyone would be the wiser. Cops never get here'n less than 10 minutes."

She dropped one of those tiny airline-size bottles into the paper cup. "On the house."

Little Beard walked it over, opened the bottle and poured the amber liquid into the paper cup. He breathed in the rising vapors. "Huh. Gonna have to buy this stuff."

I stood up carefully, gasping from the pain in my hip. I took the bourbon, and the younger woman showed me to the restroom in the back. Utilitarian and clean, it had a shelf over the sink I could set my cup on.

I stared in the mirror. The right side of my face had swollen into a purplish red blossom. Some filling had settled under my right eye, the color a shade darker than my bruised cheek. I unfastened my jeans, and pulled them down just enough to see my hip.

"Very nice," I said, inspecting the damage.

More of the same bruising and swelling. I made no attempt to fasten up the jeans. It would hurt too much. I grabbed the cup, poured in a finger of water and drained it empty. Closed my eyes, and waited a few beats.

I washed my palms with warm water and soap. Stung like hell. Zipped up and moved slowly from the restroom back to the cashier counter. I could hear a siren in the distance.

* * * *

Officer Delmot, of the King William County police department, sat on the bench seat of his police cruiser finishing up the mugging report. He asked me a couple more questions about the guy who'd assaulted me, then set his clipboard down and shifted in his seat so he faced me.

The bridge of his nose appeared to have been broken at some point and weariness dragged at his face. But his brain worked fine and his voice was crisp.

"The description you gave me of the assailant is textbook methamphetamine addict. The teeth and gums in particular. We call it meth mouth."

My fingers traced the swelling on my face. "He had so many sores." An involuntary shudder rippled through me.

"Those people, they pick at those scabs. Can't leave themselves alone, think they have bugs under their skin. One guy down here had to have his arm amputated, he'd gotten it so infected." He paused, drawing in a breath. "Miss Latrelle, I know you had an unpleasant experience. But consider yourself lucky."

Delmot seemed to focus on something in the distance I couldn't see. "You saw his teeth. Meth addicts smoke the stuff, corrode their teeth. When they're high, they're wired in a way you and I can't begin to understand. Grinding their teeth to stubs while believing they're king of the world."

He pulled some mint Lifesavers from his shirt pocket. Offered me one, which I took. He peeled the foil and paper back to expose a second one for himself.

"When they come down, they're depressed, exhausted. Guy hit you, probably wanted money for another pipeful. Doesn't cost much, but meth addicts aren't exactly adept at holding down a job. You're lucky Mr. Hethmink drove into the lot when he did."

So that was Little Beard's name. Officer Delmot had taken him aside in the ABC store, questioned him, while I sat in my chair wishing I could have another shot of Wild Turkey. Wishing I could go home to my apartment in Laurel.

"You going to be all right driving back to Colonial Downs?"

I told him I would and picked up my tote bag, glad I'd had my Master Card to purchase the fifth of Wild Turkey nestled in my bag along with the cashless wallet. I didn't want to hear any more about meth addicts.

I eased out of the cruiser, grateful when Delmot watched me until I was safely in my Toyota with the door locked and the engine running. Grateful my worst vice was the occasional one-beer-too-many or a double shot of bourbon.

Memory sliced through me. That burnt out shell, those sores. I yanked the car into drive and headed for Colonial.

12

I dug around in the glove box and found a pair of dark glasses before driving through the Colonial stable gate. Fortunately, the guard was to my left and couldn't see the mess on the right side of my face. The glasses hid the shiner. The Celica's digital clock read 4:30, just about feeding time.

I found Lorna in the dirt-floored feed room studying the sheet I'd pinned to the cork-board, listing which horse got what supplements. She'd already loaded feed into eight buckets and had left a sticky molasses fingerprint on the supplement paper. Without looking at me, she said, "What do you want the Yellow Jacket's horses to have?"

Apparently my nickname had stuck. "Don't let her hear you say that."

"Hey, I'm cool." She gave a little gasp. "What happened to your face?"

I explained about the meth head and found myself studying her reaction, hoping she'd never done speed.

"Bad scene. I saw one of those dudes back when I...before I got clean. Gruesome dude, had all those sores, like you said. People I hung with didn't smoke that stuff. Like smoking death."

I nodded, my gaze dropping to the floor.

"Does it hurt real bad?" Her voice filled with concern, her hands grasping a container of the seaweed supplement, Source.

"I'm okay. Let's finish doctoring up these buckets. We'll feed the two new ones straight grain, check them out afterwards. See what we've got."

We hauled the sweet-smelling buckets, making sure each supplement went to the right horse. Lorna grabbed an armload of buckets leaving me with less to do.

I reached Stinger's stall last. He pinned his ears and snapped at me, his "get away from my food" reaction taking over before I had a chance to give it to him. I got a rake and shook it at him. He backed off, and I dumped the feed in his tub and got out of the way. He dove in and smashed the tub against the wall as he ate.

Lorna's eyes darted between me and the horse as he grabbed the bucket edge with his teeth and tried to rip it off the wall.

"Look at him! And you with that rake. Place looks like a loony-bin."

Stinger lunged at the gate. I hopped backwards, landing on my right foot, stifling a cry from the pain that shot through my hip. I could feel Lorna glance at me, sense the question forming. "The meth head kicked me. And no, it's not broken, and I don't want an X-ray."

Lorna closed her mouth, got the hose and started topping off water buckets, wisely deciding to leave Stinger's for later.

Bobby Duvayne appeared around the corner of the barn's passthrough aisle. The bucket Lorna was filling overflowed, sending sheets of water into Imposter's stall. Lorna's gaze never left Bobby as he walked toward us.

"Lorna! The *water*." I hobbled toward her, but she shut the hose off and took a half step toward Bobby.

"Hey," he said, his voice soft, his attention only for Lorna. "Got some cold beer and a bunch of chicken to grill if you wanna come over to my barn later." He finally noticed me. "You should come — What happened to your face?"

Lorna started to fill him in and I moved away.

"So you want to go over for chicken?" Lorna called to me.

"Yeah. Got some stuff to check on first." I left them and went up to the racing office to see if anyone would let me use a computer to look up Amarilla's horses. I found a parking spot in front of the blue-framed glass door that had a green-and-white "Secretary's Office" sign over it. I dug around in my glove box and found a bottle of Ibuprofen inside and shook out three capsules. Slipping them into my pocket, I headed up the short cement walk. I was in luck. The door wasn't locked, and a lone secretary sat at a desk behind the beige counter plastered with red-and-white NO SMOKING signs. I knew the woman, Dana. She usually worked in the racing office at Laurel.

"Nikki, hi…My God, what happened?"

I was going to have to put a bag over my head. No makeup made could hide the day's damage. I gave her a brief version and asked about the computer.

"Well, we're not supposed to…" She continued to stare at my face, fascinated. "Does it hurt real bad?"

"Yeah, it's pretty bad." I gave her my best forlorn look.

"Come on behind the counter, I'll set you up. What do you need?"

"Brisnet?" I'd used the acronym for Bloodstock Research Information Services.

She brought up the website, and I keyed in Stinger's name on the pedigree page. He was by an obscure stallion, but his dam was by the good Maryland sire, Two Punch, also respected as a sire of mares that produced winners. Other sons and daughters out of Stinger's dam had some wins and appeared to favor the dirt.

Next I opened the past performances page. Stinger's last 10 races were way too close together, with unnecessary morning speed workouts between each one. No wonder the horse looked wrung out. I'd see how he came through the race before talking to Amarilla. Finally, I pulled an early program to see Stinger's odds and who he was up against.

Amarilla had entered him in a forty-thousand-dollar claiming race, meaning Stinger and the other horses listed in this race could be bought, or "claimed," for that amount. Only a licensed trainer or owner with that much cash in their Colonial racing account could claim a horse. Forty thousand was a lot of money, and with Stinger's past performances, I couldn't imagine anyone taking him.

His odds were pitiful. Thirty-to-one longshot. The program listed several good horses. Stinger might beat them. *If they fell down.*

My head began to throb so I went over to the water cooler and downed the Ibuprofen. The scent of chicken, fries and grease worked its way under the swinging doors from the hallway. The kitchen must be cranking up for the dinner crowd. Since vans, grooms and horses had been arriving steadily over the last few days, the Latino family that ran the kitchen would probably have a full house that evening.

I sank back into the computer chair and looked up Amarilla's filly, Daffodil. Her pedigree and race record astonished me. She was by the excellent turf sire, Theatrical, and out of a mare by the Maryland sire, Smarten, another solid stallion whose progeny loved the turf. When I'd seen her, I noticed her long barrel and legs. A big, tall filly, she had the look of a horse that might prefer to run on the grass.

I pulled her last ten starts. A three-year-old, the filly had run eight times, no wins, and every single start on the dirt. What were her handlers thinking? An idiot would know to try her on grass.

"What's wrong?" asked Dana.

I must have groaned. "This horse in my barn, she's bred for the turf. You ever heard of this trainer, Marjolsalina?"

"Margo what?"

"Never mind. Look at the pedigree."

She left her desk and inspected the computer screen from behind my shoulder. "I see your point. Does the owner have a problem with the turf?"

I didn't know, but I needed to find out.

* * * *

A worn gas grill sent a thin plume of steamy smoke into the air by the Duvayne shedrow. The scent of chicken and tangy barbeque sauce drew me across the open ground to our neighboring barn. Several well-used plastic lawn chairs, two coolers and a hay bale draped with a clean white saddle cloth were assembled on the red Virginia clay next to Bobby's barn.

Lorna lounged in one of the chairs drinking a beer. Her jeans encased her legs like a glove, her hooded velour jacket unzipped to reveal a milky curve of breast that swelled from a deep V-neck. Sable sat next to her in a stretchy black tank, despite the cooling temperature. The sun, low in the western sky, cast horizontal rays that reflected off their aluminum beer cans and outlined the muscles beneath the smooth dark skin on Sable's arms.

"Hey lady," said Sable. "Lorna told me you got beat up. You all right?"

"I will be."

Will Marshall, his back to me, faced Bobby who used a long-handled fork to turn the tasty smelling chicken sizzling on the grill. A bowl of red sauce with a brush handle sticking out sat on the ground nearby.

My sharp interest in the food surprised me. Must be a survival thing.

Bobby wore a red apron with black lettering that read, "Riders Do It With Gentle Hands and a Big Stick."

I itched to peek under his apron, a part of me I rarely owned up to.

Will glanced at me without commenting on my face, opened a blue cooler and handed me a beer.

Lorna drained her can and Bobby moved in, pulling another one from the cooler. He popped it, and handed it to Lorna. Stood close, watched her drink it, his leg touching her thigh. Heat in his eyes.

A train wreck waiting to happen. Will caught my eye and shrugged. It was Lorna's call. Maybe all I could do was pick up the pieces.

A plate of baked beans, salad and four chicken thighs later, I lay back in Bobby's plastic chair with my eyes almost closed, trying to ignore my pain and the heat building between Lorna and Bobby. They'd been lounging side by side, their chairs pushed close together.

Sable had left, and now Will stood up, stretched and threw his second and last beer can into the trash barrel. He'd pulled the skin off his chicken, had about a tablespoon of the sugary beans and a lot of salad. His skin was clear and his eyes shone green like the ocean. Must be that healthy diet.

He paused at my chair. "Get some sleep, Latrelle." He dropped his voice. "Maybe get Lorna out of here too."

This broke my lethargy. I straightened up to respond, but Will was already walking away, leaving me keenly aware that three's a crowd.

"Lorna, we should probably get going." I eased out of the chair, careful to put more weight on my good leg.

"I'll bring her home in a little while." Bobby's long fingers were resting on Lorna's shoulder.

"We have to get up pretty early, you should probably come now."

She rolled her eyes, her mouth tightening slightly. "I won't be long."

Bobby stood up, facing Lorna. "Besides, she needs a ride in the Cobra."

He was still wearing his apron, but now he loosened the ties and pulled it off.

With a quick intake of breath, Lorna's eyes widened. Bobby leaned toward her, pulled her out of the chair. Hands on her shoulders, he turned her so she faced away. He pulled her in so her buttocks pressed against the thick bulge in his jeans I'd glimpsed for an instant.

Lorna trembled. I had to get out of there. Leaned over to grab my tote bag, and when I straightened, Bobby's arms encircled Lorna's waist. He kissed her cheek near her mouth.

I could feel the tease in my own body, the desire to turn the mouth and find his lips. She did, and Bobby placed the fingers of one hand lightly on her chin, pulling her mouth closer, sliding his tongue in.

Abruptly, I turned to leave, but a magnetic pull had me and I made the mistake of looking back. Bobby's knowing eyes were on me as he kissed Lorna. A hot rush of desire hit me, and the son-of-a-bitch knew it.

Amused triumph glittered in his brown eyes.

13

I hurried back to my barn, retreating through the middle aisle, relieved at the distance and solid brick walls between me and that sexual quicksand. I leaned against the framed opening to Hellish's stall. As if sensing my poor state she pushed her silky head against my shoulder, and I breathed in that warm, satisfying horse scent. Stroking her velvet muzzle, my fingertips seemed to draw solace from the filly.

How bad could Bobby be? Was I overreacting? Though vulnerable, Lorna was an adult and her sexual adventures were really none of my business. But still…

I got a mental grip, telling myself there'd been too much stress that day. Moved down the row of stalls to the two newcomers, Stinger and Daffodil. I clipped a lead shank to Stinger's halter and led him into the aisle way. The other horses perked up, pushing heads over stall gates, curious. Racehorses don't usually come out in the evening and, being creatures of habit, the gang was eager to know what was going on.

"Just checking out your new buddy," I said. Hellish nodded, no doubt a coincidence. But I'd learned never to be certain of anything with these animals.

The heavy, rumbling purr of Bobby's Mustang rippled the evening air. He must be leaving with Lorna. Trying to ignore the sound, I turned back to Stinger.

The horse stood a little over 15 hands high, small for a Thoroughbred. But a lot of great racehorses had lacked height. The gelding's real problem, in my eye, was his previous trainer wearing him down to a nub. His flanks and belly narrowed and drew up to an extreme. No fire in his tired eyes. His coat could have been glossier. If I hadn't seen his past performances earlier, I'd have had one of the vets look at him.

I'd beef up his feed, add weight and muscle building supplements like creatine. This horse would only jog between now and his race three days away. Realistically there wasn't enough time between now and Sunday to accomplish much change in his condition, but going easy with him might save him from further damage.

I jogged him up and down the shedrow, watched him move, and detected no unsoundness. The rhythm of his clip-clops in the dirt was smooth and even. I still wanted to get on him in the morning, give my body a chance to read the physical nuances before deciding if he should race, but I'd probably run him, ride him myself. I didn't want some hot jockey abusing the little gelding if he got tired in the stretch.

Daffodil was a whole other animal. She had strength, polish, and fire in her eyes, like Hellish. "We're going to put you on the turf, young lady," I said, staring into her liquid brown eyes.

A deep exhaustion settled over me. I left any more decisions about horses for the morning, and headed for the cottage, where I soaked in a hot bath. Above the bathroom window's café curtains, the quarter moon hung over the darkened tree line, the silver slice of evening-pie a bit wider each night in its slow transformation to a harvest moon.

I used a lot of soap and water but couldn't rinse away the memory of the meth addict. His rotten breath, crazy eyes.

Slippers sat on the bathroom floor fascinated by the drops and splashes of bath water. I climbed from the tub and he pounced on a trickle of water pooling on the floor at my feet. I briskly toweled everything not bruised, slathered on some body lotion and found myself thinking about Bobby. A man as addictive as methamphetamine. Was I jealous?

With that thought I trudged to my bedroom and went to bed with the cat.

* * * *

I woke up after midnight thinking I'd heard something. Slippers lay curled in a tight ball at the end of my bed, snoring. I crept from my room, ears strained for a foreign sound. The cottage was empty. Lorna hadn't come back and the quiet seemed almost relentless. I gathered up Slippers and burrowed back into bed, finally falling into a restless sleep.

The rooster went off at 4:35 A.M. Somebody should adjust that bird's timer. Outside my bedroom, I could see Slippers wedged against the cottage door, as if hoping to squeeze through the crack between the door and the frame. Probably wanted to be with his chicken.

I staggered from bed noticing my aches and pains had lessened with sleep, then stilled as I felt the emptiness. I knew without looking that Lorna had never come back, then told myself as long as she showed up for work on time, I wasn't her keeper.

I arrived at the track before six, the air crisp and chill as the moon lowered in the western sky. No sign of Lorna.

Ramon tottered behind a wheelbarrow piled precariously high with dirty straw. "We need help. Too many horses. Lorna not here?"

His barrow hit a bump and a mound of dirty bedding fell to the ground. He muttered something in Spanish. The words were foreign, the meaning clear.

I got the first horse out, a rangy bay mare, put a good gallop in her, cooled her out myself, and rushed to the next horse. Ramon ground through the dirty stalls, stopping to help me tack up a few of the more difficult horses. I rode Stinger out to the track where he balked for a moment at the entrance, but gave in as if he'd accepted resistance was futile.

Something about the horse's hind end felt a bit jammy, but after a quarter mile or so of jogging, he warmed right out of it, the stiffness melting into fluid movement. I kept him at it for a mile, then turned to go in and could almost feel his astonishment at not being pushed to go farther, faster. I took his tack off and cooled him out. Still no sign of Lorna.

I was mad. When the track closed for the half-hour break, I marched across the grass and clover to Bobby's barn. The morning dew left rings of wet on the hems of my jeans. I didn't see the Cobra, but the man who'd argued with Bobby the day before was talking to a track vet whose truck idled nearby. The vet climbed into his truck and left. The man stood watching me as I approached. He appeared close to six feet, was big and beefy, reminding me of a bull. Thick arms and shoulders, and the slightly protruding gut I noticed the day before.

"Hi, I'm Nikki Latrelle. I was looking for Bobby?"

The man hesitated, maybe swallowing a comment about my bruised face. He smiled. "Bobby's not in yet. I'm his dad, John Duvayne."

We shook hands. "What do you want with Bobby?" His voice held a southern drawl with a redneck undertone. His features were coarse. Hard to believe Bobby's refined bones and stunning beauty had sprung from this man.

"He sort of went off with my rider last night, and I need her back."

"Sorry about that, boy's hard to control." Worry appeared in the man's eyes, but his expression suggested resignation. "They should be along soon."

"Her name's Lorna. Pretty redhead. Did you see her last night, or this morning?"

"Bobby has his own apartment over the garage, so I couldn't tell you." He turned, searching for something. Probably any distraction. "Break's almost over, I have to saddle up two horses…"

"Sure," I said. "Me too. And I've only got one rider." The man looked irritated by my retort. Yeah, well too bad.

Next on my list was Hellish and like Stinger, she planted her feet at the entrance to the dirt mile-oval. Only with her it was a "make my day" kind of resistance. She froze beneath me, motionless, tense, an act usually preceding detonation.

"Damn it! I've got four more horses to get out, I'm sore and I don't have time for your shit." I knew better, but whacked her with my crop.

She exploded straight up, all four legs high in the air. When we hit the ground, she bolted onto the track, heading straight for the inside rail, veering away at the last instant. I lost a stirrup and hung to one side, gripping her mane like a lifeline. She plunged her head between her legs, pitched her hindquarters into the air. The ground came at me fast, hard.

I just lay there, not because I was hurt so much as mentally beaten. A man who'd been standing by the rail with a stopwatch ran over to see if I was injured. I sat up, brushing the sandy dirt from my jacket. Told him I was okay and felt tears on my face. An outrider flew by in pursuit of Hellish. *Good luck with that.*

I began the long trip back to the barn, muttering to myself like a deranged bag lady, especially when the track megaphones blared, "Loose horse on the track, loose horse on the, nope, horse is on the grounds. Near the receiving barn."

That meant she'd ricocheted off the track at the other end, near the racing office and the stable gate. I prayed she wouldn't get out on the main road.

Always embarrassing to walk on the track. People stare, they know you got dumped. They're not unkind, just truly glad it was you and not them.

"The horse is contained, the horse is contained."

Relieved, I kept slogging through the heavy shifting sand, and when I finally dragged myself onto our shedrow, Lorna stood there with a big grin on her face.

"Hey doodarina, need some help?"

I closed my eyes, ready to ream her out, only I realized she'd slurred her words. Beer? I peered at her. No, not beer. Her eyes were round and dilated as saucers.

"Lorna, what'd you do last night?"

She smiled a big slow smile, swaying slightly. "Bobby." She glowed with sensuality. "Oh, man. He's awesome."

"I don't want to hear about that. Did he give you drugs?"

"No, wait. L'me tell you. S'got magic hands. Made me…"

Apparently words couldn't describe his abilities. "Lorna —"

"Did me all night long." She shivered at the memory.

"Lorna, shut up!" I glanced at Ramon walking toward us. He didn't need to hear this stuff. She swayed again and Ramon rushed over to steady her.

"*Madre de Dios*. What wrong with her?"

"Too much beer last night," I said quickly. But Ramon shook his head, maybe seeing what I did. And if Ramon could see it, what would happen if security came by on their regular rounds? Lorna was still on probation and if someone like Investigator Cormack saw her, she'd be peeing in a test cup faster than you could say "screw me."

Lilly Best came around the corner leading Hellish. "I got her," she said. "Doesn't seem like she hurt herself. Think she was just having herself a good time."

"Thank you," I said. Lorna started singing some tune with the refrain, "All night long." She stumbled and giggled.

I had to get her off the backstretch. "Ramon, can you put Hellish away and feed? Don't worry about the supplements, just give them grain."

"I can do. But the horses, they not go to track?"

"I can't help that." Jesus, I hadn't gotten Daffodil out, and Imposter stood there waiting patiently for his turn, and another gray mare.

I grabbed Lorna's wrist and dragged her toward my Toyota. "Get in the car."

"But I have to ride, and Bobby's over there. I was gonna —"

"Get in the fucking car!"

14

Lorna's shoulder pressed into the passenger door, her red curls crushed against the window. She'd fallen asleep just outside the stable gate, hardly stirring since. Up ahead, the Cheswick Victorian and the ancient oak growing alongside came into view. The tree climbed to the sky, the leaves dappling green, orange and red as the oak readied for winter. I drove the Toyota under the oak's massive limbs, continuing uphill to the cottage.

"Lorna, wake up. Time to get out."

A plaintive moan, then she seemed to sink into a heavier sleep.

I poked her shoulder. "You've got a bed inside. Come on." I shook her, and not too gently. She grumbled as I pulled her from the car and led her to the cottage. Inside, I guided Lorna to her bed and left her to sleep it off.

In the kitchen, the wall clock's hands crept past ten. No point in rushing back; the track had already closed for training. Good thing Colonial's first races were still two days away. I didn't feel up to selecting and administering pre-race drugs for Stinger, saddling him in the paddock. All that stress. I'd had enough.

I drew a bath, hoping to relax and ease the pain still throbbing in my hip. Soaked there a while, then crawled onto the living room couch, where I must have nodded off. I felt a presence and cracked one eye open. Lorna stood at the end of the couch, her expression wary.

"Guess I screwed up, huh?"

"Pretty much." I sat up, yawning, my glance cutting to the kitchen clock. After one. I'd really passed out.

"Are you, like, gonna turn me in?"

Memories of the morning snapped me fully awake.

"If I was going to do that, I wouldn't have brought you home. Jesus, Lorna. What were you thinking? I had to get those horses out by myself." I took a deep breath. Letting loose a tirade would only make matters worse. "We've got a long meet ahead of us, Lorna. I can't do this by myself. I need to know I can depend —"

"You can, you can. I screwed up last night. Won't happen again." Her fingers jerked and twisted at a lock of hair. Her upper lip quivered.

Jeez, now she was going to cry. "Look, we'll work it out."

She nodded hard and swiped at her eyes. I was trying to think what to say next when my cell rang from the depths of my tote bag. I snatched the bag, rooted around, found the phone, staring at the number. Jim. Probably wanting an update.

"Jim —"

"What the hell's going on? That security guy, Cormack, called me. Said we had a horse loose on the backside this morning. Said he couldn't find anyone but Ramon at the barn. At nine-thirty! Where were you? Who got loose?"

I held the phone away from my ear as Jim's voice grew louder and louder. Lorna, who could hear every word, was hugging herself, her face dismayed. She mouthed, "I'm sorry."

I turned my back on her and started explaining about the mugging and how Lorna'd come down with some kind of flu bug that morning. I hated the excuse and the lie, but the whole truth wouldn't help.

Mollified, but doubtful, Jim said he would drive down the next day. "You still haven't told me what horse got loose."

Cringing. "Hellish."

"That freak. You'd better get her in line, Nikki. Cormack's talking about ruling her off."

"No, he can't!"

"Guess that's up to you. What about this Chaquette woman?"

I gave him a brief account, glad I'd researched the horses and could talk like I wasn't a total screw up, even if I felt like one. Had to do something about Hellish.

"Any chance we could get Mello down here? Ramon's kind of over-loaded now we've got two extra horses."

He waited a few beats. "I can bring Mello down with me. If he'll come."

I could hear a smile in Jim's voice. He knew I wanted Mello because the octogenarian had a magic effect on Hellish, and Jim knew the man would follow Hellish anywhere. Mello had it in his grizzled old head that Hellish was a reincarnation of 1940s champion Gallorette. Instead of insisting Mello was crazy, Jim had offered the mysterious phrase, "Mello knows things." I was still trying to figure out what that meant. Something to do with "second sight."

"See you tomorrow, Nikki." He didn't need to say things had better be ship shape. For Jim, the horses always came first. He'd given me a chance in Virginia, and I'd paid him back by screwing up. My future depended on the stable sailing smoothly forward. I might not get a second chance.

* * * *

We drove in the stable gate at four-thirty the next morning, and went right to work. We dumped the light breakfasts I'd measured up the night before into feed tubs, then scrubbed out water buckets, filling them fresh.

Ramon showed up at five, his eyes widening to see us both so early. Rolling out the wheelbarrow, Ramon and Lorna grabbed pitchforks, working the shedrow, mucking one stall after another. I loaded up the after-training lunch. Thought about Stinger a moment, then added the body-builder creatine, along with electrolytes and other essential minerals.

The excellent airway-opener, Clenbuterol, would probably enhance the horse's performance, but as a restricted medication, its administration had to be stopped four days before he raced. I didn't expect Stinger to end up in the test barn where state officials automatically sent the first and second-place finishers of each race, but in Virginia they had a sneaky habit of drawing in an additional control horse, testing it for drugs too — usually the-favorite-who-ran-amazingly-bad, or the-long-shot-who-ran-shockingly-well.

You never knew for sure, and with my luck they'd pull in Stinger. If he tested positive for Clenbuterol in Virginia, I'd be fined heavily, and given "days." Days I wouldn't be allowed to work or train at the track. Days I'd get no income. Days that would get me fired. If by some miracle the horse won a little purse money, they'd take that away, too.

I put the pricey Clenbuterol back in a locked cabinet. By six, I'd taken Daffodil for a test drive around the shedrow, discovered she had a tender mouth and decided she'd go well on a snaffle bit. Lorna climbed on the patient Imposter, and together we rode the dirt path that wound through the pines to the track entrance nearest our barn.

Daffodil was all class, no questions asked. I put her into a gallop, and she thrilled me. Took her awhile to get those long legs in gear, but once she did she seemed to float across the heavy dirt and sand. Beside us Imposter's hooves churned frantically as he fought to keep up.

Lorna stole a couple of glances. "Wow, is she the real deal, or what?"

Yet I wasn't surprised when after five-eighths of a mile the sink-and-pull action of the deep track began to wear on Daffodil. She struggled for air, losing momentum, confirming my belief she'd prefer the firmer surface of the turf course.

We got seven horses out, leaving Hellish in her stall to think about her evil ways. I'd try her the next day, praying Mello would come and work his magic on her before that. I jogged Stinger a mile and put him away, then hand walked Hellish around the shedrow. Lorna kept glancing at her watch, fidgeting with her hair, asking me more than once what time the boss would arrive.

When Jim showed up around ten, relief settled in as I saw Mello's light brown skin and grizzled mat of hair through the Ford's passenger window. The two men climbed out, Jim tall and stooped, his gray hair covered by the inevitable baseball cap. Mello stood slightly shorter, his frame bent with age.

I snuck a glance at Jim's shaggy brows, a barometer I used to gauge his moods. They didn't look especially thunderous; maybe he'd forgo a lecture. Not that Jim said much. He liked monosyllables. In small doses.

"Miss Nikki." Mello touched his worn felt cap in greeting, then nodded at Lorna and Ramon. A neatly knotted bow tie decorated the collar of his threadbare shirt, the ensemble topped by a shabby jacket, probably manufactured when Gallorette ran in the previous century.

Hellish heard his voice, thrust her head over the stall gate and nickered repeatedly.

A long silence stretched between us until Jim said, "Let me see the new ones."

Lorna's shoulders sagged in relief. Did she think I'd ratted on her? Ramon got busy with the rake. I brought Stinger out first, then Daffodil, explaining my theories, waiting for Jim's comments.

He studied Daffodil a moment as I held her lead shank, then put his hand on the high point of the filly's hip, sliding it down the outline of the long sloping bone. He nodded to himself.

"You've got a good eye, Nikki."

A glow of pride touched me, and I hoped it didn't shine too pink on my cheeks.

"Woman sounds difficult over the phone. Is she?"

"Ms. Chaquette? She's pretty tough."

"Hear she's got money, likes to run her own show." Jim pulled his cap off and ran a hand through his thinning hair, his eyes never leaving Daffodil. "Told me she doesn't like turf racing. Brought her stock up from South America to avoid the grass."

Moron. "Could you talk to her, Jim?"

"Nope, you're in charge."

Oh great. I chirped at Daffodil and put her away. When I came out Jim was talking to Ramon and my peripheral vision caught Mello's red bow tie disappearing into Hellish's stall. How did he know her so well?

Edging over to her gate, I found Hellish with her head stretched over

Mello's shoulder, the old man crooning nonsense. Hellish bowed her neck, using her chin and throat to gently pull Mello into her chest, an action that spoke volumes about trust and love. Me, she barely tolerated. Her brief attention after I'd fled Bobby and Lorna the previous evening was a rare show of affability.

Motion caught my eye. A black SUV rolled to a stop next to Jim's truck. The words "Virginia Racing Commission, Operations and Enforcement" were painted on the side. Broad-shouldered Jay Cormack eased out from behind the wheel, using the running board to help his disproportionately short legs reach the ground.

With that southern drawl I'd heard the day they buried Paco Martinez, he said, "I'm looking for a man goes by the name Mello Pinkney."

He caught my quick glance toward Hellish's stall. What was this about?

Cormack's small legs moved him to Hellish's stall gate faster than I'd thought possible. He peered inside.

"Mr. Pinkney?"

Mello shuffled from the stall. "Yes, sir."

"You working here as a groom?"

Mello's eyes darted from Jim to me, and I didn't know if his trembling hand was age or fear. "Yes sir."

"Mr. Pinkney, you're a convicted felon. Virginia Racing Commission doesn't license employees with priors."

I opened my mouth to protest, but Cormack turned on me. "Miss Latrelle, could I see you over here for a minute?" He motioned me toward his SUV, and after I followed him, lowered his voice so only I could hear.

"You've got a rogue filly on the grounds, and now a convicted felon." The ticking of the vehicle's cooling engine punctuated his words. "Thought any more about what I said outside that church?"

"Not exactly." Hadn't I made it clear I'd never rat on a fellow jockey? What had Mello *done?*

Cormack gave me his best cop stare. It didn't hold a candle to Maryland's chief racing investigator, Offenbach, but unnerved me just the same.

"Now might be a good time for y'all to think hard. I still need information about cheating. Drug abuse."

He hadn't mentioned drugs before. My imagination, or did something beneath the hard facial exterior plead for my co-operation? Maybe he was new to the job, in over his head. My sympathy evaporated with his next words.

"I might forget about your filly running wild yesterday, unsettling people's horses, causing complaints. Might even overlook the old man's conviction...if you was to comply."

"That's blackmail!" My fingernails bit into my palms as heat flushed my face.

Jim, Lorna and Mello stared at us from the barn. Ramon had gotten so busy with his rake he was down at the far end cleaning someone else's shedrow.

A chilly breeze rustled along the gravel path, blowing bits of trash and straw. Cormack leaned over to remove a piece of baling twine that had hooked itself onto one of his highly polished shoes.

"Not blackmail, Miss Latrelle. This is a deal I'm offering you. But if you accept, don't try slackin' on me. I'll *know* it." He made a light whistling sound between his teeth. "You're in a position to help us. Something's going on, something bad."

Mello had moved back to Hellish's stall, and the filly's chin was resting on his shoulder. *Oh, for God's sake.* I turned back to the relentless gaze of the investigator with his soft voice and metal-hard mind. I couldn't see a way out.

"What is it you want me to do?"

15

"First, don't say a word about this to anyone." Cormack's eyes, cold and shallow, flicked over Lorna and Jim where they stood watching us. His cop-stare was improving with use.

Ramon pretended to ignore us from the far end of the barn, and Mello had gone to ground in Hellish's stall.

"You tell 'em," Cormack gestured toward the barn, "I gave you a warning, that Mello Pinkney's conviction is over 60 years old and we're going to ignore it. For now."

Curiosity drove my tongue. "What did Mello do?"

I didn't really expect an answer, but Cormack paused, appeared to consider my question. "Reckon you've a right to know. This was long before my time, back in the forties."

When Gallorette was piling up victories and winning Mello's young heart.

He continued, "Pinkney's father was a sharecropper here in Virginia. The son, Mellonius, you know him as Mello, was up north working at Delaware Park racetrack and Belmont. There was an altercation." Cormack's gaze shifted to the ground. "The landowner killed Pinkney's father. Mellonius retaliated by beating up the landowner."

Who could blame him?

"Property owner was white. Back in those days he wasn't even charged, but Pinkney received an assault conviction."

"That's disgusting. You'd use that as blackmail?" My opinion of Cormack plummeted.

The man astonished me by grinning. "Nah." Then, with an effort, he wiped off the smile, put the cop face back on. "But I will rule off that crazy horse of yours. She could hurt somebody."

This guy's personality was as mismatched as his legs. "Fine. But what am I supposed to do?"

The investigator relaxed a bit, leaned against the hood of his SUV. "What I said before. Keep an eye out for anything peculiar with other riders. Stopping the favorite. Carrying a battery. Anyone appears to be on drugs."

I'd seen a jockey or two pretend to ride-out the favorite when in reality he had a stranglehold on the reins. But the stewards usually caught it if they reviewed the race film carefully. Or if someone gave them a tip. I'd never seen anyone with a "battery," a small device like a miniature cattle prod used to make a loser win. Of course, that was the idea. You weren't supposed to see it. How would I…then the obvious hit me.

"I don't have access to the male jocks' room. I won't know what's going on in there." The cold breeze picked up again as a cloud scudded across the sun, darkening the stable area. I fumbled with my zipper, trying to close my jacket.

Cormack's lips compressed into a dismissive line. "I know that. But we have more girl riders each year. I need to keep tabs on everyone."

So, he had a spy among the guys already. Of course he did.

"And Ms. Latrelle, keep an eye out for anyone in trouble."

"In trouble?"

"You know, like the Martinez boy."

An increasing chill prickled at my hands and face. I shivered, pushing away the memory of Paco collapsed in that hallway. "I'll do what I can. Could I ask you a question?"

He rubbed his forehead, squeezed his eyes shut a moment, then nodded.

"Lorna and I got here Tuesday evening and set up the shedrow. We drove out of here after nine, and there were police all over the road. We saw a body, saw the guy's face." I paused. "It was horrible, like melted wax. Was that someone from the track?"

Cormack straightened. Worked his lower lip between his teeth. "Police think it's a murder victim. Someone dumped the body. Maybe drug related. Victim's still unidentified. Management's hoping it wasn't anyone from here." He stared off toward the horizon a moment. "Now let me ask you a question. Who clocked your face?"

I'd almost forgotten how I looked. The swelling had gone down and it didn't hurt much. I told him about the mugging, and his teeth got going on his lower lip again.

"Methamphetamine's a nationwide problem," he said. "Got it here in southern Virginia." He exhaled slowly. "You say that man's face looked like it melted?"

When I nodded, he said, "Might have been a lab fire. These people cook up pseudophed with some nasty chemicals to produce meth. Stuff's real volatile. Blows up, torches everything in its path. Local county hospitals get a lot of burn victims. Most of 'em don't have insurance. Gets real messy."

A Dumpster truck lumbered toward us, heading for a nearby manure container. The engine whined as the driver reversed, grinding the rig back, stopping inches from the metal container and slanting the truck bed to the ground. The driver hopped from the cab, hooked the winch cable to a loop on the nose of the container, then climbed back in the truck. With metal shrieking, and gears moaning, the machine dragged the container onto the truck.

Cormack gazed at the bare spot where the container had been. "Too bad law enforcement can't use one of them things to clean up the meth problem." He rubbed at the corner of one eye and yawned.

In the colder air, a hot fetid steam had begun to rise from the rotting manure. The driver shifted into gear, the truck lurched forward, and just like that, the whole smelly mess disappeared around the corner.

Something tugged at my peripheral vision. Bobby Duvayne walking along the shedrow toward Lorna. He'd pulled his glossy brown hair into a ponytail, enhancing the finely molded bones of his face. A beaded woven-leather strip adorned his neck. Faded blue jeans hugged his long muscular legs. I felt like whimpering.

When I glanced at Cormack, his eyes were studying the newcomer. Bobby spoke to Jim and shook my boss's hand. Lorna, practically vibrating with excitement, stepped closer to Bobby, touching his arm, then his hand like she couldn't stop.

Cormack shook his head.

"What?" I said. "Is there something we should know about him?"

"Tell your girl there to be careful." A deep weariness appeared in the investigator's eyes as he sighed. "Police think young Duvayne might have some connection to a multiple homicide happened a while back."

"Homicide?" Oh, God.

"The way I heard it, two friends of his were killed. Duvayne might've been at the scene or know what happened. But he's never talked. Police think the murders were drug related."

Why didn't that surprise me?

Cormack pulled out a slim leather wallet and a pen. His manicured fingers selected a business card. "This is my private number." He scribbled it down. "Far as anyone's concerned — and especially young Duvayne over there — we've been discussing your filly and Pinkney. You got that?"

His words faded against the noise inside my head. *Homicide.* The question wouldn't wait. "Who was killed?"

But I already knew the answer and felt a dizzying surge of panic.

"Cheswick boys." He pushed his card at me. "You're staying in the cottage where they used to live."

16

Sitting in a blue side-chair in the women's lounge, I struggled to pull on my paper-weight racing boots and suppress mental questions about Bunny Cheswick's boys. I squeezed the second boot over my heel, staring at the spacious and comfortable jockeys' quarters.

In September of 1997 a group of Virginia horsemen had won hard-fought legislation to return pari-mutuel wagering and live racing to the Commonwealth. By that time, women jockeys had come a long way. When Diane Crump rode that first race at Hialeah back in 1969 she'd been forced to change in the public ladies' room nearest the paddock.

Whoever designed the Virginia track had acknowledged women riders weren't going away. Instead of the narrow lockers I struggled with at the older Maryland tracks, Colonial's large dressing room had a long wall of pale blue dressing cabinets, each with a rod for hanging clothes, a large well-lit mirror, and a counter with cabinets underneath. The clutter of shampoo, cans of mousse, moisturizers and a pink cosmetic bag might seem incongruous with the tough sport of race riding, but we were female and needed our hair products.

I slipped on Amarilla's silks, closing the Velcro strip down the front before tucking them into my white nylon breeches. The body or "jacket" of the silks was a rich brown, the sleeves and collar an iridescent yellow. The program described the knifelike design stitched at chest level as "crossed gold swords." Looked more like yellow-jacket barbs to me. My riding helmet, snug in a matching yellow cover, lay on a wood table next to me. I poked a finger at the brown pompom adorning the top.

Over the outside loudspeaker I heard the track announcer calling the fourth. My race would be soon. Ready or not, Sunday had come at me like a church collection plate, and I had to give Stinger what I could. Saturday evening I'd studied tapes of his last few races, noticing his habit of gunning to the lead early, then burning out in the stretch. I'd have to see if I could get him to relax and save some fuel for the finish.

Kim Kravel, and another rider I didn't know, came into the lounge giggling and carrying paper sacks from the jock room's kitchen.

"Hey, Nikki," Kim said. "You in the fifth?"

I nodded and pulled my helmet closer to make more room for the two women as they sat at the table next to me, pulling sandwiches, drinks and napkins from their brown bags.

"Didn't you have one in the first?" I asked Kim.

Her freckled face lit up. "Yeah, horse named Will Not Be Denied."

"And he *wouldn't*," Kim's companion said.

"You won?"

Kim swallowed a bite of turkey-on-rye. "Yeah, he…"

A taller, bony girl wrapped in a damp green towel walked from the shower area at the room's other end. Her dark hair hung in a wet mat about her shoulders. Susan Stark.

I hardly recognized her and wondered if her appearance had quieted Kim. "Painfully thin" would be an understatement. Her cheekbones looked sharp enough to cut bread.

Kim stared, a smoldering anger heating her eyes. "You almost cost me the win, Stark."

The skeletal girl wrapped her towel tighter, glaring at Kim. "My horse drifted. Sorry if he got in your way."

She didn't sound sorry, and I hoped a fight wasn't brewing. I put my hands on the edge of the table. Never hurts to be ready to go.

"Had a hole big enough to drive the starting gate through, and you fucking blocked it. I had to go five wide. You cost me a lot of ground, and I know why."

Stark's dark eyes cut to the floor. She turned and moved toward her dressing cabinet.

But Kim had just gotten started. "You're so starved you couldn't even steer the damn horse. If you want to kill yourself, that's your business, but stay the hell out of my way!"

"Easy, Kim," I said.

"Well she shouldn't have gotten in my way." But her voice had softened to a grumble.

Stark swung a cabinet open, snatched a carryall, then slammed the door shut. She didn't say anything else. She grabbed a hairbrush from her bag, but her hand trembled and she dropped the brush, then had to steady herself on the counter after leaning over to grab it from the floor.

Weak and thin. Anorexia, or were drugs involved? The girl was in trouble. Should I tell Cormack? He could still rule Hellish off and make trouble for Mello.

"If you're in the fifth, you'd better get a move on." Kim pointed at the wall clock.

My fingers worried Amarilla's pompom as a rush of race nerves punched my stomach. I'd probably never be anointed with one of those slick names like "The Ice-woman," or "Cool Hands Nikki." Still, I needed to stay focused. I took a long slow breath, then dashed for my tube of gel, and slicked back my short, spiky hair in less than five seconds.

I slid my helmet on, locking my hair in place. I'd have a nasty case of helmet head later, but no stray strands would whip my face in the meantime. I bolted from the ladies' lounge into the main hallway, where three guys riding in the fifth headed for the paddock.

Outside, the previous day's cold front had left the air crisp. Breath steamed from the nostrils of a big bay that marched past, dragging his groom around the oval paddock. I glanced at the four horses already circling. Stinger and Ramon hadn't come in yet.

Amarilla Chaquette stood in the grassy center with a tall, flamboyant man who smoked a brown-and-white pipe decorated with carved ivory curlicues. Amarilla and her companion wore brown felt hats sprouting canary-yellow feathers, the style suggesting an Alpine shopping spree. The colors woven through the man's richly-textured tweed complemented Amarilla's flame-gold velvet suit worn beneath an ankle-length fur vest.

"Just taking in the scenery, or riding the four horse?" Will Marshall had pushed through the door behind me.

"That's the owner, the woman with the big sunglasses."

Amarrilla's pipe-smoking companion turned sideways, revealing a magnificent belly. As he marched across the manicured lawn to speak with another man, Pipe Man's stomach extended so far ahead it appeared to be leading him.

"Somebody should put a leash on that thing!" Will said.

I snickered, then noticed Pipe Man speak to a tall guy who looked familiar. Their conversation appeared urgent. Then I remembered, Chuck Cheswick, our landlord. The father of the murdered boys.

Ramon led Stinger into the paddock, and my attention narrowed to a pinpoint. I could almost feel the horse's anxiety. The way the veins popped on his skin told me his heart pounded as wildly as his eyes stared. The little gelding knew he was going to run.

I hurried over to stall four, where Lilly Best, who'd offered to help out, stood waiting for the valet to bring the saddle and girth.

"Little nervous," she said, eying Stinger as Ramon led him past.

"I think he hates the whole business. Owner put him in. What he needs is a rest."

Lilly nodded.

All nine entrants had arrived and were parading around the paddock. Across the grass oval, a crowd crushed against the railing, intent on Daily Racing Forms, track programs, cups of beer and the horses. A small child waved his arms and crowed from the shoulders of a man, causing a horse to skitter sideways.

Amarilla had joined Pipe Man, who appeared to speak sharply to Cheswick. My landlord rushed away toward the grandstand, his long stride appearing ungainly as if the length of his legs had forced his hip joints to work too hard for too many years. The paddock judge called, "Put your horses in," and the grooms began to lead the animals into the saddling enclosures. Though cranked, Stinger kept a tight lid on as he stepped into his slot. Two doors down, a flashy looking gray reared, then kicked the stall wall, the crack loud and ringing. From the grass, Amarilla stared at me as if I'd committed a crime. What was her problem?

The valet showed up, and he and Lilly smoothed the folded saddle towel onto Stinger's trembling back, placing a rubber pad and my tiny saddle on top.

"This girth's too big." Lilly glared at the valet. "Get a smaller one."

The man dashed toward the jocks' room, and my stomach did a lovely series of flips. No pressure here.

Somehow, they got the horse saddled in time for the paddock judge's call of "Riders up!" and before I knew it, I was out on the track moving Stinger into a gentle warmup.

As the race was a six-furlong sprint, the tractor had pulled the starting gate to a point exactly three-quarters of a mile before the finish line. From the paddock I jogged Stinger the wrong way, heading backwards up the home stretch, keeping the gate far away, catty-cornered across the mile-oval. Stinger didn't need to be confronted with the rattling steel monster any sooner than necessary. I listened to his body. He seemed fluid enough, but I still wondered why Amarilla had entered him in such a competitive race.

When a horse runs for a $40,000 claiming tag, there's bound to be some good horses in there with him. The two and the eight were co-favorites. Neither had run for a tag before, their past performances listing only non claiming or "allowance" races. In the track vernacular, these two were "dropping down."

The two horse, the flashy gray, floated by us on long loose legs. He carried a healthy amount of flesh and a gleaming eye. The ever changing numbers on the tote board declared him the favorite. I searched the field and spotted the eight horse, now picked to run second. A sturdy bay, so dark he appeared black. Damn, he looked good, too. I patted Stinger's neck.

Will came alongside on the six horse, an unassuming bay with dull past performances. "Can your horse run?" he asked.

"Not really," I said. "What about him?"

"Like a potted plant." He booted the horse into a slow gallop and left us behind.

"Come on, Stinger. Let's get this over with."

The assistant starters loaded us up fast. One horse tried to bust out of his stall, others thrashed about. When it grew quiet, the starter hit the switch. The gate crashed open.

Stinger was out of there quick as a wink, rushing for that early lead. We lay about fourth. I took a long, slow hold and steered him over toward the rail, neatly covering him up with the front runners, leaving him nowhere to go. Relax, little dude.

We raced down the backstretch and headed into the turn. Some of the riders started making moves. No whips, just more body action, arms, backs and seats pumping the horses. The gray moved alongside me, crowding me into the rail. I sat chilly, asking for restraint, and Stinger listened, allowing the favorite to go by. I waited. Then waited some more.

We were through the turn, at the top of the stretch, lying about sixth, when I asked him. Stinger turned on the speed, rushing to the heels of the gray just ahead. I planned to use the favorite and hoped he'd live up to his short odds. He did, shoving his head into a nonexistent hole next to the rail, hammering through it. Mental "*Yes!*" as Stinger drafted in his wake.

We'd saved ground, and I still had some horse under me. We lay second, the wire coming at us fast. I asked Stinger for more, but the gray opened up, leaving us behind. The black horse loomed in my peripheral vision. No! My hands and legs got busy scrubbing Stinger out. He dug in, holding head-and-head with the black for a few strides, but at the wire the second-favorite shoved his head forward, leaving us third by a whisker.

Damn. We almost had the place. But hey, we were supposed to be last. I eased Stinger, slowing to a canter as Will and his potted plant caught up with us.

"How'd you manage that, Latrelle?"

I just grinned, too busy sucking air to say anything. Wasn't every day a plan worked so well. I really had Stinger's number. I pulled him down to a jog and turned toward the waiting grooms.

Amarilla stood behind the rail, near Ramon, her eyes boring into me. What kind of trouble was I in this time?

17

Ramon held Stinger while I dismounted. He'd dressed up to bring the horse over for the race, wearing a crisp white shirt, neatly pomaded hair, and pants as tight and black as a matador's.

"This horse, he run a little, no?"

"Yeah, he can." I loosened the girth and pulled the saddle from Stinger, who tried to scratch his sweaty head against Ramon's shoulder. The poor horse had been running steadily for almost two years. Who knew what he might do with some time off? I searched for Amarilla's yellow velvet, but the woman had disappeared. I needed to find her, convince her about Stinger. Daffodil, too.

"Excuse me, Ms. Latrelle?" A small man with wet lips and a false smile stood next to me. He clasped his palms, as if in supplication. "The Baron and Ms. Chaquette would like you to join them for a drink in the Baron's suite."

I stared at the guy a moment, taking in his pointy nose, weak chin, and the way he fluttered like a baby bird. The word flunkey came to mind. He was probably over thirty, but I worried he might cry if I declined his invitation.

"Sure, I guess. After I change." And do something about the helmet head.

"Wonderful, wonderful," he said, rubbing his hands together. "Take the elevator to the fourth floor. Ask for the Baron's suite. They'll know who you mean." He nodded several times as if agreeing with himself, then scuttled off. His diminutive form disappeared into the crowd.

"That man, he loco." Ramon twirled an index finger near his temple before leading Stinger away.

I double-timed it back to the dressing room and took a quick shower, glad I'd brought a decent pair of black pants and a nice pink sweater. I fluffed my short layered hair, grabbed my makeup case and swiped on some mascara. Stared at the other tubes and compacts. Nah, took too much time.

The sixth race went off as I walked through the grandstand's ground floor. I passed through the crowds swirling around betting windows, banks of simulcast monitors, and fast food take-out stands. Gamblers who'd laid money on the sixth pressed close to the monitors, their voices rising, urgent and excited as the horses rocketed around the track outside.

"Bring him home, Jose!"

"Come on two, come on two, come on and bring me the money!"

The air around me tightened. On the monitor, the horses had reached the top of the stretch.

A man snapped his fingers, his body weaving in time as he called for his pick.

A woman in a short red skirt started shrieking, "Do it Iron Man, do it!"

Jeez, sounded like she was having sex. The finger snapping grew louder, the voices rose to nonstop yelling as the horses tore down the stretch to the wire.

During those last seconds, the losers filled my ears with shouts of disappointment and anger. The few who'd gotten lucky were delirious, intoxicated with winning.

The way the woman in the red skirt screamed and threw herself at her male companion, I didn't have to look at the monitor to know who'd won. I hoped for her companion's sake he could perform as well as Iron Man.

Up ahead, elevator doors slid open. I made a dash for them, busting inside before they closed. The other two passengers needled me with irritated looks before they got off at the third floor. The elevator rose to the fourth and tricked me. The two doors making up the back wall of the elevator opened onto a foyer and left me facing backwards. *Stupid elevator.*

Beyond the foyer, a handsome wood bar dominated the center of a large, crowded room. Waiters ferried trays of drinks to the tables and chairs spread about the dining area. The scents of grilled steak, beer, and freshly sliced lemons-and-limes mingled in the air.

A maroon carpeted corridor, lined with doors to what must be the suites, stretched to my left and right. I moved to the left, read the nameplate on the wall next to the first door. Virginia Thoroughbred Association.

"Ah, Ms. Latrelle. Come, come." The little man scurried toward me from a few doors down, motioning with a flapping hand. "They're waiting for you." His soft dark hair, cut in short layers, reminded me of feathers.

I followed him down the hall. Inside the suite, Amarilla held court in a yellow velvet jacket and pencil skirt. Her fur vest draped the back of a nearby chair. She sipped a martini and spoke to a woman with salon-blond hair in a snappy black-and-white knit. A cloud of smoke circled next to the sliding glass doors that opened onto a balcony overlooking the track. The Baron puffed his pipe and listened to a craggy-faced man with tortoiseshell glasses. A NO SMOKING sign hung on the wall next to them.

About ten people stood with drinks or small plates of food in the rectangular room. Framed prints of racing scenes decorated beige walls. An upscale crowd, men in sharp suits, thin women coiffed, perfumed and dressed in expensive outfits.

The little man clapped his hands. "Your attention, please." His eyes darted about until the room grew silent. "Miss Nikki Latrelle."

Everyone stared. I felt like Cinderella at the ball, only without the gown. Wished I'd taken the time to use the tubes and compacts.

"Nikki." Amarilla's brilliant smile warmed her eyes, finally allowing her beauty to surface. *Now*, I could picture that face on a magazine cover.

"Everyone," she said, "this is the jockey!"

In response, there were smiles, murmurs and one woman actually applauded. Had they watched the wrong race?

"I have told everyone here," said Amarilla, "this is Stinger's best race in quite some time. I am very pleased." She turned to the little man. "Pemberton, see to her drink." Then she turned back to the salon-blond.

I told Pemberton I'd take a bourbon and water. I needed one.

The little man minced to the bar near the entry door, spoke to the bartender and motioned me over. "Don't mind her. Spoiled rotten. Extreme beauty, you know."

"You work for her."

"Heavens no." He rolled his eyes. "I work for the Baron. I'm his... secretary."

More like lapdog, but the guy was being nice to me and I liked him for that, even if his spice-based cologne made my eyes water.

"Your drink." He thrust an icy glass into my hand. "Allow me to introduce you to the Baron. It's Baron von Waechter." He paused and gave me a look to make sure I listened, then pressed his palms together. "Helmut Vindenberg Stahlkaur von Waechter."

Sounded like a mouthful of rocks. Was I supposed to be impressed?

"You don't know the name? Oh dear. A very, very important man. A German *baron*. Owns the most prestigious stud farm in Virginia." He cocked his head, as if listening to an imaginary flourish of trumpets. "And the company, Gilded Baron?"

"Sorry, haven't heard of it." Never heard of the stud farm either.

"Surely you know the famous bourbon distillery?" Pemberton's eyes rolled. "It's what you're drinking!"

I'd had better bourbon. This was loaded with sugar, covering a raw under-taste. I raised my brows, parted my lips. "Yeah. Wow. Can't wait to meet him."

Pemberton ushered me over to the baron, made introductions, and scuttled away. I shook the big man's hand, trying not to choke on the cloud of smoke gushing from his nostrils. Silver haired, he had gray-blue eyes the color of a glacier hanging over the ocean.

"Miss Lotwall, you have made our Amarilla quite happy."

"I'm glad she's pleased," I said, ignoring his mutilation of my name. Were Amarilla and the Baron an item? The man's full sensuous lips spoke of appetites, but his ponderous belly suggested they were mostly for food and drink.

No time like now. I plunged in. "Stinger has some speed. He just needs to build up stamina, maybe have some time off. Now, Daffodil, she should be ferocious on the turf, and —"

"Ah, yes," he said. "You like the bourbon? It's Senator Vandergraft's favorite."

I'd stopped at the first over-sweet sip. "Oh, it's…wonderful."

Pemberton materialized nearby. Had an unseen signal passed between them? The little man's monkey-hand latched onto my wrist as another pungent cloud of smoke spewed out the Baron's nose.

"Why don't we speak to Ms. Chaquette about the horses?" Pemberton said, turning me to face the front of the room.

"A pleasure to meet you," I called over my shoulder. The Baron dismissed me with an abrupt nod.

Pompous ass. Amarilla sat next to her fur vest talking to a short-haired brunette wearing brilliant diamond earrings. The ex-model held a fresh martini with two empties on the table. Maybe she'd downed enough that I could talk her into running Daffodil on the turf, convince her to give Stinger a rest.

Pemberton pulled out a chair and I sat opposite Amarilla at the round table.

"Oh, you're still here?" Amarilla asked.

The shorthaired woman extended her hand to shake mine. "Katherine Crosby," she said. Up close she had shrewd eyes. "Liked the way you used the favorite in that race. Nice riding." She glanced at Amarilla. "Girl knows what she's doing."

I'd been handed a golden opening and dove in. "Ms. Chaquette, I wanted to talk to you about Daffodil and Stinger."

The smoky eyes narrowed, the lips compressed. "What about them?"

Katherine sat back, lit a cigarette and watched with interest.

"Your filly's got turf written all over her," I said, leaning forward, warming to the subject. "Her pedigree alone —"

"No. You are the assistant trainer. You do not decide."

Her response seemed to amuse Katherine, who took a long pull on her cigarette, then exhaled. The smoke drifted past one cheek, curling around a diamond earring before dissipating in the air.

She tapped ash into a dish. "What does the trainer say?"

"Jim Ravinsky? He agrees with me." I directed my words to Amarilla. "Filly's built for the turf."

"Is the Kentucky Derby run on the turf? No. The New York Filly Triple Crown? No. They are not. Good horses run on the dirt."

She said it with such finality, I swallowed an immediate retort. Ignorant woman. After the animal's care, the first rule is to run a horse where it can win. Amarilla's tunnel-vision irked me.

"She's 0-for-8 on the dirt, building up a terrible record," I said. "She's devaluing her future as a broodmare."

Katherine leaned forward, her eyes lit with anticipation.

"You dare to argue with me?" An ugly scowl darkened Amarilla's beauty. She jabbed a sharp, red fingernail at me. "You. Do not. Ever. Do that again. You understand me?"

The room had grown quiet. Eyes were on us. Like a big ship, the Baron steamed toward us.

"Amarilla, dearest, what has upset you so?"

"The young woman does not know her place," Amarilla folded her arms across her chest.

Had I landed in some alternate universe? What was wrong with these people? The Baron was as phony as his lousy bourbon and Amarilla had such delusions of grandeur I almost felt sorry for her. Almost.

I stood up, shoving the chair back. "You know what? I'm gonna check on Stinger. He just ran his heart out for you, lady. You've run the poor horse half to death. He needs a break."

"You're dismissed." Amarilla's voice, shrill and loud.

"She means you're fired," Katherine said, a gleam in her eye. "At least for today."

"Fine!" I said and marched out the door.

18

Dense clouds crept over the backstretch, shutting out the late afternoon sun, drawing the dark in early. A damp chill saturated the air, promising rain as I drove toward our barn.

Lorna, who'd watched my race on the kitchen monitor, stood waiting for me to park the Toyota. She came over, looking for a high-five.

I didn't have one to give her.

"What's your problem?" she asked. "That little dude really rocked. If that Yellow Jacket hadn't worn him down to a nub, he could've won the thing!"

"That Yellow Jacket just fired me."

"No way. Is she crazy?" Lorna's gold brow ring disappeared into her curly bangs.

"What am I going to tell Jim?" I kicked a stray bucket. "Amarilla's such a bitch."

Lorna wanted the details and I poured them out.

"Oh, man, you're gonna lose Daffodil?"

I nodded, once again envisioning that classy blond horse flying down the lane on the turf, sailing under the wire well ahead of the pack, winning big. Wasn't meant to be.

Mello ambled around the corner of the shedrow leading Stinger, whose head hung low. Fortunately, the octogenarian holding the horse's lead shank rarely managed more than a fast shuffle. Mello wore a bright green bow-tie with his shabby suit-jacket. The skin around his eyes crinkled like mahogany-colored leather.

"How is he, Mello?" I said, stepping into the shedrow for a closer look.

"He be fine. You in trouble again, Miss Nikki?"

Lorna and I exchanged glances. Either the track grapevine moved excessively fast at Colonial, or Mello really did have a sixth sense.

"Why do you ask?"

"I knows when things be wrong. You got that shadow hanging round you again."

Some intuition. I probably looked miserable. I grabbed a rake and began tidying up the dirt aisle. I didn't believe in auras or any of that mumbo jumbo. *Did I?*

"Lorna in the shadow, too," Mello said as he led Stinger past us.

My movement with the rake stopped. Did his insight go beyond my altercation with Amarilla? Jim believed Mello could see into the dark that shadowed evil. My thoughts rushed back to Cormack's warning about Bobby and the double-homicide. I'd been so self-involved with Stinger's race, I hadn't even told Lorna what Cormack had said. Not that she'd listen.

The redhead's eyes had widened. "What do you mean, Mello?"

The old man stopped Stinger at a red water bucket hanging on the wood railing and let him drink his fill. Hot horses and cold water don't mix, but the gelding had cooled out past the danger stage where only brief sips were allowed.

The old man's dark eyes settled on me. "Miss Nikki, you remember I knows about the evil?"

I nodded.

"There's some powerful bad 'round here and you girls best be careful." He stared into the dense woods, then chirped at Stinger. As they moved away, he mumbled, "I knows things, deed I do."

Lorna had paled to sheet-white. "I wish he wouldn't do that. Gives me goose bumps."

"He's a little weird, but in a good way. He might be on to something." The air moved gently, bringing the scent of rain. I paused to gather my thoughts and searched the low-lidded sky overhead. Slow, heavy drops punched tiny craters in the dust outside our shedrow. Graphite clouds looming to the west sailed rapidly over the backstretch and let loose sheets of water. Puddles formed, gutters gurgled, and the metal roof overhead drummed like thunder.

Instinctively, Lorna and I backed up against the inside wall. "Lorna," I said, "I need to tell you something."

She shrank away from me, eyes widening. "What?"

"When Cormack was here yesterday, he told me..." I swallowed. "You know how we wondered what happened to Bunny's boys?"

She nodded, her expression wary.

"They were murdered. Both of them. The police think Bobby might have been involved..."

Lorna's fingers pressed her lips flat. She shook her head.

"Not like he hurt them or anything." I spoke fast. "More like he knew something and wouldn't tell. But he's trouble, Lorna. Cops think Bunny's sons were killed because they were involved in drugs, and —"

"That's a bunch of crap! You're...jealous. And that Cormack, he's an asshole. Bobby would never.... Screw this, I'm not listening to you."

A breeze gusted from the west, driving cold rain under the shedrow's roof. Lorna pulled her jacket tight and plunged into the downpour through the rail opening, running hard to the right, then ducked back under the rail and darted down the middle aisle. Toward Bobby's barn.

My recent fiasco with Amarilla hadn't taught me much. I'd handled Lorna even better, sent her running straight to Bobby. Would she confront him about the Cheswick boys? Would she be in danger? I leaned against the wall, rubbed my temples. I still had to call Jim, tell him about Amarilla.

I heard comforting clip-clops as Mello and Stinger moseyed around the corner. They paused at the red bucket, but the gelding turned his head away. If you do it right, a horse usually fills up on water about the same time he finishes cooling out.

I stepped over and stroked Stinger's neck, then out of habit knelt down and ran my hands over the knees and ankles of his front legs. I didn't feel any abnormal heat and stood up. Mello put Stinger in his freshly bedded stall and the horse went right to his hay. Good boy. I didn't want to lose him.

I found my cell and pushed Jim's speed dial. His gruff voice reached my ear pretty quick.

"Saw the race on simulcast, Nikki. Did a good job with that horse."

"Ms. Chaquette fired me."

"What? What the hell happened?"

Jim remained silent until I finished my tale. "Damn owners," he said. "You're my assistant. She's going to have to fire me too." I heard a sigh and there were a few beats of silence. "Chaquette might change her mind. See what she says in the morning."

I told Jim I'd let him know what happened and disconnected.

Mello seated himself on a dilapidated wood bench that at one time had been painted green. Now peeling and faded, it still held a few spots of bright pigment that matched Mello's bow tie. I eased onto the bench next to him. We sat in companionable silence, watching the driving rain, taking a breather before starting the round of evening feed.

Beyond the grass and Virginia clay, the forest canopy swayed against a dark billowing sky. The wet wind scattered red and orange leaves, layering a soft carpet onto the forest floor. Water streamed down the tall native evergreens, leaving the air heavy with the scent of pine. Was Lorna safe with Bobby?

Mello stood up abruptly and stared into the forest. Gusts of wind swirled more leaves and rocked the pines gently. I started as a darker shadow pushed among the pines. A figure emerged in a black rain slicker. Long hair plastered against a pale white face. A glint of steel behind.

That dreadful man again? Yes, and still dragging a shovel.

I sprang from the bench and grabbed a nearby pitchfork, stepping close to Mello. "I've seen him before. He came out of the woods the night we arrived. Scared everybody half to death." I should've asked Cormack about this guy.

"Don't fret, Miss Nikki. He won't hurt you."

"Easy for you to say."

"Hey mister," Mello called out, "you be mighty wet. Why'nt you come up here out of the rain?"

I got a tighter hold on my pitchfork, whispered, "I don't want him up here. He's nuts."

The man stopped, his haunted eyes empty holes. He pulled his shovel forward, leaning on the handle for support. Raindrops worked to clean wet earth from the metal blade.

The guy had been out digging in this rain? He was crazy as a loon and appeared to have an object tucked under his arm the size of a cantaloupe.

Mello leaned over the rail, drops of water glistening in his tightly curled hair. "You have any luck today, mister?"

"They know. They all know. But they won't tell." His voice a soft wail beneath the wind.

"Won't tell *what*?" Exasperation sharpened my voice.

The man leaned the shovel against his hip and slowly pulled the object from the crook of his arm. Something white smeared with mud. He held it out in both hands, then let it drop to the ground.

Yuck, a skull. Human? No, the jaw too long, the teeth those of a grazing animal. A small horror crept between my shoulder blades. I whipped out my cell phone to call security, but Mello placed his hand on my arm.

"You don't need to be doing that, Miss Nikki," he said softly. "Man ain't dangerous. His heart's broken, is all." His hand swiped at the rivulets of water on his forehead. "You find what you're looking for, mister?"

The man's eyes cleared and focused on Mello a moment. "Thank you for your kindness. I'm still searching. And I will find the place they put her."

Beside me, Mello made the sign of the cross. A stronger rush of wind undulated the trees against the sky, and a spray of rain doused my face, the smell of sodden earth and decay strong in my nostrils. The man nodded at us and walked away down the side of the barn toward the gravel road.

I was definitely going to ask Cormack about this guy. He couldn't be wandering around Colonial like this without people being aware of it.

On the ground the animal skull glistened in the rain, its empty eye sockets staring.

19

After evening feed, I stumbled through the rain over to Bobby's barn looking for Lorna, only to see taillights and hear the heavy rumble of Bobby's Cobra leaving the racetrack. In the dim light I could make out two figures in the front seat. He must've had Lorna with him. I tried her cell but the call went straight to voice mail. I couldn't think of a message to leave and disconnected.

On the drive back to the cottage, wind buffeted the Toyota, making it hard to steer and hold the road, already treacherous with downed limbs and standing water. Images of Bunny's broken dolls and dead sons seemed to spill from my head and fill the car. I didn't want to pass by her workshop, arrive at that isolated cottage, then face a night as long and lonely as the road. But I had company waiting for me on the doorstep.

Slippers and the Cochin rooster huddled together in the shelter of the cottage's doorway. The entrance was recessed in the building's thick stuccoed walls, and the animals avoided the worst of the weather. The rooster's soggy tail hung low behind him, his beak almost dragging on the stone block as he slumped in misery.

"I hope you don't think you're coming inside," I said, surprised he didn't move as I leaned over him to push the key into the lock. "What a pitiful sack of feathers." But I smiled, glad to have something to talk to.

Slippers rubbed against my leg. Unidentifiable pieces of vegetation clung to the cat's long fur. "You're a mess," I said. The cat sped into the house before I had the door open six inches.

The rooster rousted himself, shook his feathers and marched in right behind. I didn't have the heart to put him out, and after setting down my purse, I arranged some chairs and couch pillows to make a sort of pen which I lined with old newspapers. I tried to shoo him inside and finally had to put my hands on him and push him in. I discovered wet chickens don't smell very good and washed my hands.

I fed Slippers and gave the rooster some bread, which he pecked to pieces and devoured in about five seconds. I gave him more bread and then a little dish of water. Funny how you comfort yourself while tending to others.

I pulled the café curtains closed, made a steaming cup of orange-spiced tea doused with bourbon, and sipped it while soaking in a hot tub. Life wasn't so bad. Lorna should be all right. With the sluicing gutters and sighing wind providing a melancholy lullaby, I fell asleep beneath a threadbare blanket and an old comforter embroidered with faded cabbage roses.

Something crashed. I sat up in bed. A desperate cry that might have been, "braa-wuk!" sliced through the night air, followed by a sharp scream, then fumbling noises until a light came on.

"Fucking chicken! What's this McNugget doing in here?"

Lorna must have stumbled into my makeshift pen as she snuck into the house. Served her right. The lighted dial of my bedside clock told me it was only 10:45. The reasonable hour and the clarity I heard in Lorna's voice filled me with relief.

"He sort of followed me into the house," I called from my bed. "Are you all right?"

"Yeah, but this stupid chicken's been pooping all over the newspaper. It's on my shoe."

My grin was irrepressible. "You ever hear that old Stones' song called 'Sweet Virginia'?"

"Not a fan. Way before my time. You've always been stuck in childhood with your mother's music. You ought to move on."

"That may be true, but the song's called "Sweet Virginia." Has this great line, "Got to scrape the shit right off your shoes." I buried my face in my pillow to muffle my laughter.

"I'm gonna scrape it on your head." But I sensed a smile in her voice. She limped into my doorway, one shoe in her hand and one still on her foot. I was afraid she'd throw it at me, but she tossed it toward the front door, hobbled into my room, and sat on the edge of my bed, her eyes growing serious.

"Bobby said he wasn't involved with that murder. I believe him."

He'd probably lied. I could smell a musky animal scent on her, see a warm bloom in her cheeks. A drowsy sensual shine glittered from eyes I believed were blinded by love.

Slippers padded into the room and sat on the floor, his tail switching. I held my tongue. Outside the rain had eased to a gentle patter, the wind only a sigh.

"I just want you to be happy," I said.

"I know. I'm gonna clean up, get some sleep."

I nodded. The lamp in the living room silhouetted her, turning her hair into a dark red cloud, making her appear fragile, almost ethereal.

* * * *

At 9:30 the next morning, Amarilla's horses were still in the barn and I hadn't worked up the nerve to call her. Sunshine drenched the moist air around me. Deep puddles on the gravel road by the barn reflected blue sky, and backstretch workers sloshed through the mud and wet grass in Wellingtons or waterproof paddock boots.

Out on the wet track, horses galloped briskly, their hooves slicing through surface water. The tightly packed sand and dirt underneath acted as an accelerant, the footing reminding me how as a child, I loved to speed across the smooth wet sand at the ocean's edge. At ten, Lorna and I slid off the last two horses — Stinger and Daffodil.

Ramon and Mello were cooling out two gray horses, so Lorna and I continued on with Amarilla's. After a couple of turns we put them in wash stalls at the end of the barn. I adjusted the hot and cold faucets until warm water gushed from the hose, and I shampooed Daffodil's muddied coat with a big sponge. Next door, Lorna worked on Stinger.

In the chilly air, steam hung above the filly's back, a fog bank filled with the scents of soap, horse sweat, and wet fur. I used a metal scraper to remove excess rinse water, then rubbed her briskly with a rough towel. We threw on light horse blankets designed for cooling out and kept the horses moving along the barn's dirt aisle, stopping only for sips of water from the buckets we'd hung on the railing.

As the horses dried, we'd fold the blankets a little more, exposing the horses' necks, then withers, and backs, rolling and gathering the fabric bit by bit until the blankets hung over just their hips.

Lorna stopped her horse a while later and tossed the gelding's blanket over the rail. She ran her hands over his back and chest.

"Stick a fork in him. He's done." She led Stinger into his stall.

We started in with brushes and combs, then polished and massaged their coats with new towels. We cleaned their feet with metal hoof picks, then did their legs up with poultice, liniment, or bandages depending on the need. After all that, it was time to feed lunch, and after that, Lorna and I collapsed onto Mello's wooden bench.

Just then, an elegant black-and-silver car waded through the mud and stopped at our shedrow. Looked like a Rolls.

"Dude's driving a Bentley," Lorna said. "Is he, like, a chauffeur? He's got that little cap on."

I stared through the shiny windshield. A gold badge adorned the cap worn by a man in a starched white shirt. He stared straight ahead, his eyes hidden beneath the hat, his body stiff and formal behind the Bentley's wheel. Something yellow moved in the back seat. The rear door opened and a vast arrangement of long-stemmed black-eyed Susans, with a small set of human legs beneath, worked its way out of the Bentley.

Pemberton's sharp little face craned to the side as his arms adjusted their grip on the flowers. He wore a dark wool suit and tasseled loafers. Mud and grit seemed to leap from the ground and cover the shiny leather before he'd taken two steps.

"My beautiful *shoes*!" He shifted into a tiptoe-hustle and made for the opening in our wood railing.

"Who is that?" asked Lorna. "Looks like a baby bird."

"It's that Pemberton guy, works for the Baron," I whispered, and grabbed a new towel.

The little man sped into the shedrow and began stomping his shoes on our aisle's dry dirt. In his arms, the flowers nodded their velvety brown-and-yellow heads in time with his beating feet. He stared at his shoes and the mud peppering the cuffs of his suit pants. Dismay filled his eyes.

"They're *Ballys*. A present from the Baron!" Serious eye roll, then he collected himself. "Here," he said, thrusting the black-eyed Susans at me. "These are for you, from Amarilla. She hopes you will accept her apology." His voice lowered, taking on a gossip's intimacy as he stepped closer. "This is what she does. Gets mad, sends an emissary to fix the damage. Lucky me, I got the job."

"I was just about to call her," I said, handing him the cloth with one hand as I folded my other arm around the flowers.

"A towel! You're so handy." He paused a moment. "By the way, you're not fired."

The air I exhaled felt like it'd been held too long. I breathed in the mingling odors of manure, sweet feed, hay, and tangy liniment with newborn appreciation.

"May I?" Pemberton asked Lorna, then collapsed on the bench next to her. He rubbed his shoes, streaking the white cotton with dirt. "Nikki, have pity on me. Say you'll take the job back."

"Sure," I said, still clutching the black-eyed Susans.

Lorna gave me a "I can't believe you caved" look as Mello ducked out from under Hellish's stall gate carrying a dandy brush and a plastic baggy of red-and-white striped peppermints. He wore his green bow tie.

Lorna threw a dark look at Pemberton and stood up. "Let me get you a bucket for those flowers." She took the flowers from me and marched toward the feed room.

Mello eased next to Pemberton, his dark eyes watching the diminutive man clean the Ballys. A glimmer flickered in the old man's eyes.

"Yes, indeedy," he said to no one in particular.

Pemberton slapped his forehead. "*The Invitation.*" His hand dove into the inside pocket of his suit jacket, rippling his green and pink silk tie. He pulled out a thick cream-colored card and handed it to me.

It read, "Cocktails. In Honor of Ms. Amarilla Chaquette. The Baron Helmut Vindenberg Stahlkaur von Waechter. Saturday, November 1st. At Five O'clock P.M. Vindenberg Hall."

There were no directions, as if the farm were so famous no one could possibly be unfamiliar with its location.

"Where is this place?" I asked, staring at Pemberton and Mello. Quite a pair — sitting on the same bench, both on the outer edges of society, and wearing green ties that matched perfectly. Pemberton pulled out a ballpoint and wrote directions on the back of my invitation.

Lorna came from the feed room carrying a red bucket stuffed with the flowers. She headed for the water hose and stopped abruptly as Bobby emerged from the barn's center aisle. A look passed between them.

He wore his jeans faded, his hair loose. A leather jacket partially covered a black T-shirt, and a large antique gold cross set with rubylike gems glimmered from his chest.

"Hello, Bobby," Pemberton cooed.

"Hey, Pem," Bobby said.

To my knowledge, Mello had never seen the young man before, but he stood up quickly with an almost fearful recognition. His hand shot out and grasped Bobby's arm. "Your people. They be Taskers?"

Bobby's eyes widened. He turned slowly, facing Mello. "My mother...was a Tasker."

Bobby seemed so nervous. The usual cockiness in his tone changed when he mentioned his mother. I couldn't see his eyes as he faced Mello, but his voice held a lost quality. I glanced at Lorna. She seemed as much in the dark as I was.

"I knows that cross." A tremor cracked Mello's voice.

Bobby touched the gold jewel. "It belonged to my mother."

"Lord have mercy," said Mello, and backed away.

20

The week rushed by in a blur of wind-whipped manes and half-mile poles. I put long gallops into Daffodil each day. She thrived on the work, her coat blossoming with dapples. Hellish generally behaved herself and remained sound. The racing secretary stirred my interest when he wrote an allowance race made to order for Hellish. Though Lorna hung with Bobby, she seemed to stay out of trouble and be happy.

The Baron's party was Saturday night. Friday evening I stared at the assortment of work clothes in my closet. Yeah, *right*.

I grabbed my keys and headed for the mall outside Richmond, where I found a pair of silky black pants and an empire top with flounces the sales woman insisted looked "striking." I had my doubts, but the mall was closing so I made the purchase. I called my Baltimore friend, Carla Ruben, from the car. Carla knew style like I knew horses. After I reached her, I described the top.

Carla's voice had a warm blend of confidence and sexuality. "Empire and ruffles are in this year, though you'd do better in that minimal nineties look. You've got those gorgeous blue eyes that need a strong red, electric blue, or —"

"Black-and-turquoise animal print," I said. Like I'd forget the advice of a hot-hunk-magnet like Carla.

"Good. Just fix your hair, wear the lipstick and remember to walk into the party like you own the place."

Easy for her to say. She was a stunning blond with a matching body. Men stumbled when she walked by.

"Right," I said.

"Met anyone down there?"

"An irresistible bad-boy. He's too young and has the hots for Lorna." I slowed the Toyota, easing off the Richmond beltway onto Route 64. Above the tree line, a bright star blazed on the horizon. Probably a planet, like Venus.

"Good for Lorna. How's Hellish?"

Her question was more than idle curiosity. I'd sold Carla an interest in Hellish, after she fell for the haughty chestnut.

"The racing secretary wrote a starter allowance that's got Hellish's name on it. I think we should enter."

"Go for it! But remind me, what's a starter?"

An SUV's headlights filled my rear window. I put on my blinker and moved to the slow lane. The guy driving the vehicle made a rude hand gesture as he blew by.

"Asshole."

"What?"

"Never mind," I said. "A starter is an allowance or non-claiming race. But it's only open to horses that have run for a specific claiming price."

"And this one fits Hellish because…"

"It's for horses that have run for $5,000 or less. Remember, right before I rescued her from that slaughter house, she ran in a $5,000 claimer?"

"I do, and I still can't believe anyone would let a horse go to slaughter." Carla stayed silent a few beats, but I could hear her thinking.

"So this race will be as easy as a cheap claimer?"

I shook my head then realized she couldn't see me. "No. First, the purse is too high. Second, there'll be trainers who ran good horses cheap one time to get the eligibility. Of course, they were gambling their horse wouldn't get claimed."

"And if one of those guys did lose his horse, the new owner gets to put him in. Right?"

No flies on Carla.

"I got to go," she said. "Don't forget your push-up bra."

* * * *

When I pulled up to the Cheswick cottage, a newly risen gibbous moon dwarfed the bright planet I'd noticed earlier. Outside the car, the temperature had dropped, water beads glistened on the grass, and the spicy scent of cedars floated in the night air.

I was almost to the porch when the moon threw a moving shadow onto the edge of the yard. I stopped abruptly, staring at the dark clump of cedars.

"Who's there?"

A form separated from the dense black of the evergreens. I turned to face the moonlit figure that slowly approached me. Too short and heavy to be shovel-man. Why would he be here anyway?

"Who is it?" I said, my voice splintered by fear. "What do you want?" I strained to hear the low words drifting toward me.

"Todd and Tim. I'm looking for them. Are they here?"

I recognized the lumpy figure of Bunny Cheswick. I sure hoped Todd and Tim were farmhands or maybe neighbors.

"Is that you, Bunny?" Something about the woman's hesitant movement kept my voice gentle.

She was still a moment, then moved closer. The moonlight revealed confusion in her face. "Yes, I'm Bunny…I'm Bunny."

Oh boy. This didn't sound so good.

"You want to come in the house?" I stepped forward, stretching out my hand. She clutched it, gripping my fingers until they hurt.

"Yes. I need to see Todd and Tim. Are they in there?"

"I don't think so. Who are Todd and Tim?"

"My boys. They're…" Her face was awful to watch. Realization flooded her eyes and then pain. She made a high keening sound. If I hadn't held on to her, she would have crumpled onto the wet grass.

"Come inside. I'll make us some hot tea."

I led her to the cottage doorstep, fumbled with my key, but Lorna pulled the door open from the other side.

"Lorna, Bunny here needs some tea."

She started to ask a question, saw the slight shake of my head.

"I'll put the kettle on," she said.

I got Bunny seated in one of the wooden chairs at the kitchen table and pulled some blue china mugs from the cabinet. I set them on the counter next to Lorna, worried anything I did in that cottage would remind Bunny of her children.

Bunny's hand shook as she fidgeted with the sugar bowl on the oak plank table. The lid rattled, then fell onto the table. "I'm sorry, I'm sorry."

"It's fine," I said. "It didn't break or anything."

Her voice rose to a wail. "I just forget, you see. I don't mean to. But sometimes I just have to believe they're still here."

Lorna wore a desperate expression. "Oh, look, the water's boiling." She yanked the cabinet open and grabbed the box of orange-spice tea.

I set the mugs on the counter and sat next to Bunny. "You mean your sons."

She nodded. She'd corralled her hands in her lap, the fingers tightly entwined, her lips compressed. Tears slid down her cheeks but she didn't say anything.

"You said their names were Todd and Tim?" I ignored Lorna's don't-go-there expression.

Bunny dragged in a breath. "Todd was the oldest. He'd be nineteen now. And Tim, Tim…"

"How long ago did they die?" I asked, before she broke again. Lorna looked ready to strangle me, but I had a strong sense Bunny needed to talk.

"A year ago last August. They went out to meet that Duvayne boy and never came home."

I darted a glance at Lorna. She wouldn't look at me, but the hand dunking a tea bag stopped.

Bunny's voice grew stronger. "Bobby always said they never met up. Chuck believes him, but I don't know. The police think it was drugs." Her voice trailed off.

Lorna rushed the table with two mugs of steaming tea, spoons and napkins. I hustled over to the cabinet, grabbed the bourbon bottle and dosed my cup until it overflowed.

"They were good boys," Bunny said. "Tim was only fifteen."

I could almost see the wall of pain building around Bunny, locking her in. She grew very quiet.

"Someone's coming." Lorna moved to the kitchen window and stared outside. Headlights flashed through the top of the café curtains.

"Is it Bobby?" I asked.

"Uh, no. I'm seeing him tomorrow night. Looks like Mr. Cheswick." She stole a glance at Bunny, who seemed to have grown smaller, shoulders hunched, chin almost down to her chest.

I could hear Chuck's footsteps approaching. The door shook with a loud rap. Lorna opened it.

"Have you gals seen — *Bunny*! You had me worried half-to-death." He moved quickly across the room, stopping next to her.

"She was just having some tea," I said.

"She needs to come home. This is the last place she should be!"

Bunny began to rock back and forth, her gaze firmly on the hands clasped in her lap. An odd humming noise started in her throat.

"Oh, Christ!" Chuck said, staring down at Bunny. His thick silver hair flopped on his forehead as he dug in his jacket pocket and pulled out a bottle of pills. He leaned over and set two pale pink ones in front of his wife. "Take those with your tea, Bunny. Now."

She continued staring at her hands and rocking. I thought she said, "No." A tiny plaintive sound. Lorna and I exchanged glances. I poured a big slug of tea down my throat, shivering as the strong whiskey hit me.

Chuck grabbed one of Bunny's hands, yanked it onto the table and put the two pills in her palm. "Don't make me force you."

"You *make* her take pills?" The words were out of my mouth before I knew it.

He gave me a sharp look through his heavy black glasses. "Look at her. This is what happens when she gets off her meds. I don't like making her take this stuff, but the doctors say she has to have it."

"Is it because of your sons?" I asked.

His eyes widened, but he nodded.

"It's been over a year. The doctors still want her drugged?" Why was I interrogating him like this? Maybe the strong feeling someone needed to stand up for Bunny.

"Look," he whispered. "You weren't on the psych ward. They kept her there for almost two months. She's a suicide waiting to happen." He almost sounded disgusted. He let out a long breath.

"I'm sorry, I'm sorry," Bunny moaned. Her hand moved slowly to her mouth. She pushed the pills through her lips and took a sip of tea. Her body slumped in resignation, but her eyes lifted for a second, so pleading I thought she'd said something out loud.

Chuck's long fingers grasped her shoulder. "I need to get her home." He strong-armed her out of the chair, pulled her through the cottage door, outside into the darkness.

I bolted from my seat, ready to go after them. I had to help her.

Lorna, already standing, got to the door first and blocked it. "Nikki, don't." She shook her head. "Don't do it."

I released a long breath, nodded. My need to help the helpless could get me into trouble. Maybe it was time to rein it in.

21

I drove to the Baron's party at dusk the next day, turning through Vindenberg Hall's stone entrance gates onto an oyster shell drive. The road wound past an apple orchard, greenhouses, and acres of pasture enclosed by five-board fences. The setting sun cast a clear gold light onto the fields, which gave way to manicured shrubs, neatly pruned trees and varieties of miniature evergreen I'd never seen before.

I came around a last curve, astonished to see an enormous castle looming behind a circular drive. Austere pairs of evergreen trees stood guard on either side of the white stone building I suspected was new. Colorful little flags waved from its turrets. Perhaps the senior Waechters had failed to take their child to Disneyland.

I stopped behind a long platinum-colored Jaguar. A man in a gold-braided uniform approached my car window. His lips curled slightly as he took in the battered Toyota.

"You have an invitation?"

I dug into the velvet bag I'd borrowed from Lilly Best. When I found the invitation, I handed it to the man, hoping the makeup I'd used earlier still hid the last traces of my bruising from the speed addict.

The parking guy handed me a valet ticket and held my door open. As he drove the Toyota behind the castle, a black stretch-Hummer with tinted windows rolled into the driveway. Who'd want such an ominous looking vehicle?

I hurried toward entrance steps carved from stone and fell in behind the silver-haired couple who'd emerged from the Jag. She wore a full-length fur, stiletto heels. Her perfume floated behind, rich and floral.

I had on a wool peacoat, Lorna's wedge-heeled boots with rhinestones, and eau de backstretch.

As I followed the couple through a massive set of oak entrance doors, the woman's perfume mingled with a light scent of wood smoke. Inside, the ceiling soared at least two stories. The walls flanking a center staircase were hung with tapestries of unicorns and other mythical figures. Some kind of mastiff slept on a rug in front of a huge fireplace that burned logs the size of tree trunks.

Light spilled from an archway to our right, and as the older couple and I moved toward it, two uniformed maids offered to take our coats. Static electricity charged through my wool jacket, snapping my hand as

I pulled the peacoat off. A maid reached for it, her hand pausing uncertainly as clumps of gray cat fur stood at attention on the wool, tilting in her direction. She took the coat and remained expressionless as she handed me a ticket. A stray rooster feather drifted to the floor.

Five or six young men in black trench coats came through the entrance doors. Several sported gold earrings and most of them wore dark glasses even though the sun outside had set. Ostentatious, just like the Hummer they'd undoubtedly arrived in, they gave me the once over. I turned away and moved through the stone arch into a large well-lit room decorated with marble statues and ornate gilded furniture. Silken floral carpets in vibrant shades of turquoise, gold and purple covered much of the stone floor. People actually walked on these things? I dragged my gaze from the floor and checked out the crowd.

Men in dark suits or tuxedos, women in long dresses, the fabrics formal and extravagant, reminding me of the crowd from the Baron's suite, only dressier. My turquoise top looked pretty sharp with the carpets, but I was the only woman in the room wearing pants. Should I hide in a closet now?

"So, you got an invitation." The shrewd-eyed Katherine Crosby studied me through the smoke curling off the tip of her cigarette. She wore a black dress with a plunge neckline edged in gold lace. The facets of her diamond earrings sparkled, and amusement lit her eyes.

"Nice boots, baby." A Hummer guy had moved next to me. Dressed in a black suit, he wore dark glasses and a neon orange tie. He grinned down at me and gestured toward Lorna's boots. "My kind of shoe, sexy."

"You must work at the Baron's plant." Katherine's lips formed a pleasant smile, but something in her eyes made the guy uncertain.

He shifted back a step. "Matter of fact, I do. Bottling manager."

"How nice," I said.

No one attempted to exchange names and Katherine's gaze on the man remained cool and steady. He looked around the room. Probably for a way out.

"See you ladies around," he said.

Katherine's mocking expression eased as he lost himself in the crowd. She turned to me. "Great outfit, Nikki. Would you like a drink?"

"Yes," I said, "I would." Her kindness surprised me.

We threaded through the crowd to the nearest of several bars. Katherine ordered a champagne cocktail, and I asked for bourbon-and-water. The bartender had a waxed handlebar moustache and wore a tux. When he reached for a bottle of Gilded Baron, I must have winced.

"Something else I can get you?"

"What've you got?"

He winked at me, reached under the bar and flashed the label on a bottle of George Dickel. "You've got a great smile," he said, and poured a stiff one.

I followed Katherine into a knot of people discussing the upcoming stakes races at Colonial. A thin woman, wrapped in beaded blue satin, dominated the conversation. Her eyes seemed overly bright.

"Oh, yes," she said, "they're having a stake for Virginia-bred fillies. The Princess. Has a $500,000 purse. Same day as the special stake they wrote for older males, The Virginia's King."

My antennae went up. "Is the filly race on the turf?" I asked. When she nodded, I said, "How far?"

"A mile-and-a-half." Perspiration webbed her forehead, and her hands gestured excessively as she spoke. "You'll need a horse that can run all day."

Daffodil. I lost track of the conversation for a moment as I worked on an idea. What were the chances? Could I get around Amarilla? Where was the guest of honor, anyway?

"Nikki, hey."

I turned, surprised to see Susan Stark behind me. She had the same bright-eyed look as the woman in blue. Her voice reminded me of a rubber band stretched tight enough to snap. If possible, she looked more emaciated than the day Stinger ran.

"I don't have to worry about weight any more." She grabbed at a shoulder strap of her too-large black dress. The strap drooped halfway to her elbow. The waist hung loosely down by her hips.

"You giving up riding?" I asked, hoping that's what she meant. She was too tall and heavy-boned to make jockey weight without starving.

She blinked, her eyes moving rapidly, then leaned close, her breath hot and unpleasant. "No. I got the stuff."

"What stuff?" I asked.

"Not cheap, but man, does it work. You want to try it? You can get it here, like tonight." Her answer, a spittle-filled whisper, sent me back a half-step back. Something in her breath made my eyes water.

"Here?"

"Oh, yeah! Way cool." Dilated pupils darted under pale lids in a face blotched by internal heat. "I can fix you up."

"No. Susan, you don't want to do this." I felt like shaking her.

Katherine stared at us through the smoke of a fresh cigarette and I fell quiet.

Susan tugged at her strap again. "Of course I want to. It's the greatest, it's —"

"Ladies and gentlemen."

I knew that voice. A bell tinkled across the room near the entrance arch. Pemberton stood there, head and shoulders above the crowd. He must have climbed onto a box. His small hand clutched a bell, which he rang until the surrounding voices lowered to murmurs and grew quiet. He wore a tuxedo, its cummerbund hot pink.

"Please step into the grand hall and allow me to introduce our guest of honor, Ms. Amarilla Chaquette."

I leaned closer to Katherine. "Why the intro? She new around here?"

"Old friend of the Baron's from South America, but these people don't know her."

Guests crowded through the wide stone arch into the high-ceilinged hall. I lost track of Susan in the shuffle, but nabbed a position with Katherine just inside the hall. On the wide staircase, six ebony statues of scantily-dressed men held candelabra carved with fruits and flowers. Dozens of candles cast flickering light onto the cold stone steps.

The baron appeared at the top of the staircase, a cleverly-cut tux diminishing the size of his belly. Pipeless, he extended an arm to his side and Amarilla stepped from the shadows and joined him.

She had shrink-wrapped her body into a sleeveless brown silk dress with a low bodice. A cape of fur dyed to a rich yellow flowed from her shoulders. Her skin sparkled with some kind of glittery powder and a tiara with yellow jewels perched on her slicked-back dark brown-and-blond-streaked hair. I'd never seen her look more like a yellow jacket.

"Oh. My. God." Katherine said under her breath.

A buzz of voices and a restrained titter had Pemberton ringing his bell furiously. He raised his voice to drown the low hum of derision. "The Baron Helmut von Waechter and Ms. Amarilla Chaquette."

He set his bell down and began to clap his hands. Tight wrinkles bracketed his mouth. I felt sorry for the guy. After a slow start, the audience set up an enthusiastic round of applause. After all, they were getting free food and booze.

The baron and Amarilla swept down the stairs and launched into the crowd, shaking hands and exchanging greetings. I shrank back against the stone wall. I didn't want to talk to either one of them.

As guests wandered back into the main room, an austere grey-haired woman latched onto Katherine and pulled her away. Snatches of their conversation floated back to me, "...and that tiara! The woman's without class...."

I kept my place against the wall and finished my drink, having a grand time watching the crowd. The younger women wore dazzling strappy gowns, reminding me of plastic Christmas flowers dipped in glitter. The booze flowed, the laughter rose, and the smell of perfume and whiskey swirled around me. A waiter came by and I set my empty drink on his tray.

"Where could I find a ladies' room?" I asked. He pointed at two smaller archways opening onto corridors.

"One on the left," he said. "Go through the first room and look on your right."

I hoped I wouldn't get lost and wind up in a dungeon. I wished Lorna had come with me, but when I'd offered to sneak her into the party, she'd said she had a date with Bobby. She had it bad for the guy. Really bad.

I walked through the hall the waiter had indicated, passing wall sconces, flickering candles, and long wooden tables loaded with fancy nicknacks. I entered a room full of gilded mirrors and backless couches. I looked to the right, saw what I hoped was the bathroom door. The knob wouldn't turn. Locked. I moved into the next hall and heard voices, laughter and music ahead.

The room was wood-paneled and apparently an entertainment center. Some pop diva, wearing a few small patches of cloth, gyrated and sang on a movie screen that covered most of one wall. Leather couches faced away from me toward the screen. Guests with drinks and little plates of food lolled in the deep leather. Damn, I'd missed the food.

On one side of the room people danced to the music. Some of the women had a peculiar light in their dilated eyes and wore goofy smiles. Were all the women in New Kent County on drugs?

Susan Stark startled me by appearing at my elbow. "Did you see a cop?" she asked. "Is there a cop here?"

"Why, do you need one?"

"No," she said, eyes jittery. "I, like, can't deal with it!"

"Easy," I said. This girl needed help. The drug coursing through her must be spinning her brain like a top. As I stared, paranoia built on her face, and I thought she'd lose it in another moment. Then, just like that, she refocused.

"Hey. Meant what I said about fixing you up. Premium weight loss stuff." She nodded, a big grin spreading across her face. "Real rush, too."

"I told you, I'm not —"

She darted a shaky hand toward me. "He's right here, you can get it now."

I stared at the dancers and backs of heads on the couches. "Who's here?"

On one of the sofas a man shifted sideways. Jolted, I made an involuntary little sound.

Bobby Duvayne, fully engaged, but not with selling drugs. His hands gripped the shoulders of a pretty woman almost old enough to be his mother. She appeared to be giggling as he pressed her down into the maroon leather. Before they sank out of sight behind the back of the couch, his eyes slid to mine. Then the bastard smiled.

22

I stormed the couch. "Thought you had a date with Lorna. Remember her?"

Diamonds flashed on the neck of the woman beneath Bobby. I glared at her. "Who's this one, Bobby? Your pet pedophile?"

The woman pushed at him and tried to sit up. Bobby rolled off her and faced me. People nearby stared. A woman in black satin tugged at her date's arm, nodded in our direction. Didn't want him to miss the show.

"For God's sake, Nikki, we were just partying. Doesn't mean anything."

Bobby's paramour turned on me. "You're an intrusive little bitch, aren't you? And so provincial. Did you come from a hog farm?"

"Sure," I said. "You were the prize pig."

I shifted my attention to the real problem. At least he had enough heart to look uncomfortable. "Want me to give your regards to Lorna?" I asked him.

Bobby scanned the room, then the hallway beyond. "Is she here?"

"Of course not. She's at the cottage waiting for a jerk-off drug pusher who's going to break her heart. That would be you," I said.

Confusion filled his handsome face. "Drug pusher? What are you talking about?"

"Aren't you the one selling diet cocktails?"

"What?" Either he could really act or he didn't know. Miss Piggy fluffed her short blond hair and casually adjusted the low bodice of her emerald green dress. She daggered a nasty look at me and stalked away.

Movement from the side of the room caught my eye. A tall figure scuttled toward a door built into the wood paneling. I caught a glimpse of a black jacket and light-colored hair before the man slipped through the opening.

I studied the dancers, people on the couches. Had Susan meant Bobby when she said her dealer was in the room? If not Bobby, who?

"Nikki, let me talk to Lorna first," Bobby pleaded.

I left without answering. I had to get out of there. I looked for Susan, but she'd disappeared.

I hurried along the hall to the room with gilded mirrors. Light shone from the now open bathroom door. I slipped inside, locking myself in.

Leaning over the green-and-black marble vanity, I stared at my wide eyes and flushed face in the mirror. In spite of everything, I grinned at the enticing swell of cleavage from my push-up bra and the way Carla's permanent lipstick gleamed on my mouth. I must have a pretty good buzz on. That George Dickel was mean stuff.

I used the gold-plated marble toilet, washed my hands, and noticed a second, mystery fixture squatting in the corner. What a peculiar looking toilet. Lidless and tankless, it had a faucet on one side. I turned the handle. A fountain of water shot up from a gold spigot inside the oval bowl. I started giggling.

Someone knocked on the door. "Hello, anyone in there?" A woman's voice.

I hurried to turn the fountain off, but cranked the handle backwards. Excess water splashed from the bowl and pooled onto the floor.

Knuckles rapped impatiently before I opened the door. The austere woman who'd gossiped with Katherine stood there tapping her foot.

She started to brush past me, then stopped. "Playing with the bidet?"

"Guilty," I said. "What is that marble thing, anyway?"

"A bidet," she said. "And it's not marble, it's malachite."

Jeez, a semiprecious toilet thingy. "What do you use it for?"

She started to speak, then stopped. Her face flushed slightly.

I stared, waiting her out.

"It's for refreshing yourself…after sex, or…" she gritted her teeth, "a poo poo. Now, if you don't mind, I'd like some privacy."

"Sure," I said, stepping outside. Poo poo? I moved toward the grand hall wondering how to get my coat back. The maid probably burned it.

The mastiff still lay before the giant fireplace. I drew closer, thinking I might pet him, but he curled his lips, exposing horrific teeth.

"Maybe later," I told him and looked around for a maid.

Amarilla emerged from the party room, cape flowing, tiara sparkling. "Nikki," she called, "I've been looking for you. I have someone you must meet. Come."

Why did I feel like a wild horse who'd just been run down the canyon into a pen?

She rushed over, high heels clacking on the cut stone. Perfect make-up accentuated the tilt of her almond eyes, lovely cheekbones, and slender nose. Up close, a web of fine lines crowded the outside corners of her eyes and lips.

"He asked about you," she said, her smile sly. With a curled index finger, she beckoned me to follow her.

I did. She moved through the smoky, noise filled party room until a couple waylaid her near the bar. I caught the eye of the mustachioed bartender. He winked, busied his hands under the counter, and produced another heavy hit of George Dickel. I grabbed the bourbon, returned his wink, and rejoined Amarilla as she sailed through the crowd.

I followed her into another, smaller room. Bookcases filled with tooled-leather volumes lined the walls. A man in a fussy jacket with long tails stood leafing through a book. He glanced up, smiled, and placed the book on a shelf. Maybe late forties, only a bit taller than me, he had a goatee, curly graying hair, and eyes slightly too small and close together.

"I asked Amarilla to introduce us," he said, his accent British. He appraised me with those little eyes. "You're a jockey?"

"Yes."

"Athletic. I like that in a woman."

I threw a what's-this-about look at Amarilla. Instead of responding, she nodded encouragingly.

"I have a beautiful stud farm in Florida," the man said. "And a private jet. I could fly you down for a visit." His gaze roamed over me and came to rest on the exposed cleavage I suddenly regretted.

"I don't think so, Mr....?"

"DeSilvio," he said. "Anthony DeSilvio. I own some very fine bloodstock, stakes winners. I could mount you. With my bloodlines you could win some very big races."

The guy was about as subtle as a lap dance. Did he think I was stupid or just for sale?

"Thanks, Mr. DeSilvio, but I don't think so."

"Nikki," Amarilla said, "A smart girl doesn't refuse such a generous offer. You must —"

"Querida," DeSilvio lifted his hands toward Amarilla in a palms-up shrug, "she'll come around. They all do."

Arrogant bastard. I felt my lip curl.

The full mouth above his goatee formed a tight smile. "You'd be wise to reconsider, Miss Latrelle." He turned and left the room, jacket tails flapping behind him like dark wings.

I poured some whiskey down my throat and shivered.

Amarilla's eyes narrowed. "You fool. How long you think you be young and pretty? You will never be top jockey. You make no money." Anger, or maybe fear, disintegrated her carefully structured English. "Mr. DeSilvio, he very important man, very rich. In past, I have no money. Is terrible. You want *that*?"

She actually thought she was helping me. I felt more uneasy than offended. Amarilla had picked open the bandage covering my greatest fear. Raised memories of a time I was forced to sleep in a stall at Pimlico. Days when I'd stolen packaged snacks from fast food shops, been cold and hungry. Before Ravinsky had taken me under his wing and discovered I had a gift with horses. I had my own apartment now and money in the bank. Still, the thought of losing everything terrified me.

"I'll work hard for your horses, Amarilla, give them whatever they need. But don't ask me to be some man's toy."

"*Estupida!*" She whipped sideways, grabbed a leather bound book and threw it at me. I jumped, but the volume grazed my arm. Drops of whiskey spilled from my drink.

I whirled from her, rushed back into the party lights, rubbing my arm. The scent of ladies' perfume had grown stale, and the chimney must have backed up; wood smoke choked the air. The masculine smell of cigars made me want to gag.

Amarilla had crossed over a line I struggled to hold. Crossed it a long time ago. She'd sold her heart.

23

I elbowed through the glittering crowd of cocktail drinkers, interrupting conversations, raising eyebrows. I slowed my pace, skirted a group making a champagne toast, and crashed into Pemberton.

"Oops. Sorry, Pem. How do I get my coat?"

"Must you leave so early?" he asked.

"That bitch Amarilla…"

"Oh," he said, "*her*. She can be quite trying." He seemed about to elaborate, then looked more closely at my face. "Up the stairs, first door on your right."

I trotted up the stone steps and found a room with coats on round metal racks like you'd see in a dress shop. A maid took my ticket and handed me my coat.

I thanked her and sped back to the top of the stairs, stopping abruptly at the railing. Amarilla and the baron held court below, near the front doors, probably readying for departing guests. I beat it back to the coat room.

"Excuse me, is there a back way out?"

The maid took a moment to assimilate my words, then smiled, teeth white against mocha skin. "Sí." She stepped into the hall, pointed to the far end. "You go there…" She paused searching for the words, "little circle stairs."

"Thanks," I rushed down a hall lit by electrified candles, my wedge boots thumping on a scarlet-and-green oriental runner that probably cost more than I earned in a year.

At the hall's end a steep stone staircase wound up and down. Must be inside one of the turrets at either end of the castle. Flaming wall-torches lit my way. These, and several narrow windows cut into the stone walls, made me feel I'd stumbled into a Disney set. I scurried down one flight, giggling. The flickering lights and steep stairs caused me to stumble and spill more whiskey. Stuff was too good to waste. Bracing one hand on the wall, I upended my glass and swallowed the rest.

Landing in a circular room with hallways to either side, I went left. Bright light, voices and a rich smell of food spilled through an arch ahead of me. I glimpsed kitchen help working at counters laden with platters of hot food, but saw no exit. I kept going.

Rooms opened on both sides of the hall, washers and dryers sudsing and tumbling in one, while another held racks of sodas, glass jars of fruit juices and a large, noisy ice-machine. The rumbling of machinery pounded inside my head. Why had I chugged the last of that drink?

Angry voices drifted from a turn in the hall ahead, bringing a sense of déjà vu. Bobby and an older voice. His father?

"What were you thinking?" John Duvayne's voice, sounding incredulous, the country hick undertone more pronounced. "*Mrs. DeSilvio?*"

"I never met her before. How was I supposed to know she was Anthony's wife? Jeez, *she* came on to *me*."

Inching forward, I peered around the corner. The passage widened into a sort of walkthrough pantry lined with shelves of condiments, canned goods, boxes of crackers and nuts. The two stood at the far end. Bobby's arms were folded tightly across his chest, and angry red patches blotched his cheeks.

John Duvayne's stout legs and beefy shoulders strained against the fabric of his dark suit. Distress tightened his face. I felt sorry for the guy. Who'd want to be saddled with a wild one like Bobby? John shifted in my direction. I snapped my head back and was rewarded with a stab of pain in my forehead.

I heard John sigh. "You remind me of myself when I was your age. Couldn't leave the women alone, either, until I met your mother."

"Don't talk about her!"

"Okay, okay. But for God's sake, Bobby, be careful. We don't want trouble with DeSilvio."

What was the deal with this DeSilvio guy? I tiptoed back the way I'd come. A passage to the left led me to a tall door set in a stone arch. Mud and leaves littered the stone floor. I turned the oversized brass knob and pushed until a narrow crack opened.

A dark corridor led to a larger room, most of which lay to my left. Lights glowed, shadows moved. Male voices accompanied the sound of scraping metal and gurgling liquid.

A voice whined, "Can you believe that idiot Tucciaro sent the shipment to Jersey? It sucks we got to mix this crap by hand. There's, like, four hundred people upstairs. They all drink like fishes."

Now what? I could say I got lost. Who wouldn't get mixed up in this place?

The whining voice continued. "Then that asshole sends the boss's stash over here. Now we gotta haul it out."

I took a breath and marched around the corner straight into the stretch-Hummer gang.

"Would youse guys get a load of dis one?" The whiny guy leered at me.

I'd ridden at Philadelphia Park, knew a Philly accent when I heard one. Too late to back out now, I threw Philly Whine my best smile.

"Hi guys." I gave them a little wave.

They froze, as if my entrance had turned them into a still life titled "Men at Work." Five of them, including the neon-tie man that Katherine had run off. White shirt sleeves were rolled up. Two of the men glistened with sweat. They held a heavy-looking metal container over a rolling cart loaded with large bottles displaying Gilded Baron labels. One bottle, about three-quarters full of amber fluid, had a funnel stuck in the top. A cloying, sickly sweet odor hit me, sent my stomach roiling.

Behind them a stack of shipping boxes was covered with a tarp, the words PRODUCT OF INDIA visible where the cover failed to conceal a bottom corner.

Near me, a wide-shouldered man grasped the neck of a bottle filled with clear liquid. With a quick squint I made out the lettering on its label, "Finest Spirits, 100% Grain Alcohol."

No wonder Gilded Baron tasted so bad. They were mixing some kind of gag-sweet syrup with grain alcohol.

Neon Tie straightened from where he'd been leaning over a second rolling cart, lined with bottles that were full and capped. "Well, if it isn't little Miss Fancy Boots. You shouldn't be back here, sweetie."

"I got lost."

"Big place like this, you could disappear," Philly Whine said. "Nobody'd see youse again. Know what I mean?"

Would he know what I meant if I picked up a bottle and broke it over his head? A giggle bubbled loose through my lips. *Get a grip.*

I worked for a timid smile. "This place gives me the creeps. I just want to go home."

"How'd you get in here anyway? That door is locked," Neon Tie said.

His accent was north Jersey or New York. Nothing Virginia country hick about these men. City boys all the way.

"Maybe Ches—"

"Shut up," said Wide Shoulders, turning to stare at me.

No one argued. Probably the guy in charge. He'd pierced one ear with two gold rings and wore a meticulously groomed Fu Manchu beard.

"Didn't mean to cause trouble." My stomach surged again and I clapped my hand over my mouth.

"Aw shit, lady. You gonna be sick?"

I shook my head, dragged more air in through my mouth. "Just show me the exit, and I'm out of here."

"That," Fu Man Choo said, pointing to a metal door, "leads to the rear of the castle. Make like a ghost. Disappear." He grinned.

I'd almost reached the exit when a familiar voice reverberated in the darkened hall behind us.

"You boys sleeping? They're outta whiskey up front. Get a move — what the hell's she doing back here?"

I turned toward Chuck Cheswick. Anger darkened his face.

The Hummer men stared at the floor, except Foo Man Choo. His gaze flicked from the tarp covered boxes to Cheswick. "I was just showin' her out, Mr. Wick. She —"

"Shut up," said Cheswick. He rushed me, bent down and shoved his face too close to mine. "I don't like you. You're a busybody, got no business back here, snooping around."

My heart pumped so hard I could hear it in my ears. What had I stumbled into? I swallowed.

"Really, I got lost…looking for a way out." The air was better near the exit. That, and the fear pumping through me began to clear my head.

"She's just a drunk bimbo," Philly Whine said.

Cheswick's silver bangs flopped to one side as he swung on the younger man. "Did I ask you?" He turned back to me, pointed a finger. "I want you out that door."

But as I hurried to leave, he grabbed my arm near my shoulder.

"Listen to me." The glaring eyes behind the heavy, black-rimmed glasses locked onto me. "You stay away from my wife. Don't be giving her any ideas. Now get out!"

I was so shaky I stumbled on my way to the door, fumbled with the brass knob, couldn't help looking over my shoulder. A figure stood far back in the shadowed hallway. A man. Couldn't make him out, but could feel his stare so intensely the hairs rose on the back of my neck.

I turned the knob, yanked the heavy door open, ran into the night. The air was sharp, clean, and cold. I tried to get my bearings. Parked cars filled the flat field behind the castle. I found the stretch-Hummer easily, then my Toyota nearby. I sucked in the fresh air. Above me, the sky soared up a million clear miles, its vast dome stenciled with silver stars.

I didn't understand the logistics, but it seemed Cheswick worked for the Baron. The Baron appeared to be bottling and selling lousy, doctored booze, which the Virginia ABC might want to know about. They wouldn't want the baron pocketing all those tax dollars. This might explain some of Cheswick's consternation.

I leaned into my car, found the keys beneath the seat, slipped inside, and locked the door. My hands still shook from the adrenalin rush, from the high of a close call — like being on a horse that clips heels in a race, almost goes down, but recovers at the last possible moment. The engine turned over and my little Toyota ferried me out of there. When I turned onto the county road, I laughed. An impulsive, nervous laugh.

I'd discovered a dirty little secret. Somehow, it didn't explain the depth or intensity of Cheswick's emotions. I didn't know who'd watched me from the hall, but it gave me an eerie feeling. Something more was going on. I'd make book on it.

24

Lorna met me at the cottage door with a lost look in her eyes. "Bobby never showed." Her lower lip trembled as she spoke. "He didn't call, won't answer his cell."

"He probably will soon." What should I tell her? Surely not the truth. At least not the whole truth. I pictured Bobby on the couch with that blonde. My gaze fell to the stone step beneath my feet.

"Could you, maybe, drive me over to his house? See if he's home, or something?"

"He's not there." The words popped out before I caught them.

"What do you mean? How do you know?"

"He was at the baron's tonight. With his father. Probably a last-minute command performance."

Lorna stepped back from the doorway to let me in. She watched me closely. "Yeah? So what was he doing?"

"Uh, talking to people. Hanging with his father. You know."

"Nikki, why do you keep looking at your feet? Is there something you're not telling me?"

Slippers headed toward me. I knelt down to greet him and rubbed his forehead with my knuckles. He plumed his tail and bumped his head against my thigh.

"Bobby might have had a drink or two," I said, gathering the cat into my arms, silently swearing never to drink bourbon again.

"He could've taken me." Her voice became a soft wail. "Why didn't he take me?"

My already tense muscles knotted as car wheels crunched on the gravel outside. It wasn't Bobby. You could hear that Shelby coming a mile away. I hoped like hell it wasn't Cheswick. Surely he'd be busy with the baron's party until late.

Lorna ran to the window and stared into the moonlight. "It's that investigator guy, Cormack. Why's he here?"

I sighed. It must have been a rougher night than I realized. I'd forgotten my call to Cormack on the way home from the party. He'd been real interested when I told him about Susan, said he'd look me up first thing in the morning. Apparently he'd decided not to wait.

My cell rang. The caller ID showed Cormack's number.

When I connected, he said, "This is Jay Cormack. Wanted you to know it was me out here, didn't want to spook you gals. Anybody in there 'side from you and Ms. Doone?"

I looked around the room. "Nobody except us and...a chicken?"

There was silence on the line for a beat. "I'll be right in, then."

"Lorna, I thought you hated that rooster."

The bird perched on the back of a kitchen chair, head low, eyes half closed.

"Him and Slippers were on the step earlier. I let the cat in and that feather duster busted in behind him. I was afraid he'd peck me or something. He boogies in, flaps up there on that chair. Hasn't moved since. I put some newspaper under him."

"I can see that," I said and headed to get fresh newspaper. "Got a name for him?"

"Nope." She glanced at the bird. "He does kinda grow on you, though."

My grin was interrupted by Cormack's knock. When I opened the door, he came in, cop eyes darting around the cottage, his close-cropped sandy hair covered with a black ball cap. He circled the room, glancing inside both bedrooms and the bath.

"Evenin' ladies." He took his hat off, rubbed his head, put the cap back on, and glanced at me. "I have some questions about what you told me earlier."

"Sure," I said.

Lorna stared. "What happened?"

"It's about Susan Stark. And maybe some other stuff I should tell Investigator Cormack."

"Call me Jay, please. Why don't we sit down?" he said. "Coffee would be nice." He moved over to the wood-plank table, then leaned over the rooster and stroked the bird's breast feathers with an index finger. "Hello there, Mr. Chicken."

The rooster made an odd trilling noise and closed one eye. *Mr. Chicken*? Worked for me.

Lorna got cups out, put milk and sugar on the table, while I brewed a pot of coffee. We sat at the table with our coffee and the bird. Slippers surprised me by arranging himself in Cormack's lap.

Cormack petted the cat with one of his neatly manicured hands. "Tell me again why you think Susan Stark was on drugs."

I explained how hopped up she'd been, how she went on about some awesome diet drug. "She told me her provider was at the party, in the room where we were talking."

Cormack's eyes narrowed. "Who was it?"

"I don't know. The place was crowded. People were dancing." I avoided Lorna's gaze by staring at Cormack. "I got distracted and Susan disappeared. I never had a chance to ask her. But I will."

"Go back a minute," Cormack said. "What distracted you?"

I struggled for a poker face. "Uh, I saw Bobby Duvayne." I studied the chicken's speckled black-and-white feathers. "I saw a guy with light, maybe blond hair running from the room, through this door in the paneling. Like he didn't want me to see him. At least that's the feeling I got."

"Know who it was?"

I shook my head. "Only got a glimpse." Could it have been Cheswick's silver hair? Had the man been tall enough? Why couldn't I remember? I held my coffee mug with both hands, comforted by the warm, smooth china.

"And you say young Duvayne was there?"

"Bobby doesn't sell drugs!" Lorna said. "He was there with his father."

"Didn't say he does," Cormack said easily.

He might not sell them, but he sure handed the stuff out to Lorna.

"Jay, you did ask me to call you Jay?" When he nodded, I continued. "Susan Stark worries me. She's super thin and she had a weird odor, like chemicals. She looked almost as bad the last time I saw her at the races. I didn't say anything to you. I should have said something."

"Better now than too late." He made that soft whistling sound through his teeth. "I don't want to spook her, though. I'll see if I can get the track doctor or the chaplain to talk to her."

Lorna opened her cell and pressed a speed dial number, no doubt trying Bobby again.

Cormack gently grasped Slippers, set the cat on the floor, and stood up.

"Y'all be keeping this information to yourselves, right?"

"Yes," I said.

Lorna glared at her phone, snapped it shut, and dropped it on the table. Cormack stared, waiting.

"Sure," she said. "My lips are zipped."

Except for what she'd repeat to Bobby. But Cormack wasn't stupid. Maybe he just wanted to shake the tree, see which varmints fell out.

I followed him so I could lock up after he left. He swung the door open, revealing a night sky where scudding clouds played across the moon, and shadows moved among the cedar trees.

The shifting tree line evoked a memory. "Wait," I said. "There's something I meant to ask you. I'll walk you out to your car." I grabbed my coat from a hook and shrugged it on.

We stepped into the yard, and Cormack turned to me. "What?"

"There's this weird guy. He drags a shovel around at night in the woods next to the backstretch. A real creep. Do you know anything about him?"

"Unhappy eyes, tall and thin?"

"That's him," I said. "Who is he?"

"Mike Talbot. Not a happy story." Cormack paused by his SUV. "It's been maybe 10 years now. Nobody knows exactly what happened, but he had some kind of nervous collapse. Comes from a good family, local people. But they had trouble dealing with him. Finally had him institutionalized. For almost a decade."

"But he's out now. Is he dangerous?"

"Nah. Hospital in Richmond cleared him. Shrink says he's harmless. A cousin has taken him in, makes sure Talbot goes to the walk-in clinic once a week."

A soft breeze rustled through the evergreens, branches rising and falling. Mello had said the same thing, that Talbot wasn't dangerous.

"He doesn't look harmless. What's with the shovel?"

"Wondered that myself," Cormack said. "The man used to be a riding instructor, a normal guy, well liked in the area. He's only been out a few weeks, but we keep an eye on him. Gave him a hot-walker's license so he could work for a trainer up near the stable gate."

"Talbot said something weird to me. He talked about finding her. Do you know what that means?"

"No," he said. "But the way you ask questions I might just put you on payroll." He grinned, folded himself into his SUV and drove away.

What had driven Talbot to insanity?

The breeze worked itself into a little wind, moaning softly through the pine needles. Things moved and shifted in the dark around me. I hurried, anxious to get back in the cottage.

25

I awoke with a tongue swollen like a toad sitting in my mouth. My head felt worse than that, but after a pot of coffee, Lorna and I managed to leave the cottage before six. A warm front from the south had left the air damp and humid, the ground wreathed with fog. I drove carefully along the farm road, slowing each time gray mist obscured our path.

When the Toyota hit a pothole in the gravel drive, I groaned and Lorna grabbed her head. She'd gotten into the Wild Turkey after Cormack left. Unable to reach Bobby, she'd had no trouble finding the bourbon in the kitchen cabinet. I'd escaped to my bedroom and crawled under the covers.

"Watch those bumps," she said. "My head feels like an overripe pumpkin." She pressed fingers to her forehead. "Bobby better have a good explanation."

I admired the bravado in her voice. The previous night, I'd heard her crying after I went to bed. Better to be angry. As we rolled through the backstretch to our barn, she looked over the grounds for Bobby, while pretending not to.

Ramon had already fed the horses their light breakfast. We were met by eight pairs of bright eyes, heads over stall gates, and body language straining with an impatience to train.

"We could stay in the car," Lorna said. "They might forget we're here."

Yeah, right.

We rode the first set out, warming up the horses with a brisk jog the "wrong way" around the track. We passed the five-eighths pole, eased the horses down to a walk, and turned to head counterclockwise — racing direction.

I was aboard a five-year-old gray mare. The minute I turned her the "right way" she danced and fretted, anxious to go. We kept the gray and Lorna's bay head-to-head, and just before we hit the pole, we urged them into a speedy two-minute lick. The rail flew past us as we powered five-eighths of a mile, covering each eighth in 15 seconds.

At the wire, we stood in our stirrups and galloped the horses out another quarter mile. They blew hard as we walked back, having just moved at the speed it takes to cover a mile in two minutes. The pair had shipped off a training farm in Virginia and were hardly as fit as the owner claimed. Of course, Lorna and I weren't in great shape either.

Lorna's eyes searched the track, but Bobby had either ridden back to his barn or hadn't come out yet. He might not be around at all. Might be afraid I'd told Lorna about the blonde. But I'd let *him* have that pleasure.

We rode back to our shedrow at a conservative walk, turned the horses over to Ramon and Mello, climbed on the next two, and headed back out. Will Marshall rode alongside us onto the sandy oval. He was astride a fractious youngster.

"Mind if I ride with you?" he asked.

"Not at all," I said, taking in the sleeveless black shirt and jeans over his wiry, trim body. The morning's warmth had reduced Lorna and me to short sleeve tees beneath our protective riding vests. Sweat ran between my breasts. The stuff dripped from beneath Lorna's helmet and trickled down her temples. I hoped the previous night's toxins flushed out with the sweat.

Will's colt tossed his head high and slammed into my roan gelding, forcing Will's knee into my thigh, and a smile onto his mouth. "Looking a little rough there, Latrelle. Late night?"

"I don't want to talk about it."

"Will," Lorna said, "have you seen Bobby this morning?"

"No," he said, his lips tightening. "Don't care to, either."

"Let's move on," I said, and we eased into a gallop, Will against the rail, me in the middle, and Lorna on my right. Our pace was slower than originally intended, but Will's colt needed to learn. People at the track help each other out. It was one of the things I loved. I had no doubt Will would return the favor.

* * * *

Lorna and I were in the feed room measuring up lunch when I heard Mello's voice.

"You hurt yourself, Mr. Bobby?"

Lorna whipped past me into the shedrow. I stuck my head out the door to see Bobby limping toward us.

"Oh my," Mello said, shaking his head.

An ugly bruise marked Bobby's jaw, reminding me of the damage done to my face by that speed addict.

"What happened?" Lorna asked. She'd stopped a few feet away from him, as if unwilling or uncertain about closing the gap.

"I fell off earlier." He placed his fingertips lightly on his swollen jaw. "Grazed the rail on the way down."

He wouldn't look at any of us and I knew he was lying. Somebody goes off and hits the rail, you hear about it. Everyone would have. Lorna would probably pry out the real story.

They were a sorry pair. Lorna's eyes were puffy from crying, her skin color sickly from hangover, and Bobby looked like his horse had run over top of him. I ducked into the tack room, dug in my purse for a bottle of Ibuprofen, then offered them around. The three of us ate the pills like candy, washed them down with Coke. I returned to scooping grain into buckets and when I came out, Bobby had left, and Lorna sat on Mello's rickety green bench with her eyes closed. What had Bobby said?

"I wanna go back for a nap," Lorna said. On the way she asked me to stop by the Providence Forge Rite Aid. She wanted Sudafed.

We wasted time in the store's allergy aisle looking for the decongestant. I finally asked a girl stocking paper products one aisle over.

"You have to get it from the pharmacy," she said, stabbing a box cutter into a cardboard carton of paper towels.

"Why?" Lorna asked.

"It's the law," the girl said, struggling to pry paper towels from the box.

The man behind the pharmacy counter wore a fussy little mustache, had nervous fingers and thin, disapproving lips. Behind him white laminate shelves rose to the ceiling stacked with bottles of pills, liquid medicines and medical supplies.

"You got any Sudafed back there?" Lorna asked through the narrow opening in an inch-thick wall of Plexiglass. Probably bulletproof.

"We sell it," he said, staring at Lorna, taking in her brow ring and tattoo.

"So, could I buy some, or what?"

"You got a driver's license?"

"You gotta see my driver's license to sell me Sudafed?"

"State and federal law." He folded his arms across his chest. "It's you young people causing the paperwork and trouble."

"I don't know anything about that." Lorna twisted a lock of red hair.

"Kids use it to make methamphetamine."

"Seems like the law punishes the innocent," I said.

"You don't like it? How do you think we feel?" He leaned to the side and grabbed a clipboard, slammed it on the counter. "I have to have proof of identity, disclosure forms, copy your license number and address down." He waved a clipboard at us, white paper flapping. "I have to contact the Attorney General if —"

"Stop!" Lorna said, pulling a wallet from her jacket. "*Please*, here's my driver's license. I've got this headache. My sinuses are all stopped up."

They glared at each other a moment, then the pharmacist grabbed Lorna's license and wrote the information down. When they finished, I could see the guy had trouble handing the medicine over.

Lorna snatched the pharmacy bag and turned to me with a gleam in her eye. I could see a smart comment coming.

"Don't," I said. "Guy's just doing his job. Remember what that meth addict did to me?"

She sighed. "Yeah. But it's ridiculous to go through this bullshit." She paused a beat. "You know, almost looks like the same guy mugged you got a hold of Bobby. He didn't go off any horse this morning."

"No," I said. But why had he lied? It was time to find out more.

26

I left Lorna at the cottage, telling her I wanted to get a book at the Providence Forge library, which had hours till noon. What I really wanted were newspaper articles relating to the death of the Cheswick boys, especially any mentioning Bobby Duvayne.

Like everything else in Providence Forge, the library appeared to be caught in a 1960s time warp. It had a flat roof, that old style that's usually maintained with tar and gravel. Time and sun had bleached the parking lot's asphalt to a pale gray. Potholes pitted the surface and loose gravel spun beneath my wheels as I parked outside the library. Pushing through a heavy glass door, I spotted the librarian behind a counter. A bald man, maybe 40 years old, hunched over a computer screen, typing rapidly with intense concentration.

I stood there a moment, finally saying, "Excuse me."

He glanced up. "Yes?" His fingers still flew on the keys.

"I'm looking for information on an incident that happened a year ago August." I spoke fast, competing with the rapid pace of his fingers. "So, how would I do that?"

"Local or national?"

"What?"

"The incident, was it local or national?"

"Oh, local. I was thinking the Richmond paper…"

"What incident?" he asked, fingers still galloping along, his eyes never leaving the screen.

"Two boys were murdered."

The typing stopped as he met my gaze. "The Cheswick boys, you mean?"

"Yes. Do you know about them?"

His mouth grew prim. "Let me direct you to the Richmond *Times Dispatch*."

I wasn't going to get any gossip from this guy. He stood up and walked me over to a shelf with stacks of the newspaper.

"Copies up to one year old are here. For older articles you'll have to access the *Dispatch's* morgue on a computer." He waved a hand at several machines on a long rectangular table.

"Can you show me how?"

He did, and in no time I was typing "Cheswick" in a keyword box.

A craft show featuring Bunny's dolls and an article about a blue-ribbon rooster at the New Kent County Fair popped up. They were dated about six years earlier. So Bunny'd had a life. I studied her picture, younger, happier. The days that were no more.

Then I noticed a range-of-dates box and typed in August and the year the Cheswick boys died.

A flurry of articles came up. Staring at a photo of Todd and Tim, their life and death suddenly became real. They looked cute and bright. The younger son, Tim, looked mischievous, the way his brows raised and his lips curved in a half smile. Bunny, losing both sons. No wonder...

They'd been found in a parking lot behind a bar in Sandston, Virginia, not far from the Richmond airport. Shot at close range, suffering chest and head wounds. A picture showed two black body bags. I turned my eyes back to the rows of type.

I found nine articles in the three-month period, from August through October of the previous year. Headline news at first, they tapered down to one paragraph buried on the last page of the metro section.

Only two articles mentioned Bobby. They carried similar information, but the second expanded a bit:

LOCAL BOY QUESTIONED
IN CHESWICK MURDERS

Investigators are questioning Providence Forge resident Robert Duvayne, 18, in the August 16 murders of brothers Todd, 18, and Tim, 15, Cheswick. Duvayne allegedly met the Cheswicks at Sandston's Riviera Bar & Grill shortly before the brothers were shot to death, according to police. The shooting occurred in the bar's parking lot at 11:30 P.M. There were no witnesses. Police have not determined the reason for the shooting.

"It was a drug deal gone sour," said Riviera employee Vincent Argulie. "I'm convinced of it. They were pumped up on something, talking tough, dropping hints about some 'big deal' they were into. It's sad. Underage, all of them. The youngest hardly looked fifteen."

Argulie identified Duvayne as the man accompanying the Cheswicks, police said. Information about what role, if any, Duvayne might have played in the brothers' death is not known. Calls to the Duvayne home were not returned.

So Bobby *was* there. But *he* hadn't been shot. Had he left in time or did he know the shooters? More importantly, how could I get Lorna away from this guy?

I rolled my shoulders to ease a growing muscle tension, took a deep breath, drawing in the smell of paper, ink, and plastic dust jackets that layered the room. Time to get some newsprint on my hands. I walked to the shelves holding the last twelve months of the *Dispatch*, and dug in.

No reference to the case until late December of the previous year. A follow up article appeared with a short headline.

NO LEADS IN CHESWICK MURDERS

Bobby's name came up about midway through the article:

> Investigator Norman Jasper of the New Kent County Sheriff's Department, in a statement issued Monday, said Mr. Duvayne was cleared of involvement in the murders, and is no longer a suspect.

The report did not say why Bobby was cleared. Maybe some woman came forward saying she'd spent the night with him. Probably dragged her feet with the alibi because she was married. Be just like Bobby. At least Lorna wasn't running with a murderer.

But whatever the alibi, it meant nothing to me. Bobby knew something about those Cheswick boys. I'd lay money on it.

27

Lorna and I returned to the backstretch that afternoon to find Mello dozing on his bench, his head resting against the brick wall, a brown paper bag at his feet. He roused himself, yawned, and began humming a soft, nameless tune. The old man had a history with alcohol, whiskey in particular, but since he'd arrived in Virginia he'd been on the wagon. Living in the backstretch grooms' quarters without a car probably played a role in his sobriety.

I stared at the bag. "What you got in there, Mello."

"Miss Nikki, you don't needs to be worrying about me."

I did worry, but didn't want to say it. "It's just that I need you at your best for the horses, Mello."

"Don't you be fretting like some old broody hen. I always takes care of my horses."

I clammed up. I was hardly in a position to criticize. I still had a hangover.

"That Mr. Pemberton, now he be a gentleman. Brought me a bottle from that party last night."

"*Gilded Baron*?" My stomach churned.

Mello stretched his arm down, slid a gnarled hand into the bag and withdrew a liquor bottle. He squinted at the label. "That what it says here."

He unscrewed the cap, took a swig. "Mighty sweet, but kicks like an old mule. Yes sir, like an old mule." He sighed and rested his head against the wall again.

"Mello, didn't you say you found a grill?" When he nodded, I said. "It's warm enough we could cook outside. I brought some chicken and salad stuff."

"Sounds mighty fine, Miss Nikki. Let me get that grill."

I'd hoped to dump out some of that rot-gut while he was gone, but he picked up his bag and took it with him. No flies on Mello. The man had a gift for "finding" things, too. Like grills, rubber stall mats, and extra feed tubs just when they were needed. Oddly, nobody ever complained about missing items. Many things about Mello remained a mystery.

"Are you gonna help me scoop grain, or what?" Lorna stood at the door to the feed room.

Nodding, I stepped inside and began adding glucosamine, corn oil, and other supplements to the buckets she'd lined up.

"Bobby told me what happened last night," she said.

"Yeah?" I studied the fine print on an electrolyte box.

"He said he might've had too much to drink. Might've gotten a bit too friendly with this woman. Said you saw him."

"Huh," I said.

"So was he, like, doing the lip lock or what?"

"Yes," I said. "I interrupted them."

"Was she pretty?"

"She was old enough to be his mother." I didn't need to add "sexy blonde bombshell" to my description.

"What did they do after you *interrupted* them?"

"The woman stormed off, and that was the end of it."

"He could have been with me. Why didn't he want to be with me?"

I didn't have an answer. I gave her a hug instead.

Bobby appeared a short time later in figure molding jeans, a white tee, and a suede jacket. His mother's ruby cross glowed at his neck. I glanced at him and Lorna. All was not lost in paradise. He reached a hand to her face, his long fingers gently tucking a lock of red hair behind an ear. He traced the line of her cheek. Lorna leaned into him. I looked away.

Mello rolled his grill over, fired up the charcoal, and returned to his bench. The paper bag rested at his feet again.

The simple meal swept out the last of my hangover. Bobby, Lorna and I consumed quantities of iced coke. Mello nursed his bottle throughout the evening, and at some point his attention settled on Bobby and remained there.

A motherless boy. Could that be one of the things that attracted me to Bobby? I'd always been one to pick up strays, Hellish being my latest.

"Bobby," I said, "what happened to your mother?"

Lorna's eyes widened, Mello leaned forward abruptly, and Bobby's face had that deer-in-the-headlights expression. He stared at me a moment, then spoke in a voice so low I had to strain to hear.

"She ran out on me."

"Were you young?"

"Ten." He seemed to draw inside himself, and Lorna, who sat next to him, closed her hand over his.

"I'm sorry." I didn't know what else to say. Why had I pried at him like that? In the chair opposite me, Mello's eyes never left Bobby.

"Your Mama didn't leave you. She loved her baby, 'deed she did."

"What the hell are you talking about?"

Lorna leaned closer. "Mello doesn't mean anything. He's just been into that bourbon, is all."

"I knows things, and I knows Miss Catherine didn't walk on you."

Bobby snatched his hand from Lorna's and stood, knocking his lawn chair over. His face darkened with that angry flush I'd seen at the party. His bruise seemed to swell and grow uglier.

"Listen, old man. You don't know what the fuck you're talking about. My mother left me, snuck away in the middle of the night, and I never saw her again. I don't need you telling me what happened."

Mello cringed. He unscrewed the top from his bourbon bottle and downed a long swallow.

Bobby whirled and faced Lorna. "You coming with me, or what?"

Lorna stood without answering, passing me as she followed Bobby toward his car. She looked rattled, almost afraid.

That had gone well. What was wrong with me? I almost reached for Mello's bottle. Almost.

"Mello, please don't drink any more."

"I'd like to oblige you, Miss Nikki, but I just don't knows if I can." He sighed and stared at the amber liquid still rolling inside the glass. "Terrible thing that boy been led to believe his mama ran off."

He'd caught my attention. "What do you mean 'led' to believe?"

"Someone told that boy she ran off. I knows she didn't."

"How do you know?"

"I get my little visions, messages from the other side."

If Mello hadn't drunk so much whiskey, he might not have disclosed such doubtful information. Messages from the other side? Was I supposed to think he sat around conversing with Catherine Tasker? Then again, what did I know?

Mello began to tear strips of paper from the brown bag and watch them drift to the ground. "Then too," he said, "I got a Pinkney cousin lives here. She kept house for the Tasker family, back when Catherine was a girl. My cousin always said Miss Catherine was a kind lady and real beautiful, too."

I knew Bobby hadn't gotten those looks from his father. John Talbot's face had all the refinement of a brick. Had Bobby's intoxicating sexuality come from Catherine, as well? If so, she'd have stirred up the local male population.

"Does your cousin know what happened to Catherine?"

"She won't say, she scared about something." He set the bottle down, hummed for a bit, yawned, and closed his eyes.

I cleaned up the dinner trash, grabbed a carrot from the tack-room refrigerator, then walked the shedrow to check the horses. Stinger had taken longer than most to recover from his race stress, but tonight his eyes glowed. He'd put on some weight, too.

Next door, I admired Daffodil's glossy coat, long clean legs and elegant manner. I'd see if the racing secretary would let Daffodil work the turf course. I needed to know if she'd take to the grass like I thought she would.

Moving down the row, checking each horse, I kept remembering Bobby's anger. I understood the source all too well, but it didn't give him the right to mess up Lorna's life. At the end of the line, I stopped outside Hellish's gate.

She pinned her ears, swishing her tail like an irritated cat.

"You're such a head case," I said. "That starter allowance is coming right up and you'd better behave."

I'd made the mistake of wagging my finger at her. She bared her teeth, rushed the stall gate, and snapped at my finger. I jumped back just in time.

"*Bitch.*" I pulled the carrot from my jacket pocket and held it out. She pricked her ears, arched her neck, and warmed her eyes with kindness.

"Deceitful, too." I handed her the carrot. Her front teeth chopped it in half, her tongue rolling it back to crunch between her molars.

I could hear Mello snoring from his chair, so I stopped in the tack room, found a clean horse blanket and draped it over him, tucking the ends around his shoulders. He never stirred. I left him to sleep it off.

* * * *

I was in bed when Bobby dropped Lorna off before ten. I hadn't planned on getting up until I heard her crash into the kitchen table and break what sounded like china.

I flipped on the light. Lorna sat on the floor next to an overturned chair and the blue shards of a smashed coffee mug.

She blinked in the sudden brightness, focused on me, and began to giggle.

"Thick a fork in me. I'm done." Another peal of laughter. "Bobby done me so good."

Her slurred speech and lack of coordination said "drunk," but her expression was intent as she stared at her right leg. She tapped her thigh with a finger, then smiled.

"Lorna, what are you doing?"

Slowly, she glanced up, gave a little start as if surprised to find me standing over her.

"Stuff makes me numb," she said tapping her thigh again. Feels weird."

"What stuff?"

"Awesome shit. 'Ludes or somethin'. Makes me like I got no bones, you know?" She smiled a dreamy smile, gave me a sly look. "Bobby did some Ecstasy and man, he was all over me like he'd never stop. And I —"

"I don't want to hear that part! Are you talking about Quaaludes?"

Lorna's smile grew uncertain. "Yeah."

"This is bullshit, Lorna. This guy's gonna put you in jail. At the very least, get you ruled off."

"No," Lorna said, her voice soft. "We took the stuff because it's, like, magic sex potion. I couldn't get enough, and he couldn't give enough."

I stared at her.

Her gaze drifted away. "Bobby loves me."

"If he loves you why does he put you at risk?"

Lorna's finger still poked at her thigh, but tears fell on her hand. Her shoulders shook, then sobs filled the room.

I went to the kitchen sink, snatched a paper towel off the roll and knelt next to her, placing the towel into her hand.

"I'm not gonna let that son of a bitch ruin your life, Lorna."

She wouldn't look at me.

Damn Duvayne. "Come on," I said. "Let's get you to bed."

I knew something about the illegal muscle relaxer, Quaalude, and was pretty sure Lorna just needed to sleep it off. I waited for her to mop her face, then helped her up, got her into her room, and finally to bed.

A boy who'd been held back in my Baltimore grade school had called himself the Quaalude King. The powerful drug had been banned from the prescription market, but the "King" took the downer regularly and sold it to classmates. Rumor had it the King had a violent home life, took the pills to cope. He should have run away.

"Worked for me," I said, my words sounding hollow in the silent cottage. But Lorna had a family that loved her. She deserved better.

28

A bit groggy, but otherwise functional, Lorna stood in Daffodil's stall holding the filly's halter. She watched while I repeatedly looped a strip of white cotton under the horse's jaw and over the tongue, finishing with a knot.

Most racehorses wear a "tongue tie" during morning speed works and afternoon races. Pre-race tension, or a rush of adrenalin, often triggers an anxious swallowing reflex, causing the horse to roll his tongue back and block his air passage. A horse without air is a horse that slows dramatically, usually about the time he's supposed to be flying down the home stretch.

"That tongue ain't going nowhere," Lorna said.

"I hope not."

When Lorna pulled a set of blinkers over Daffodil's head, the double cue of tongue tie with blinkers caused the filly's muscles to tense to a marble-like hardness.

"Grab that stopwatch, Lorna. You need to get her time in case the clocker doesn't. Go stand at the finish wire."

Lorna scooted away while Ramon gave me a leg up. He led Daffodil for a turn around the shedrow. With all that equipment on, she might feel like bucking or plunging. Better to have someone at her head.

We made it to the track without incident. I warmed Daffodil up with a slow gallop, then nudged her through the inside rail-gap with my heels. I felt those long legs hit the bouncy sod, her first step onto the springy turf of a professionally maintained course. Probably hadn't seen an expanse of green since the last time she'd been loose in a pasture.

Daffodil nodded her head rapidly up and down, as if excited by the grass beneath her hooves.

"Good girl," I said, pushing her into an open gallop, aiming for the five-eighths pole. We hit the pole and I set her down, the ground seeming to rise as her tremendous stride grew long and low. *Racing speed.*

Daffodil hit the turn, banking through it like a fighter-jet before exploding down the stretch. My body screamed from the effort of keeping up — pumping, breathing, balancing. Lorna and the finish line flew at us fast, flashing by in a blur.

Breathless, I stood in the irons, asking the filly to ease back, fearing she'd run off with me. But like a pushbutton machine, she bowed her neck and collected herself into a rocking horse gallop, then slowed so she could turn and head back. No drug in the world could produce a high like the one she'd just given me.

Daffodil's performance had knocked the grog from Lorna. The redhead snapped a shank on Daffodil. "Look how fit she is! This filly wouldn't blow out a match."

Hard as I was gasping I could have extinguished a blow torch. When I could, I said, "The time Lorna, what's her time?"

Lorna looked up at me, her hazel eyes filled with trepidation. "Uh, think I messed up, didn't hit the right button till you'd passed the pole."

"That's just great, Lorna." Who was this lackadaisical, incompetent person? I stroked the fur that glistened with sweat on Daffodil's neck. My fingers left streaks where they slicked her coat, leaving the air filled with the hot scent of horse.

Nearing the barn, I spotted Amarilla's yellow Cadillac with the brown vinyl-top parked by our shedrow.

"She know you were working Daffodil this morning?" Lorna asked.

"Not exactly."

"I thought she didn't want the horse to run on the turf. She have a change of heart?"

"Not really."

"*Oh boy.*" Lorna's enthusiasm seemed inappropriate. "She's tapping her foot."

We reached the barn and Amarilla, dressed in yellow and brown leather, was indeed tapping her boot-encased foot. Her arms were crossed over her chest and a scowl transformed her mouth into something released from hell.

Didn't look promising.

"Didn't she throw a book at you the last time she saw you?" Lorna sounded gleeful.

"Why don't you—" I breathed in, rubbed my jaw. "—see if the clocker caught Daffodil's time."

She remained motionless, her glance switching back and forth between Amarilla and me.

"*Now.*"

She undid Daffodil's lead and scurried away. I wished I could go with her. I rode the filly onto the shedrow's dirt aisle and booted her inside her stall. Ramon came in behind us with her halter, and I slid off.

"That Amarilla, she not too happy," he said.

"Doesn't appear to be." I sighed and stepped outside to face the venom.

Amarilla hovered near the stall, almost buzzing. "Are you deaf? You not hear me say no turf? I try very hard be nice to you. And how you respond? Insolence!"

"Amarilla, you pay me to train the horse. It's my job to make her the best race filly I can. She's made for the turf." Hadn't Daffodil just proven that?

"You estupido, like disobedient child. I —"

"You know what? Why don't you just take your horses and make some other trainer's life miserable, because I'm done."

My outburst left her speechless. I enjoyed my little victory. It probably wouldn't last.

Lorna appeared around the corner of the barn with trainer Lilly Best in tow. "Tell 'em what the clocker said!"

"I will, if you'll stop draggin' me. Let me catch my breath." Lilly pulled her hand from Lorna's grip. Her substantial figure came to a halt as she blew air in and out.

"Who is this woman?" Amarilla demanded.

"Nice to meet you, too." Lilly ignored Amarilla's nasty scowl and turned to me. "That chestnut you worked on the turf just now? Everybody's talking 'n gawking, she was that fast."

"Lilly," I said, nodding at Amarilla. "This is Miss Chaquette, the owner."

"Got a nice horse, Miss Jacket. Stakes potential on the grass with that one."

"She run even better on the dirt, no?"

Lilly stared at me. I answered with a "beats me" expression.

"Lady, you need to get real," Lorna said. "That was a bullet work out there. Clocker said no horse has ever worked this turf so fast. And you want to run her on the *dirt*?"

"How fast she go?" Amarilla's anger dissolved into palpable, greedy interest.

We turned to Lilly. "Y'all wanna sit down first?" she said, enjoying her moment.

"Lilly," I said. "Spit it out."

"Fifty-seven flat."

"Holy shit." I clapped my hand over my mouth, afraid I might start shrieking.

"This is not unheard of," said Amarilla. "Many times I see horses race the, how you say, five-eighths, like this."

"Yeah, but this was around the cones," Lorna said.

"What is this cone?" Amarilla's frown deepened. She didn't understand.

Lilly shifted her considerable weight to her right foot, used that pla-
cating, soft Virginia drawl. "Track sets cones out — those red and white
things about yea tall?" She bent her knee a bit, lowered a hand to the
height of a cone tip.

Amarilla's foot began to tap.

"They do it to protect the turf. It makes the horses stay farther from
the rail than they would in a race."

Amarilla's foot quieted. "Yes, I see," she said. "So Daffodil, she go
farther. The time should be slower, yet she…" The scowl flew away,
replaced by a warm smile. "Yes, I see. Still…" She turned to me with a
last barb, "I prefer the dirt. I will think about this."

Lorna rolled her eyes, her lips soundlessly mimicking Amarilla's last
words.

"You do that. I've got a race to get ready for."

I left the woman to stew in this new conflict and moved toward
Hellish's stall, the first touch of pre-race anxiety like a feather on my
spine.

29

The following afternoon, I rode Hellish from the paddock for the starter allowance beneath an overcast sky. Along the rail, Carla Ruben, who'd driven down from Baltimore, stood wrapped in fur-trimmed black leather. Her blond hair, full and luminous around her shoulders, stirred slightly as a breeze kicked up. Lorna leaned on the rail next to her, her head barely reaching Carla's shoulder.

They gave me a thumbs up, but I could see they were nervous. They each owned a piece of Hellish, and owners get jittery before their horses run.

Hellish's muscles rippled, her veins clearly defined beneath her slick red coat. She was pumped. As we cantered away, she pushed hard into the side of the pony that accompanied us.

The pony's rider, a Native American with one glass eye, cursed softly. "Thinks she's the queen bee."

He jerked the strap that ran through the ring on Hellish's bit, giving the filly's mouth a reprimanding snatch. Hellish bared her teeth at him, then mercifully behaved.

After the mob of racehorses, ponies and outriders finished the warmup, we formed a ragged line behind the red-coated outrider leading us toward the starting gate.

Each horse approaching the row of narrow metal stalls was required to have run for a tag of five thousand or less, and reading the Form earlier, it didn't appear any had shown much improvement since they ran that cheap. Except Hellish. A work she'd put in at Laurel a few weeks earlier appeared an aberration on the page. She'd produced a work almost as sensational as Daffodil's. The track handicapper had made her the morning line favorite. Made me glad she was in a race where no one could claim her.

I practiced my breathing, hoping to keep the tension under wraps. I'd never raced Hellish, and comments like, "unruly at the gate," and "difficult at the start," peppered her past performances. Of course I'd worked her from the gate in the morning, but Hellish knew the difference between the morning and the afternoon. I'd never seen her this cranked.

We'd drawn the four hole in the field of eight. Will Marshall had the outside post, and next to me Susan Stark, looking weak and skeletal, had drawn the three spot.

Assistant starters loaded the first three, then one took Hellish's strap from our one-eyed pony man. Hellish allowed him to lead her to the four slot, but planted her feet, refusing to go in. I booted her gently. She reared, plunging backwards.

The lead guy hung onto her head while two other assistant starters carefully joined hands behind her. Their arms formed a band and they pushed it against her hindquarters, encouraging her to move into the gate. I could feel her back hump behind the saddle. I grabbed mane and held on as she let loose a series of vicious kicks.

The two men leapt to safety. The guy at her head reached in his pocket and pulled out a tong. I might not know everything about this filly, but I knew if this guy clamped her ear with a nasty tool resembling a pair of pliers, somebody'd get hurt. Bad.

"Don't use that!" Frantically, I worked my fingers under the elastic bands that held the silk's sleeves tight against my wrist. I withdrew a small carrot. "Try this."

The guy rolled his eyes and ignored me.

"Please!"

He aimed the metal tool for Helllish's ear. One of the guys who'd been behind, appeared down by my side. I remembered his name was Danny.

"Give it to me," he said, grabbing the carrot.

Quick as a wink, Danny was at the filly's head, muscling Tong Man out of the way. He showed Hellish the treat. She pricked her ears and followed him into the gate. Danny climbed up on the side rail and held her head.

"Thanks. You'd better give her the carrot," I said.

"But she's about to break!"

"You want a fit in this cage?"

He gave her the carrot.

I prayed she'd have time to swallow the thing before we broke. If it lodged in her windpipe, we had no chance. Lady Luck smiled on us, because the seven horse balked and it took a while to wrangle her into the stall.

Danny was patting Hellish's neck with one hand, holding her bridle with the other. He grinned, suddenly, "She got it down. You're good to go."

They loaded Will's horse. The one and the two fussed in place, their jockeys yelling, "No, No, No!" to the head starter who stood nearby clutching the gate's remote control. He waited for that one nanosecond of quiet. It came, the bell rang, the gates crashed open and Hellish exploded like a rocket.

A six-furlong sprint, but still, I tucked her behind the front two runners, trying to cover her up until the top of the stretch.

Susan Stark blew by us, her horse rank, its head in the air, evading the bit. Out of control, the horse grabbed the lead. She'd burn herself up, but I had my own problems. Two jockeys ranged their mounts beside me, and one of the Belgado brothers closed in behind, boxing me in. I should have expected it after Hellish's speedy work.

I bided my time, took a quick glance behind. Will Marshall, on the eight horse, ran near the back of the pack. He was the only one I was worried about. His horse had posted some good speed figures in the past, and you never knew when a horse might jump up and run the race of its life.

Still boxed in, we hit the turn. I waited for an opening. None came. Dirt from the metal-shod hooves of the horses ahead sandblasted my face and goggles. I pulled a dirt-caked set from my eyes, leaving it to dangle beneath my chin as I whipped new ones from the top of my helmet.

At the head of the stretch, Hellish made a move. I had to stand in the irons, take a hold to keep her from clipping heels with the horse ahead of her.

"Give me room!" I screamed. The jockeys ignored me. Damn. I'd buried myself on the rail.

Will's horse appeared outside the pair that pinned me in. No obstacles in her path, his filly flew by.

Son of a bitch!

On the lead, Susan's horse ran out of gas, forcing the jockey directly before me to swing wide or slam into Susan's filly.

A tiny hole appeared, big enough for Hellish's head. Not her body. Screw it. I pointed her head at the hole and she shoved it in. She pinned her ears and drove forward until her big shoulders wedged apart the horses on either side. She saw daylight, and we were gone.

Only Will raced ahead of us, the wire coming fast. But I sat on a keg of dynamite. "Now, Hellish!" I screamed. She blew by Will like he was on a stick-horse. We flashed under the wire a good length ahead. My fist pumped the air.

"Yes!"

I stood in the stirrups, felt tears stinging my eyes. My hand stroked Hellish's neck. "Thank you," I whispered, and gathered the reins. It took a while to pull her up. We were halfway down the backstretch before I got her slowed to where I could turn her toward the grandstand.

Something was wrong — an ambulance on the track before the grandstand, an outrider leading a loose horse toward the waiting grooms. People standing and kneeling by a jockey sprawled on the track.

The silks aren't green. Will wore green. The sudden need to make sure it was anyone but Will caught me by surprise. But who?

I had to get to the winner's circle. Everyone would be waiting there. I put Hellish into a canter and headed back. We approached the medics, outrider and ambulance.

Susan Stark lay crumpled on the ground, not moving. The group hovered around her and lifted her onto a stretcher. *Like Paco.*

The sense of déjà vu chilled me. Hellish moved on past. I almost pulled her up, the need to be with Susan strong. I had to shake myself mentally to remember what I was doing. A no-show for the win picture would only anger the stewards.

Why hadn't I said something to Cormack sooner? I could have kept this from happening!

"Nikki?" Ramon trotted through the deep sand after me, holding a lead shank. "Where you going?"

With no guidance from her rider, Hellish headed around the track for the gap closest to her barn. We'd already passed the winner's circle. I turned her back toward Ramon.

He stared down the track to where they'd loaded Susan into the ambulance. "How bad she hurt?"

"I don't know."

Lorna and Carla waited in the dug-out winner's circle. Behind them a shoulder-high semicircle of brickwork supported a wrought-iron fence painted teal. Fans lounged on the concrete apron behind, leaning on the railing above us, waiting to watch us enjoy our minute of fame. Jim stood near Lorna. He'd made the long drive to watch my race. His unexpected visit comforted me. He wore a big grin and I couldn't help but smile back. But why did Amarilla stand next to him? She looked… happy?

Ramon positioned Hellish sideways for the picture, the humans crushed shoulder to shoulder in front of the wall, wearing big smiles as the camera flashed. I slid off Hellish, removed the saddle and Ramon led her away. Lorna slapped my palm halfheartedly. Carla hugged me and I breathed in that fresh citrus scent she liked to use.

"What happened to Susan?" My voice had cracked as tension closed my throat.

"She passed out, just slid off the horse," said Lorna. "She never made it to the wire."

Carla studied my face. "Lorna told me about that girl. It's not your fault, Nikki."

Amarilla put her hands on her hips. "Of course it not my Nikki's fault. She the winner!" Then she stepped in and hugged me, like we were best buddies. Her pungent perfume gave me a faint wave of nausea.

"You must come to the suite. We drink, no?" Amarilla's breath smelled like vermouth. She must have already been into those martinis.

"I gotta weigh in," I said.

"Nikki." Carla's hand brushed my arm. "You look like you could use a drink. I know…" she gestured toward the ambulance driving off the track in the distance. "But how often do you win a race?"

"Yeah," Lorna said. "Carla's never won a race."

"A small celebration, then. Everyone comes." Amarilla clapped her hands.

"Sure." I headed for the scales with my saddle, thinking of Susan, so concerned with the weight. Why had she been so stupid? Taking that damn diet cocktail.

The next set of runners caught my peripheral vision as they headed from the backstretch onto the big oval for the eighth race. Like nothing had happened. To Susan…or Paco. Who would be next? Lorna?

I had to find the bastard selling this poison.

30

I sat at a table in the Baron's suite with Lorna and Jim. Carla's long shapely legs were molded in black leather pants as she walked over from the bar and handed me a tall citrus-vodka with tonic.

"I know you like bourbon," Carla said, "but what he's got is unacceptable."

I glanced at the bartender. He polished a glass with a white cloth behind an array of liquor bottles and cans of soda. An amber bottle of Gilded Baron stood among the gin, vodka and scotch. The glass on the counter, abandoned by my friend, must be filled with the odious syrup. Carla knew the service industry better than most. She sold wholesale meat to hotels and restaurants and understood the importance of quality.

I sipped the vodka. "Thanks."

"I can't imagine why they'd serve such an inferior product." She tossed her blond hair, dismissing the baron's bourbon.

Amarilla played hostess and stood close to the plate-glass window near the far end of the room. She spoke with a man wearing tortoiseshell glasses. I'd seen him during my previous visit to the suite. Amarilla snuck a couple of peeks in our direction.

Carla wore her standard shrink-wrapped white top that almost screamed, "Are these breasts great, or what?" She'd accessorized with black-and-silver jewelry. It was probably killing Amarilla to see a woman just as beautiful, only younger. Nicer, too.

Lorna and Jim worked on beers and were recapping the race.

"The way she busted open that hole! It was, like, totally awesome!"

"Has ability," Jim said.

"Yeah, then she blew past the eight horse like he was stuck on a merry-go-round pole. She was, like, dust on the horizon!"

"Let's not forget the great ride Nicky gave Hellish." Carla raised her glass to me.

I felt the tingle on the back of my neck from someone staring. Investigator Cormack stood in the suite's entrance, his hands holding a wool cap. He caught my eye. I downed more vodka.

He approached the table. "Can I have a word, Miss Latrelle?"

The room fell silent as I stood and walked out to the corridor with Cormack. He turned toward me, paused, his familiar soft whistle sighing through his teeth.

"Susan?" My voice cracked again.

"Sorry, Nicky." Cormack's hands twisted his cap. "She was dead before they got her in the ambulance. They're going to do an autopsy, but the symptoms before she went — feverish, unable to get air — sound like the report I got on that Martinez boy. You saw him, right?"

"Yeah, I saw Paco." I squeezed my eyes shut a moment. "The day he died. He could hardly walk he was so out of breath and weak. Disoriented." Damn it, I was gonna cry.

"Medics think Susan's heart stopped." Cormack pulled a snowy handkerchief from his jacket pocket, his hand holding it out to me, neatly manicured as always.

I wiped my eyes, blew my nose on the starched fabric. Oddly, I wondered about the protocol. Was I supposed to launder it before I gave it back?

"Remember anything else about that night at the party? Someone you saw, something you heard?"

"No," I said, staring at his shiny wing-tip shoes, the handkerchief wadded in my hand. I could feel his cop-stare on me.

"Might as well go on back with your friends, then. Y'all think of anything, call me, hear?"

"I will," I said, raising my eyes to meet his. "I probably want to get this son-of-a-bitch as much as you do."

His lips formed an odd smile before he turned and moved toward the elevators. I headed back to the suite. Chuck Cheswick stood a short distance down the hall. He headed toward me, his eyes never leaving my face, his expression unreadable.

"Didn't know you knew Investigator Cormack. Your visit social or business related?"

"I'm sorry," I said. "What do you mean?"

"It was a simple question, Miss Latrelle, but I didn't expect you'd answer. You might think about keeping that inquisitive little nose out of business that doesn't concern it."

Was he threatening me? "I'll mind my business, if you'll mind yours. Excuse me." I stepped around him and made a beeline for the Baron's suite, relieved when Cheswick didn't follow.

I walked into the room and the conversation stopped, glasses pausing midway to lips. The half-dozen or so people in there stared at me, their eyes filled with the question.

I shook my head. "Susan Stark didn't make it."

Lorna set her beer down so hard, foam and brew spilled onto the table. She seemed to leave us mentally, her focus aimed inward. I hoped she was pondering the role Bobby and his drugs might have played in Susan's death.

But Amarilla's reaction surprised me. Her hand covered her mouth. The lines around her eyes creased with distress.

She sat at a table farther back, still in the company of the tortoise-shell guy. She stood abruptly, moved to the plate glass at the end of the room and with her back to us, appeared to stare at the track.

I walked across the carpeted floor, stopping next to her.

"You seem awfully upset," I said. "Did you know Susan?"

"The jockey?" Her voice sounded weak.

"Yeah. She was at your party."

She rounded on me, her eyes widened with fear. She *knew* something.

I stepped closer, not caring that I invaded her space. "Susan told me someone at that party gave her a special diet drug. I think it killed her. Would you know anything about that?"

"Paco," she spoke softly, almost to herself.

The overcast light pouring through the window silhouetted her long tall figure, stirring a memory. Suddenly I recognized her. The lone woman, shrouded in a long coat, hurrying down the glistening sidewalk outside Paco's memorial service.

"You were at Paco's funeral," I said. Amarilla shook her head in denial. "I *saw* you. In that brown raincoat. You were there. You knew him, didn't you?"

"My little Paco." Her voice quivered. "He die, like this Susan. Is my fault." She grabbed my arm as if to steady herself. She mumbled words in Spanish. Something about evil and death.

"Why do you call him *your* Paco?"

Several guests who'd gone to the betting windows returned to the suite, their conversation loud and boisterous, no doubt fueled by alcohol. A few feet inside, they picked up on the funereal atmosphere of the room, their voices quickly sinking to a murmur. Their arrival seemed to snap Amarilla from her trance-like state.

"You said it's your fault, why?" I asked, anxious to keep her going.

Amarilla's expression grew wary. She shook her head, backing away from me. "I don't know. I not say any more." She turned and beat it back to her tortoiseshell friend. The man pulled out cigarettes and a lighter, had both of them lit up and puffing away in no time.

I turned and stared out the window, not seeing much. Amarilla was afraid of something. Or someone. It had been there in her eyes. Maybe Paco hadn't gotten his drugs in Maryland, maybe he'd gotten them right here in Virginia…like Susan.

I wouldn't get anymore out of Amarilla, so I moved back to the table with my friends, pulled out a chair and picked up my vodka.

"What was all that about?" Carla asked.

"Nothing important." I didn't want Paco or Susan's fate open for speculation.

I needed to think.

"Amarilla looks like a herd of wild horses just ran over her," Lorna said. Her gaze flicked sideways. "Oops, speak of the devil."

"Nicky," Amarilla's low voice in my ear, her breath smoky. I turned to find the defiance that usually flared from her eyes had dimmed, leaving her expression almost humble. "You a very good horsewoman. I let you decide. You want Daffodil on the turf, is okay." Then she walked away.

"She changed her mind just like that?" Lorna stared after Amarilla. "What got into her?"

"That woman," Carla said, "is upset about Susan's death, isn't she?"

"That's part of it." I searched mentally for a change of subject.

Jim sat across from me sipping his beer. His shaggy grey eyebrows knitted together as he studied the Colonial Downs condition book.

"Jim, what's the deadline for entries on that Princess stake?"

He stared at me. "You want to nominate Daffodil to the stake?"

"Yeah. I mean, don't you think we should?"

His mouth curved into a smile as he thumbed through the book. He turned the corner of one page down and handed it over. "Filly should be good in there, but you'd better step on it," he said.

I grabbed the book, stared at the print. It listed The Virginia Princess Stake, the race's conditions, nomination fees, and weights. The race wasn't that far away. Had I missed the deadline? Then I found it, "Entries close November 4." Wasn't today…?

"What time is it?" I asked, my words almost a shriek.

"They'll be taking entries another hour yet," Jim said.

I shoved my chair back and hopped up. "I better get over to the racing secretary's office." Jeez, if Amarilla had waited any longer to make up her mind, I would have missed the entry.

Before I turned to dash out, I spotted Cormack's hankie, crumpled and damp on the table. I'd managed to forget about Susan's death for a moment. The memory of her limp form on the racetrack rushed back, hard and sharp. I scooped up the rumpled linen and stuffed it in my pocket, before bolting from the room.

31

That evening, a gentle drizzle left the asphalt wet and slippery with fallen leaves. As I drove Lorna to the cottage, an emotional seesaw lifted me high on the thrill of Hellish's win, before plunging me back to the tragedy of Susan's death.

I'd squeaked under the wire with Daffodil's nomination to the Princess Stake, given Hellish a thorough once-over, and fed eight horses. Now, the day's events overwhelmed me. I wanted to retreat to the cottage and bar the door.

We bumped along the Cheswicks' gravel road, approaching Bunny's workshop, where from inside, lights glowed dimly into the darkness. I slowed the Toyota. Through the shop's rain-streaked windows, we could see Bunny sitting at her work table, her shoulders sagging, her eyes closed.

"That woman's in a world of hurt," Lorna said. "Losing her sons like that."

"Not to mention that nasty piece of work she has for a husband."

"Wonder how she stands living with him?"

"Maybe, she doesn't have a choice." I hit the gas, speeding away from Bunny's workshop. I pushed away the image of those broken dolls, thinking a hot bath would be nice. Then I'd just pull the covers over my head.

As we climbed from the car, the scent of pine hung heavy in the air, the evergreens glistening with moisture. An unidentifiable heap on the cottage's stone step turned out to be Slippers and Mr. Chicken, waiting to be let inside.

"That McNugget is confused," muttered Lorna. But in the porch light her eyes were bright with amusement.

Inside we performed the evening pet ritual, spreading newspaper behind the rooster's chair, and filling two ceramic dishes decorated with blue letters that said KITTY. I'd picked up some chicken feed at the local Southern States store, and the rooster had finally stopped eating the Iams cat food. Lorna appreciated this, as watching Mr. Chicken gobbling feed from a bag labeled "poultry by-product meal" usually produced comments like, "Dude, you're so gross."

We heated some tomato soup, made toast with melted cheese, and sat at the kitchen table eating off mismatched crockery. The bright expectant eyes of the two animals watched our every move.

"These two are, like, so spoiled. What's this chicken gonna do when we leave?"

"Maybe we'll take him with us," I said. I didn't know how to help Bunny, but at least we could rescue the poor rooster.

"Nuh uh." Lorna shook her head. "Why would we do that?"

"Cheswick might put that bird's head on a chopping block, or something." A chill nudged through me. I pushed from the table, taking my plates to the sink, running hot water over my cold hands.

* * * *

For almost a week the barn's training went according to schedule. Lorna and Bobby kept a low profile, Mello stayed off the booze, and I waited for the results of Susan's autopsy. The Princess Stake was set to run as the under-card for the Virginia's King Stakes the following Saturday, only a few days away.

That afternoon, the sun shone bright in an Indian summer sky outside Hellish's stall, the air dry and warm. I knelt in the yellow straw next to my filly's left front leg, my fingers reading the residual heat in her ankle. Cold hosing and poultices hadn't been able to remove it, and I might have to spring for the cost of some X-rays. This was not a problem. I felt giddy as I pulled a check from my pocket for about the tenth time. The Colonial Downs bookkeeper had handed it over that morning.

"What are you grinning about?" The sun silhouetted Will's lean figure where he stood at the entrance to Hellish's stall.

"I've never held this much money in my life." I stared at the sharp black ink on crisp green paper. "Six thousand, eight-hundred and forty dollars!"

"Wanna take me to dinner?" Will's green eyes lit with laughter.

"Are you kidding?" I said. "After I pay off my partners, there won't even be enough to cover my debts." I suddenly hoped he'd offer to take me out, then realized it wasn't necessarily for the free meal.

"What's going on with her ankle?" he said.

I hid my disappointment. Our conversation moved on to joint injuries and track gossip. But when Will put his hands on Hellish's ankle, the hard strength of his long fingers seemed to brush against me. I felt heat blossom in my cheeks and was relieved when I heard Lorna bang the feed room door.

"Nikki, you ready to feed, or what?"

Will took this as a cue to leave, and as Lorna and I got on with the evening chores I tried to shake the sense of a lost opportunity.

Bobby drove Lorna away in his Cobra about the time I finished filling the last water bucket. The heavy rubber hose I dragged back to the hydrant left snakelike patterns in the dirt. The aisle fell deep in shadow as the sun sank toward the horizon. I sat on a hay bale, my back against the barn's brick wall, and watched the sunset gild the canopy of the nearby forest. When the treetops darkened, I roused myself and headed to the track kitchen for dinner.

When I came out, night had settled in, but instead of going home, I went back to our barn to rub Daffodil. Anything I could do to make her happy, I would. I strongly believed in the old track adage, "A happy horse is a winning horse."

I grabbed a rubber curry comb, its flat rectangular surface stippled with hard little knobs, able to massage and clean simultaneously. Mello appeared outside the stall gate and began to hum "Camptown Races," as I set to work.

Like most horses, Daffodil bobbed her head in blissful appreciation as I curried the front of her neck and chest.

"How you doing, Mello?" I asked.

"Ain't dead yet, so I guess I be just fine. You be wanting to use a dandy brush now," he said, studying my progress.

I grabbed the soft-bristled brush and whisked away the dust raised by the currycomb. Last, I picked up a clean rub rag and began to polish.

"Gimme that rag, Miss Nikki. I shows you how to rub that horse." I handed it over and watched him perform his magic. The filly seemed to vibrate with energy under his touch and in the dim light from the overhead bulb, her long elegant body gleamed with a soft luster.

When we were finished, I put the tools away in a small wooden grooming box, set the kit in the tack room and locked up. Mello and I stepped from the shedrow into the dark. An almost full moon climbed the eastern sky, and more stars appeared as the dim glow in the far west hardened to midnight-blue.

"Moon be full by Saturday," Mello said.

I wondered what effect, if any, it would have on Daffodil's performance. Many horse people followed "The Sign," a zodiacal tracking of the moon's path through the constellations. Calendars tracing the moon's journey could be found in publications like *The Farmer's Almanac* and *The Blood Horse*. Some breeders religiously used the position of the moon to guide them as to when, or when not, to perform such stressful events as weaning a foal from his mama.

"You believe in astrological stuff like 'The Sign'," I asked.

"Yes indeedy. You don't be ignoring The Sign. The moon be a powerful force."

"Huh." I stared at the silver disk. The word "lunatic" flitted through my head. I hoped the full moon wouldn't stir up that lost soul, Talbot, again.

"Gettin' late, Miss Nikki. I be turnin' in." He headed toward the gravel drive that would take him to the grooms' quarters.

I should have left too, offered him a lift down the road, but the clear night, the moon, and the stars that seemed to swirl around it, kept me rooted in place, my eyes fixed on the lights in the sky.

When I first heard the noise in the woods, I told myself it was deer or some other wildlife rustling through the undergrowth. Only it kept heading toward me, the noise growing, until I heard a pattern — a slow progress forward, punctuated by pauses. As the source drew nearer, I heard labored breathing and a sound like an animal in pain.

"Who's there?" I backed into the shedrow, my hand closing on the handle of a rake. Probably only Talbot. Even Mello said he was harmless. A moan, distinctly human, seemed to stir the cool air. Someone hurt, hunching toward me. My gut told me it wasn't Talbot.

Movement at the edge of the forest. I clutched the rake and rushed closer to the form that appeared to crawl from the underbrush. A man lifted his face in the moonlight. His features contorted with pain. Filthy, shirtless and smeared with blood, I could see he'd wadded his shirt into a ball, one hand pressing it to his stomach. The fabric appeared darkened and wet.

"Stop moving," I said. "I'll get help." Jesus, where was my cell?

"Nuh," he mumbled. "Tell," he closed his eyes against a rush of pain or weakness, then rolled to his side.

I dropped to my knees, put my face close to his. He smelled like sweat, blood, and fear. I knew this guy. The stretch-Hummer gang. I remembered a whiny voice...Philly Whine.

"What is it?" I asked.

"Dead...girl. Tell, meh..."

What was he saying? I had to get help. I started to rise, but a hand shot out and gripped my wrist — the hand that had clutched his bundled shirt. The cloth peeled away, revealing a dark hole in his abdomen.

He grimaced hard, his hand losing its grip on me. He seized up, then collapsed loosely into the ground.

"*No,*" I heard a voice moan, realized it was my own.

From somewhere in the woods a dim light appeared, as if it were a flashlight and a hand kept the beam covered. Then a bright flash played over me, momentarily blinding me.

32

I rolled away from the searching light, sprang up and ran a wild zigzagging path to my car.

"Help!" I screamed. "Somebody help!"

Reaching the car, I crouched next to the side away from the woods. I kept low, opened the Toyota's door and snatched my phone. Slammed the door shut again. I wanted as much metal as possible between me and that person with the light. They probably had a gun!

In the distance, the beam flicked off. Twigs and branches snapped as someone rapidly retreated into the forest.

I hit 911 and babbled to a dispatcher about the injured man. The words "murder victim" burned my throat, but I didn't voice them. My hands shook so bad I kept missing the disconnect button. When I finally cleared the line, I punched in Cormack's number. The relief I felt when I heard his voice disintegrated what little control I had left.

"He's dying! You gotta come to my barn."

"Slow down, Nikki. Who's dying?"

"Philly Whine." I could hear my voice rise in a wail, but had no ability to control it.

"Is this person still alive?"

"I don't know."

"You call 911?"

"Yes, but —"

"Stay put," he said. "I'll send a guard down from the gate. Be there in ten."

He ended the connection, and I stared toward the woods. I should go back to that man, help him. I didn't want to.

The deep thrum of Bobby's Cobra vibrated in the distance, heading in my direction. I ran toward the sound of the tires spewing gravel as the car swept alongside my barn. Before Bobby could cut the engine, I yanked his door open and he and Lorna listened open-mouthed to my disjointed recounting of the wounded man. The three of us ran back to the spot where the stranger still lay. He seemed to have shrunken into the ground, to almost be a part of it.

Bobby knelt, feeling for a pulse on Philly Whine's neck. "Oh, man… wait, I feel something!"

A moan escaped Lorna as she pressed the knuckles of one hand against her teeth.

The moonlight revealed one side of Philly Whine's face. Though smeared with dirt and covered with a three-day-stubble, I could see the cheekbones and jaw formed a strong profile. It was a face that didn't go with a whining personality. Would help get here in time?

A faintness washed over me as my mind absorbed the violence done to this man. His abdominal wound exerted an almost gravitational pull. I averted my gaze, afraid to look.

"Someone's out there!" Next to me, Lorna's voice sounded unnaturally high. Her eyes, round and terrified, were fixed on the woods, maybe a hundred feet to the left of us.

The murderer? I didn't see anything in the woods, but heard sirens piercing the dark air. Thank God. I turned to the sound, willing them to hurry, but they were still some distance away. Where was the security guard Cormack promised to send down?

Moonlight glinted on metal, causing Lorna to shriek. Mike Talbot pushed brambles aside with his shovel as he emerged from the woods. He shuffled close, his attention fixing on the inert man. Talbot mumbled some words I couldn't make out. His eyes rose to Lorna and me, finally coming to rest on Bobby, who still knelt on the ground next to the man I hoped was still alive.

Below me, Bobby's long hair had fallen forward, partly covering his face. His features, revealed in the murky light, were beautiful, almost feminine.

Talbot's mouth went slack, his expression changing to dazed recognition.

"Catherine?" Talbot's voice barely whispered. A tremor shook his body, while his face blanched as if he'd seen a ghost. "Catherine," he repeated, his voice growing urgent. He rushed the few steps to Bobby, jerking to a stop when the younger man screamed.

"Get away from me, you crazy old man!" Bobby rose swiftly to his feet, clenched a fist in Talbot's face. There was nothing feminine about the wide shoulders, narrow hips and bunched muscles outlined beneath Bobby's tight clothes.

Talbot shook his head, as if trying to clear his vision, then emitted an anguished cry, almost a keening sound. He spun, ran across the grass, and stumbled into the woods.

"Jesus." Lorna stared after his retreating figure.

Catherine. He must mean Catherine Tasker, Bobby's mother. I felt dizzy, suddenly nauseous, and staggered a few steps before dropping to my knees. I vomited up dinner as cop cars and an ambulance careened around the edge of our barn.

* * * *

I sat in an unmarked Kent County police cruiser, my hands grasping a Styrofoam cup of coffee someone had given me. Detective Greg Anderson glanced at me with eyes devoid of kindness, before he continued typing something into the computer sitting on his lap. He had a narrow face, bladed with sharp bones, his lips tight and thin. Outside the cruiser, crime scene technicians flooded the area with bright light and yellow tape. Uniformed officers and technicians with various types of equipment swarmed the immediate area, while flashlights glimmered deep in the woods.

The injured man had been rushed away in the ambulance — on a stretcher not in a bag.

Cormack stood to one side talking to some cops. Bobby had been driven away in a sheriff's car. Was he a prime suspect? Lorna spoke with a second detective. They stood next to a white squad car. Large dark letters spelling "Sheriff," outlined in gold were painted on the side of the car. I studied these things, not wanting to revisit mental tapes of Philly Whine's near death. Would he make it?

I sipped the hot coffee, remembering instead the expression on Cormack's face when he'd first seen Philly Whine — the horror of recognition, transforming into anger. No question he knew the guy, but when I'd asked about it, Cormack didn't answer. The county detective who sat next to me now had taken over, steering me away, saying I needed to answer questions.

Anderson's hard face turned back to me. "Tell me again where you'd seen this man before."

I took a breath, stared at my knees, ran through the story again. "He was with a group of guys came in a stretch-Hummer. I got the impression they worked at the baron's bottling plant."

"Did the victim appear to be under any duress?"

"*Duress?* No, he was just one of the guys."

"Sounds like Atkins," he said, but like he was talking to himself.

"Was that his name?" Weird, putting a name to the guy.

"Yeah, Rick Atkins."

"Who is he?" I asked.

"Never mind, Miss Latrelle. You think someone was pursuing Atkins?"

"What I already told you. I saw this light flicker. Kind of glowed a little, like maybe the guy shielded it."

"Why do you say, 'guy'?"

"I don't know. I just assumed…"

"Tell me what you know, not what you assume." His eyes held no warmth, but maybe he was just reacting to the attempted murder.

I told him again how I must have shrieked. How the light shone on me, then shut off before the person retreated.

Anderson grilled me awhile longer, pushing me back over ground we'd already covered, forcing me to visualize the hole in Atkins' gut, until I felt as nutty as Talbot.

My rendition of Atkins' words really frustrated the detective.

"Meh?" he repeated, shaking his head in confusion. "Was he trying to say a name?"

"I don't know!" I wanted to throw myself from the cruiser, run shrieking into those woods, until I lost myself in the night.

The detective gave me a sharp look, as if he could read my unraveling thoughts. He sighed and massaged the side of his neck with one hand. "We're done for now, but —"

Bobbing lights in the woods grew closer, until the officers holding lamps finally reached the forest's edge and worked their way onto the open grass. Anderson unfolded himself from the car and hurried to them. So did Cormack and the second detective. Lorna trailed behind.

I plunged from the tin-can cruiser, stumbled, then breathed with relief as the night air slid into my lungs, calming me as I jogged to catch up. I passed Lorna, my focus on the police ahead.

A tall young cop, with closely barbered hair, was speaking. "Lot of activity in those woods. We're gonna have to wait for daylight to complete the search. Got disturbed ground cover and broken branches. Someone's been digging with a shovel." He paused, one hand pressing into the small of his back, as if he had an ache there. "We lost the blood trail. Can we get a canine unit out here?"

"Be here at six A.M.," Anderson said. His next words to Cormack sounded accusatory. "I want to find this guy Talbot. When you're not letting that wacko run loose in your woods, where does he live?"

"He has a room in the grooms' quarters, but he's not there, we already checked."

Anderson seemed to intimidate Cormack, who shifted restlessly, his nervous whistle working through his teeth.

Exhaustion swept over me as the last traces of adrenaline evaporated. I'd heard enough. "Are you done with us?"

The men swung around, Anderson starting as if surprised to see Lorna and me standing behind him. I thought I saw Cormack's lips quiver in an almost-smile.

"No." Anderson turned his back on us.

"No ma'am," said the second detective, his face kinder than Anderson's. "We need you to come into the station and make your statements."

"*Now?*" It was almost midnight.

"Surprised you wouldn't want to cooperate, Miss Latrelle, considering the seriousness of this crime." Anderson was such a hard case.

"Fine," I said. "But can we do it soon?"

"Won't be more 'n ten minutes, ma'am," said the other detective. "You and your buddy here," he gestured at Lorna, "can come with me. I'll drive y'all in shortly, get those statements all fixed up, and have you back in no time."

Lorna sagged to the ground, sat cross-legged and dropped her head into her hands. "What do you think they're doing with Bobby?" she asked me, her voice barely audible.

"I don't know." Instead of sitting with Lorna, I used the time to walk to Daffodil's stall, worried the commotion had upset her. I should have known better. She'd pushed her head into the aisle way and watched everything with bright curiosity as if the event had been put on solely for her entertainment. A few doors down, Hellish snaked her head into the shedrow, pinned her ears at me, then withdrew into the darkness of her stall.

"Same to you," I said.

My hand moved to Daffodil's neck, fingers stroking the satin fur. How weird that Talbot had called Bobby by the name "Catherine." Talbot must have known Bobby's mother.

Under the bright generator-driven lights, it looked like the cops were starting to close shop. Maybe I could get the hell out of there soon. I prayed Philly Whine — Atkins — would make it. Would he be able to explain what happened in those woods?

33

I woke up a little after five-thirty, raised up on one elbow, and squinted at the bedside clock. Why hadn't the alarm gone off? Then I remembered. The man crawling from the woods…

The previous night had been so long and miserable, I hadn't set the alarm, hoping to grab an extra hour of sleep. I sank back into the bed, but horses jogged in my head, nickering for food. I moaned and threw off the covers.

By the time the sheriff had driven us back to the cottage it had been after one o'clock. We'd never heard if Atkins was alive or not. I sat up fast. *Damn.* What had I been thinking, letting that cop drive us home? My car was still at the backstretch.

I got Lorna up. After lightning fast toothpaste, hot water, and soap, we struggled into our track clothes, gulped down coffee, and fed Slippers and Mr. Chicken.

"Are my eyes as puffy as yours?"

Lorna peered at me. "You ever seen a blowfish?"

"Never mind," I said.

In the distance, a truck engine turned over and idled, probably down the hill at the main house. We were always gone before the Cheswicks got up. Maybe it was old Chucky getting ready to drive booze around for the baron. Maybe he'd give us a ride.

"Nuh, uh," Lorna said when I mentioned my plan. "Don't want to go anywhere with that weirdo."

"He might go right past the track. Won't hurt to ask."

We herded the rooster and cat out the door, grabbed our coats, and scooted down the hill, following the sound of the engine.

A barn, its double-doors folded back, lay almost hidden among a stand of cedar and holly trees near the old Victorian. Apparently it served as a garage for the big panel truck that idled inside. Exhaust fumes, heavy and acrid in the cool morning air, curled out of the building. Gravel crunched, and Cheswick's tall figure loomed through the smoke.

"What are you girls doing here?"

"Uh, there was an incident at the track last night. We ended up here without my car. Any chance you could give us a lift?"

Cheswick straightened. "Wha —" He cleared his throat. "What incident?"

Lorna and I exchanged a look. "I don't know," I said. "Some man got hurt or something."

"Yeah," said Lorna. "And in the confusion, we sort of ended up without a car."

"You gals are something." He might as well have said "bimbos." He shook his head, pursed his lips like something tasted bad. He stared at us a moment, his eyes narrowing. Mental gears were clicking. For some reason it made me uneasy.

He nodded to himself. "Okay. Get in."

Lorna stepped behind me, making sure I'd climb into the truck first, be stuck sitting next to Cheswick. I could have do-si-doed and skipped behind her, but that would have been kind of obvious.

The truck's cab smelled of stale sweat. Overpowering that scent was the sickly-sweet stench of Gilded Baron. Lorna cracked her window as Cheswick shoved the stick shift into gear. We bounced and swayed along his pothole-ridden drive like bobble-head dolls until reaching the county road.

An uncomfortable silence filled the cab for the first few miles. Cheswick broke it.

"Who got hurt? Backstretch worker?"

"No." I said. "Some guy came out of the woods."

"What woods?" Cheswick's jaw tightened.

"Um, the ones next to our barn."

"That's descriptive."

"Sorry." I drew the word out. "The large stand of trees behind the very last barn at the far end of the backstretch."

"Jesus Christ," he muttered and grew silent.

We'd just passed through Providence Forge when the truck's radio phone crackled and a voice squawked for Cheswick. He swung his long arm forward and grabbed the handset.

"No, I got people with me. What?" He sighed. "For God's sake, that was supposed to be this afternoon. Yeah, yeah, I'll be there." Cheswick slammed the handset into its cradle. "Short detour."

The dashboard clock read almost six-thirty. Now I'd be even later. A few miles before the turn into Colonial, Cheswick made a right onto an unfamiliar road.

"Where we going?" Lorna asked.

"Just take a minute." He glanced at us, light from the glass windows reflecting off his glasses, making it impossible to read his expression.

The road rolled on and on, looping this way and that. Woods crowded up to the gravel shoulder on our left. A huge golf course lay to the right. When its perfectly mown lawn gave way to a mass of evergreens, the road was swallowed by deep woods on either side. We rounded a turn and passed through a chain link fence. Razor wire stretched across the top. A two-line gold-and-red lettered sign read:

GILDED BARON BOURBON
Bottling and Distribution

Lorna wrinkled her nose. "Smells like somebody cooked up a vat of rotten horse feed."

Long gray buildings occupied most of the large blacktop lot. A row of panel trucks lined up near the fence on one side. We rolled past a building sprouting ventilator stacks that spewed white smoke into the air. Soot and grime stained the block walls below.

"Must be that corn whiskey fermenting," I whispered.

Cheswick ignored our comments, turned the truck right and headed toward one of the last buildings with a sign that said OFFICE.

A plate glass door flew open and Bobby Duvayne dashed out, his face red. John Duvayne pounded right behind him. The older, stockier man caught up with Bobby and shoved him hard from behind. Bobby stumbled, tried to regain his balance, but his father grabbed him in a bear hug, pinning the younger man's arms. John lifted Bobby off his feet, displaying the immense strength promised by his thick muscular body. He threw his son onto the pavement like a rag doll.

"No!" Lorna screamed.

Cheswick sped the truck forward, slammed on the brakes and jumped out. Lorna flew out her door. I scrambled to keep up.

John wielded his legs like tree trunks, kicking Bobby repeatedly. The younger man scooted along the pavement on his hands and knees. He tried to get up, but was no match for the successive, vicious blows. Bobby drew himself into a ball, protecting his head with his arms.

"Take it easy, John." Cheswick shouted, moving forward as fast as his awkward hips and exceedingly long legs would allow.

The kicking stopped, but blood smeared the dark pavement and dripped from Bobby's face. John's back was to us as he yelled at Bobby.

"You gotta step up, boy. Do your job. I tell you to drive the shipment, you drive it!"

Cheswick reached John and grabbed at his shoulder. "We've got company," he hissed.

John shook him off. "Boy thinks his car and all that just appears.

Doesn't want to do the job. Thinks he's too good to —" John's mouth clamped shut. He'd glimpsed Lorna and me behind Cheswick.

Bobby raised his head, saw us staring. His face, pale with shock, flushed a deep pink.

Lorna rushed over to him, but he turned away. "Get them out of here." His voice sounded thick. He took a long breath, then spat red saliva onto the blacktop.

"Come on, ladies. We're leaving," Cheswick said.

"Bobby!" Lorna wailed, her arms outstretched toward him.

"Leave me the hell alone!"

"You heard him." Cheswick grabbed Lorna's arm, jerking her away from Bobby.

"Get your fucking hand off her," I said quietly, surprised by the dead calm settling over me.

The tall man laughed. "Aren't you the tough girl. Tougher than this pansy." He flicked a derisive glance at Bobby. "Get in the truck." He let Lorna go with a push toward the panel truck.

I stood my ground, staring at him in revulsion. I didn't want to go anywhere with this man.

"Please, just leave." The strangled voice came from Bobby. The enormity of his humiliation overwhelmed me.

My eyes met Lorna's, and without a word, we both headed for Cheswick's truck. The three of us climbed in, the tall man cranking the engine.

He drove to the rear of the last block structure and stopped. Looked like the back end of the building was a body-shop. Some vehicles sat in bays and a man was covering a section of a liquor truck with masking tape. Nearby, a guy in a safety mask fiddled with a spray gun. Buckets of paint sat on the floor.

Cheswick climbed from the truck and spoke quietly to one of the men.

I turned to Lorna. "Are you all right?"

Her shoulders sagged, and one hand fidgeted with her watch band. "I can't believe his father did that."

"He'll be okay." Liar.

"He told me to leave him alone."

"He was upset, Lorna."

A few men walked to the back of our truck. I leaned toward the driver's side-view mirror, but all I could see was the razor-wire fence behind us and a forest of tall pines, with oaks and poplars, dressed in the same curling orange and brown leaves as the woods near our barn.

The truck swayed, then lifted up as if a weight had been removed. A moment later, the men walked by the driver's window carrying a pallet covered with a tarp. Something about the tarp and the shape beneath it seemed familiar, only Cheswick appeared outside the window and glared at me before I could work out the memory.

"What are you lookin' at?"

"Nothing." I scooted back across the seat toward Lorna.

Cheswick got in, put the transmission in gear, and drove alongside the building. Above us, the roof had ventilator stacks, and exhaust fans roared from the block sidewall. The whoosh of acrid air worked into the cab, making my eyes water.

Cheswick hit the gas, and the truck sped forward, circling back by the office. There was no sign of Bobby or John Duvayne, only a dark stain on the asphalt.

34

Lorna and I stumbled through the rest of the morning in a daze. We arrived at the track so late, three of our eight horses never got out for exercise. Mello fussed around us like a broody hen, and I had to reassure him several times that I was okay, that the evil of the previous night hadn't hurt Lorna or me. At least not physically.

After finishing up, I took a breather on the stable bench, drinking Diet Coke and munching on prepackaged cheese-and-crackers. Nearby, Mello held Daffodil's lead shank while she grazed on grass and clover beneath the warm Indian summer sun. With the Virginia Princess Stakes only three days away, I'd squeaked in a strong gallop on the filly just before the track closed.

Deciding Daffodil had grazed enough, Mello led her into the shedrow. Her chestnut coat gleamed, her bright eyes glowed with health.

Lorna stepped from the feed room with a can of soda and paused to study Daffodil. "She looks better than we do."

"Anybody would." I rubbed my neck, trying to work out a kink.

Daffodil moved past, her hooves stirring up little puffs of dust, the dry earthy scent mingling with the smell of liniment.

"Any word from Bobby?" I asked.

Lorna's lips compressed. "No. They weren't over there," she said, referring to the Duvayne barn. She twisted her watch band, then inspected a hangnail. "Groom said Bobby and the bastard never showed up this morning. Apparently Mr. Dick-Head called and said just to walk everything around the shedrow."

"So Lorna, how do you really feel about John Duvayne?" The sharp look I got told me she wasn't amused.

Across the way, a gust of wind stirred tree branches, and yellow crime scene tape fluttered at the edge of the woods. When we'd arrived earlier, K-9 dog handlers were reloading two bloodhounds into cages on a truck.

"Wonder if they ever found Talbot?" I said.

"You think he shot that Atkins guy?" Lorna stopped worrying her hangnail, and stood up.

Talbot didn't strike me as a murderer. "I don't know who shot Atkins, but —"

Lorna stepped forward and peered over the aisle rail. "Isn't that Cormack's ride?"

I rose and moved next to her. A shiny black SUV displaying the logo of the Virginia Racing Commission rolled alongside the barn. It stopped, and Cormack climbed out. Lines of exhaustion road-mapped his face. He gave us the once over. "Everything okay here?"

I shrugged. "Did the Atkins guy make it? Who is he? I got the feeling you know him."

Cormack's gaze shifted to Lorna.

"I'll start the feed," she said.

I'd never known her to be so incurious. She'd been through so much, maybe she didn't want to know.

Cormack stood outside the railing. He leaned forward and set his hands on the wood. The nails were dirty and one was broken. Never thought I'd see the day.

"Atkins is in a coma, and yes, I know him. He's a good man. The rest is need to know, and you don't need to know."

So why was Cormack here? "Any luck finding Talbot?"

Instead of answering, he said, "Tell me again what Talbot said to young Duvayne."

I dragged in a breath, played the mental tape. "It's dark, just the moon. With Bobby's long hair, Talbot seemed to think he was a woman. Calls him Catherine. Like it's a question. Then Bobby yells at him. Talbot realized his mistake, sort of cried out, took off into the woods."

"Catherine Tasker. Is it possible?" Cormack glanced at the crime scene. "He have that shovel with him?"

"Yeah. Is what possible?"

"Never you mind," he said. A slight glint appeared in his eyes. He straightened from the rail with more purpose.

"You girls watch your backs. Don't go anywhere alone. I'll be in touch."

Oh, great. Like I needed further unnerving. "Why shouldn't we go anywhere alone?"

But Cormack stretched one of his short legs up to the sideboard of the SUV, hopped inside, and drove away.

* * * *

Two days passed with Lorna increasingly frantic about Bobby's absence. She phoned him incessantly, but got no response. She even confronted John Duvayne at his barn.

"I wouldn't piss him off, Lorna. That guy's dangerous," I said when she came back to our shedrow with tears of frustration wetting her cheeks.

"Easy for you to say. You don't know what this is like!"

She had a point. "Okay. So what did Duvayne say?"

"He told me Bobby's fine, that what happened the other morning is family business, not mine. He wouldn't tell me where Bobby is. I can't stand this."

I gave her a hug. My attempt to comfort her seemed to crack what little control she held onto. She burst into sobs and collapsed onto Mello's bench.

"Is this a bad time?" Will, his green eyes dark and intense, stood outside our shedrow with the mocha-skinned exercise rider, Sable. The last few days, Sable and Lorna had taken to eating lunch in the kitchen after the morning rounds were finished. I couldn't help but notice Sable's high cheekbones and taut, muscular figure.

"Gonna have live music and a barbeque at the track tonight to celebrate the big race tomorrow." Sable pretended not to notice Lorna's red eyes and wet face. "I got free tickets. Will's gonna go. You two wanna come?"

"I guess," Lorna said.

"You should go," I said to her. "I'm going to take it easy tonight. Got that race tomorrow."

"What she means," Lorna said, wiping her face with a tissue Sable had pulled from her pocket, "is she wants to stay here at the barn, obsess about the stakes race, and mother Daffodil to death."

Will grinned. "She's got your number, Latrelle."

"That's pretty much the evening I had planned."

Sable sat next to Lorna, put an arm around her shoulder. "Come on, little sister. Do you good."

"All right," Lorna said, and late that afternoon she wedged herself into the back of Will's Mini Cooper.

Sable sat up front next to Will, where she leaned close, then laughed and touched his arm. I wondered if there was something between her and Will. I turned on the stable radio for company, and tried to shake off the blues as they drove away.

Did I have feelings for Will? Or was it just the week-long string of disturbing events had me searching for new answers?

35

I grabbed a hot dinner at the kitchen, some sort of chicken smothered in mushrooms, onions, and peppers. After a chocolate bar for dessert, I walked back to the barn.

The moon, now rounded to a full globe, rose in the eastern sky. Dew glistened in the grass, melting into dark streaks on my leather boots. The warm temperature of the last few days still held, leaving the air mild, almost sensual.

An old Grateful Dead song was drifting from the radio when I reached the shedrow. My Mom had played the album when I was little. I knew the lyrics.

"Driving that train, high on cocaine," it went. *"Casey Jones you better watch your speed —"*

I clicked off the radio as a familiar rumble sounded in the distance. Bobby's Mustang.

A moment later his headlights swung around the corner. When he shut down the engine outside our shedrow, I hurried over, curious. Anxious, too. As Bobby opened the door to get out, the Cobra's dome light revealed a livid bruise on one cheek. Paler streaks of green and purple colored the skin beneath his eye.

"It's not that bad," he said, catching my expression.

"Where have you been?"

He shrugged. "Around."

Hard to ignore the flat, muscular abdomen beneath the black T-shirt. Even hurt, he moved with the grace of a dancer.

"Lorna's not here," I said.

"I know." He smiled. "She's at the barbeque."

A glitter in his eyes instilled a discomfort that put me on the offensive. I stared at his damaged face.

"Your dad do this sort of thing often?"

He raised his hands defensively. "Easy, lady. I'm already bruised." He walked around the hood of his car, stopping a few feet from me.

Of their own volition, my eyes dropped to the bulge in his jeans. *Damn it.* The man was dangerous. Even with his bruises and one lip slightly swollen, he was drop-dead gorgeous in the moonlight.

I tried to distract him. "Why would your father do that to you?"

"I guess I just drive him crazy sometimes." He moved closer. "Anybody ever drive you crazy?"

I took a step back.

"Knew you were afraid of it," he said, a smile playing on his lips.

"Just...go find Lorna." Jesus, I could drown in those brown eyes. My mouth felt dry, but other parts didn't.

He moved nearer. "Never been close enough to really see you before. You know you're beautiful, don't you?"

I shut my eyes. He made my legs weak, opened channels for Mother Nature's insistent whisper, *"You know you want to."*

I shook myself mentally. "This how you came on to Lorna?"

"No," he said, pushing a lock of his hair back. "Lorna came after me. You're different, like a wild horse running the prairie, won't ever let herself get caught."

Bobby grew still, studied me a moment. "Think you need a firm hand."

Desire hit me like a freight train. Bobby nodded, as if he could see the heat, smell the smoke, touch the fire.

"Come here." He grasped my wrists, pulled me into him, put his warm mouth over mine, slid his tongue between my lips.

Something ignited inside, made me whimper, lock myself against him. His hands moved to the small of my back, drew me closer. His erection pressed against me, hard electricity burning through the denim of my jeans.

What was I doing? A dizzying sensation shot through me, leaving me slick, aching, and pliable.

Bobby pushed me down onto the hood of his Cobra. Stars pulsed in the sky above, roared white-hot through my veins. Somewhere in the stables, a horse nickered. Bobby unfastened my shirt, ripping a few buttons in his haste. He pushed my bra up. Warm lips and wet tongue found one nipple, fingertips on the other.

I lay moaning, with my back pressed into the smooth metal, still warm from the hot engine. I felt drugged, the moon smiling down, Bobby hard and urgent. He unsnapped my jeans and went for the zipper.

Was I finally going to do the deed? *Not like this.* Not on the hood of this man's car. Not with Lorna so crazy about him.

"No!" I struggled beneath his weight.

"Don't stop now," he gasped. "Please."

"No! I don't want this."

He tried to slide his tongue over my nipple again.

I squirmed, got a hand free, and smacked him, realizing only as palm slapped flesh I'd hit the nasty bruise on his face.

Bobby put a hand to his cheek and rolled off me. "You bitch!"

"I didn't mean to hit you there. But you wouldn't stop."

Tears glistened in his eyes, dispelling the drugged-with-desire glaze. He stood over me, one hand clenching into a fist.

I flinched, tried to scrabble backwards.

He hesitated, exhaled a breath, then extended an open hand toward me.

I shrank away from him.

"It's okay," he said, "just trying to help you up." His cocky arrogance and swagger seemed to evaporate.

I waited a beat and took the offered hand. He pulled me to my feet. Hurriedly, I attempted to straighten my clothes, my fingers searching hopelessly for two buttons missing from the front of my shirt. The smell of engine oil and wax saturated my clothing.

Bobby took a step away, and in the moonlight some emotion flooded his face. "Shouldn't have done that," he said. "But there was something about the way you looked at me…at the plant the other night. Made me want to come after you."

Looked at him? How? Like I wanted to rescue him? Like I understood his pain? "Has he always beaten you?"

His head came up, and he moved a step back. "No. You've got the wrong idea. He's okay. It's me. I disappoint him and stuff."

"I'd hate to see what he'd do if you really pissed him off. He's got no right." I could feel myself taking up for a stray again, feel the anger that abuse always stirred in me.

Bobby's gaze drifted to the ground. "You don't understand. It was hard for him when my mom ran off."

"Not as hard as it is for you when he beats you. That's what happened to you when you said you fell off and hit the rail. Isn't it?"

"Yeah." His voice was so low I could barely hear him.

Overhead, a nightbird flew across the moon, a dark silhouette, the flapping wings loud in the still air.

"Did he hit your mother? Is that why she ran off?"

He stared at me, his mouth open. "I…don't know. I don't remember."

I watched him, questions crowding my mind.

"Don't look at me like that," he said. "All full of pity. That's bullshit. I got a feeling you've been down the same road. The way you're afraid of sex, afraid of me."

We glared at each other in the silver light.

"So my dad knocks me around sometimes. What's your deal?"

I wanted to tell him. My own self involvement? Or did I imagine owning up might help him in some way?

"I lost my mom, like you."

His eyes widened fractionally. "She ran out on you?"

"No." My voice harsh, condemning. "She died, left me with her new husband."

"Oh." His teeth pressed his lower lip a moment. "He hit you?"

"He had other interests."

"Whoa. He didn't like —"

"I ran off before he did." Fear still rattled my voice. Memories of running in the dark along Park Heights Avenue near Pimlico racetrack, of what really happened before I escaped. I pushed them away, focused on Bobby's words.

"I figured. It's why you seem like that filly, loose on the prairie, still running. So, you've never been…caught, have you?"

I'd never thought of my virginity in such lyrical terms. Maybe the man ran deeper than I'd thought.

"Hey, I could still take care of that for you." But he said it with a grin, his voice lacking sexual undertone.

Without warning, I liked him. Absent the swagger and excess testosterone, I felt myself warming to the person, felt myself grinning.

"That's not gonna happen," I said.

"I know. Friends?"

"Sure." I slid my arm around his waist, giving him a brief squeeze.

"Thanks." He smiled, closed his fingers lightly over my hand.

"*Bobby?*" Lorna rushed at us. Her eyes held a wild light and her hands were balled into fists at her sides. "What the hell's going on?" Arriving on foot, wearing her Nikes, we'd never heard her coming.

Bobby and I jumped apart. Could we look any more guilty? Well, yeah, if Lorna had arrived a few minutes earlier.

"It's not what it looks like," Bobby said, moving toward her.

That was lame. But what can you say that doesn't make it worse?

The betrayal in Lorna's eyes crushed my heart. This wasn't fixable.

"Lorna —"

"Don't." Lorna held up her hand, staring at my disheveled clothing. I'd forgotten the torn buttons. My shirt gaped open, revealing my bra.

"Damn you. Damn both of you." With a little cry, she whirled and ran. Bobby started after her, but she screamed over her shoulder. "Leave me alone!"

"She's too freaked," I called to Bobby. "Give her some time." I wasn't sure there could be enough time.

A shadow moved on the shedrow, shifting into human form as it stepped into the moonlight. *Will*. Great, how much had he seen? As he walked closer his expression was unreadable.

The pounding of Lorna's Nikes made me turn. She ran down the gravel road, as if heading for the other barns. Then she veered into the woods.

"Lorna, don't go in there!" I took off after her, Bobby on my heels.

"I'll get a flashlight," Will called from behind.

I entered the woods on a diagonal, hoping to head Lorna off, and promptly fell over a fallen tree limb. I went down hard on my palms and one knee. The limb got Bobby, too. He crashed beside me.

In the distance I could hear Lorna's progress — the snapping of twigs, the rustle of branches, the tread of feet — some of it muffled by pine needles, all of it speeding away. In the murky light it would be almost impossible to chase her. As Bobby and I stood up, the beam of Will's light found us.

"Wait up. I brought an extra flashlight." Will reached us and held it out.

"You're a regular boy scout, aren't you?" Bobby said, brushing leaves and dirt from his clothes.

"Thank you, Will." I took the extra light. "Lorna was pretty upset about —"

"She had reason to be." Will turned away from me. "We should spread out," he said over his shoulder. "You might as well stay with Bobby. Keep calling her name, so we can hear each other." Then he moved away through the underbrush.

"Lorna," I called, my voice weak.

"We are, like, so busted," said Bobby. "How long do you think she was standing there?"

"Let's go," I stumbled ahead through the underbrush. "Lorna," I shouted. Damn everything. I groaned out loud. What had I been thinking?

I'd *known* Lorna and Bobby were a train wreck waiting to happen. Christ, they'd been heading for it since the day they met. I'd just never envisioned myself as the oncoming train.

36

The smell of damp earth and rotting leaves hung heavy in the air as Bobby and I blundered through the woods. A massive cloud bank worked its way across the night sky, obscuring the moon and making it harder to see. Will's occasional cry of, "Lorna," echoed through the trees somewhere to our right.

Between the police, bloodhounds, the escaping Atkins, and Talbot's shovel, there were too many broken branches and too much disturbed ground for any hope of following my friend's trail.

"Lorn-*aah*." Bobby's voice rang out before evaporating into the dense woods.

I shook my head. Here was Bobby searching so hard for Lorna, when she'd spent the previous two days desperate to find *him*.

"So Bobby, where were you all that time Lorna was looking for you?" In the dim light I had trouble reading his expression as he hesitated next to me.

"I had to drive a shipment to Jersey with this other guy. Then we hauled some stuff to the Canadian border. We never stopped, just kept driving."

"For your dad?"

"No," he said quickly. "For the baron. My dad manages the distributorship, but it's the baron's company."

"So you were shipping what? Liquor?"

"Well, yeah. I guess."

"You guess?"

He threw me a sharp look. "It's company business."

Striding ahead, he left me behind. I ran, caught up, and grabbed his shoulder just as the moon broke briefly through the clouds.

"Then tell me about the Cheswick boys."

In the silver light I could see the color leave his face. He stared at me, silent. I wanted him to speak.

"You were with them the night they died. You have a part in that?"

"Jesus Christ, no! They cleared me of any involvement."

"Yeah, I heard. But you *know* why they died."

"No." He kept his eyes wide and honest appearing, but something shifted in them, a blink that wasn't quite a blink. "I *don't* know, and this conversation is over." He stalked ahead.

The air around me grew cold and darker, as a pattering sound rattled the dry leaves overhead. I glanced up, and drops of rain stung my face. I should have known Bobby would never answer my questions.

"We'd better go in," he called over his shoulder. "Too bad Boy-Scout Will didn't think to bring a cell phone. For all we know, Lorna could be trying to reach us."

I didn't think Lorna was trying to call anybody. I remembered that betrayed look in her eyes.

Bobby stopped walking and shouted, "Will!" A voice called from the right, and the two men yelled back and forth until Will drew close enough and used our light as a beacon. I didn't want to see the judgment in Will's face, either, so I turned and started back.

The rain came down harder as I navigated around a fallen tree trunk that blocked my path. A huge old thing, it must have come down in a storm. I didn't remember it from earlier. Had I headed in the wrong direction? I glanced back to see if the guys were following and stepped into open air. I fell into loose dirt and mud, my flashlight flying from my hand.

"Nikki!" Will cried. "Are you all right?"

"Yeah, I fell into a hole or something. Over here." I found my light, then shined it around me. I was in a dug-out rectangle about two feet deep and six feet long.

"Aaah." I scrambled to my feet and climbed out of there.

"Jesus." Bobby stared down from where he stood on top of the log. "That looks like a grave! Is there anything…in it?"

"Just Nikki, apparently." Will came around the end of the log. His flashlight illuminated the hole.

A creeping sensation made me shudder. Dirt covered the back of my jeans and cold wet denim pressed into my skin. "Talbot's been digging graves?"

"Why would he?" Bobby asked.

"Let's get out of here," Will said.

We moved away from the grave, trudging through the underbrush in silence. Was Lorna out here somewhere? Cold? Wet?

Ahead of me, the downpour soaked into fallen leaves, the smell of decay growing stronger. Moss at the base of a tree glistened in my flashlight's beam, reminding me that water poured on Colonial's turf course, too. If it rained all night, the racing secretary could take the race off the turf, run it on the dirt. I'd have to scratch Daffodil.

Maybe it would be just as well.

Wiping water from my forehead, I took a deep breath. Screw that attitude. I'd worked too hard, and was gonna ride that filly with everything I had. My shoulders straightened as I hurried forward. Will and Bobby scrunched through the undergrowth behind, while distant lights from the Colonial backstretch glimmered through the woods ahead.

Clearing the trees, I broke into a run for my car and cell phone. I punched the numbers for Cormack, and once again felt relief when I heard his voice.

"What now?" He sounded weary. No doubt his dictionary featured a picture of me next to the word, "trouble."

"It's Lorna. She got upset and ran off into those damn woods. I searched with Will Marshall and Bobby. We can't find her."

He was silent a beat, but I thought I heard teeth grinding. "How long she been missing?"

"About two hours."

"Y'all spent all that time in those woods looking for her, without callin' anyone?"

"Well, yeah."

"Stay the hell out of there! Where're you now?"

"At my barn." Jeez, he didn't have to bite my head off.

Cormack's sigh drifted through the cell phone. "Stay put. I'll be right there."

The rain stopped a few minutes later, and the three of us left the cover of the shedrow where we'd been waiting. Bobby bumped Will with his shoulder, causing the jockey to stumble.

"Watch it, asshole," Will said.

"Wanna make me?"

Oh for God's sake. Didn't we have enough trouble? Thankfully, Cormack's SUV pulled up. The investigator used the running board to work his legs to the ground.

"He looks pissed," said Bobby.

"Know just how he feels," Will said, shooting a glare at Bobby.

I walked closer to Cormack, hoping the men's animosity wouldn't escalate into a fistfight. They hung back, leaving me to talk to the investigator on my own.

"I'm really scared about Lorna."

"Y'all should be worried about yourselves, too. Goin' in there like that." He gestured toward the forest. "Real bad idea." He shook his head then muttered, "Of all the damn places to go."

Places. My memory clicked on like a forgotten light switch. Those trees behind the razor-wire at the plant, so similar to the ones we stared at now. My words came out fast.

"What's on the other side of these woods? Do they back onto the baron's bottling plant?"

Cormack's head jerked, but he didn't say anything.

"So they do?"

Cormack walked a few steps farther away from Will and Bobby. He motioned me to follow. "Keep that piece of information to yourself." He kept his voice low. "There's a major investigation goin' on relating to that place, and you're so damn nosy you're gonna mess it up, or get yourself killed."

"What?" Surely he exaggerated.

"That man you met at the baron's party, the one that almost died?"

"Atkins?"

"Yeah, him. He was an undercover cop for Virginia's ABC Bureau. One of the best." Cormack paused a moment, cleared his throat. "Somebody found out he was nosing around and tried to kill him. That clear enough for ya?"

"Oh my God! Did the baron —"

"We don't know who's responsible for shooting Atkins. We know they're sellin' bootleg whiskey out of that place and..." His mouth clamped shut.

"It's more than just bootleg whiskey, isn't it?"

He gave me a sharp look, then shook his head. "We're not sure what all's goin' on over there."

Especially since Atkins had passed out before he could tell me anything. The thought brought a short gasp.

"What?" Cormack said.

I swallowed, sucked in some air. "The person in the woods, with the flashlight. Do you think they saw Atkins trying to speak to me?"

Cormack's lips twisted. "You'd be hard to make out in the dark. You shoulda thought of this before Lorna ran off. What upset her, anyway?"

"Uh..." He didn't need to know about that, did he?

His gaze dropped to my open shirt, then quickly back to my face. "Never mind." He paused a beat. "I'll call the county boys, see if they'll get up a search team."

"Don't they have to wait twenty-four hours or something?"

"Probably." His face held the same frustration I felt, but I could almost hear his mental gears grinding. After a moment he broke into a smile. "Remember those dogs?"

"Won't they have the same restriction?"

"They would, but a drinking buddy of mine has a search and rescue dog. Let me call Andy, see what he can do."

About twenty minutes later, a man arrived in a pick-up truck. The interior light showed a long-haired black-and-white dog lounging on the seat next to him. Leaving his truck lights on, Andy got out with his dog. Tall and thin as a stick, the man's rugged jeans were belted with a tooled leather belt. High heeled cowboy boots adorned his feet. I wished him luck in the woods with those things.

After examining the items of Lorna's clothing available in the tackroom, he chose her protective vest. I showed him where I thought Lorna had broken into the woods.

The worried eyes of the fluffy dog reflected my mood as he snuffled Lorna's vest. Andy gave him some kind of hand signal and the dog put his nose to the ground. He must have caught the scent, for his tail wagged furiously, and he bounded away into the woods, leaving Andy to lumber behind.

"How's he gonna keep up with that mutt?" I asked.

"Don't you worry. That dog finds anything, he'll take Andy to it."

My body sagged with exhaustion.

"Let 'em search," Cormack said. "You can't do any more here."

"Okay." I was too tired to argue.

Will left with a curt nod in my direction. Bobby squeezed my hand and rumbled off in his Mustang. The crunching of Andy's boots grew fainter as he followed the dog deeper into the woods. I prayed the mutt would find Lorna.

Before someone else did.

37

I read the blue card on the kitchen counter.

Dress Code for Virginia's King Day.
Business attire is to be worn.
Men's shirts must have collars.
Absolutely no athletic wear or jeans.

Boy, these southerners sure like to get dolled up. The card had been distributed to the entire backstretch a week earlier, but things being what they were, I hadn't bothered to read it. I dumped my coffee into the sink, double-timed it to my closet, and snatched the outfit I'd worn to the baron's bash. I could end up in the clubhouse after Daffodil's race.

The bureau's mirror reflected a wild-eyed woman with dark racoon rings under her eyes. One hand clutched a hanger full of clothes, the other covered her mouth as if to restrain laughter about to rise out of control. How insane to worry about dress codes when Lorna was missing. When I faced maybe the toughest race of my life.

I sank onto the bed, feeling dizzy. It would have helped if I hadn't been awake half the night, lying in the empty cottage, contemplating tangled relations and broken friendships.

I had to get going, and still clutching the clothes, I stuffed Lorna's rhinestone boots into a bag, grabbed my purse and keys, and headed for Colonial. When I pulled up to our barn, Will stood under the shedrow roof dressed in his riding gear.

I had mixed feelings about his presence. Had he witnessed my performance on the Cobra's hood? There was something honest and clean about Will. His opinion mattered. I left my car, trying not to look sheepish and could feel his assessing gaze. I waited for a smart remark.

"Did you hear from Lorna?" he asked.

"No." I'd hoped he might have news. At least he hadn't brought up my go-round with Bobby. Maybe he hadn't been there early enough last night.

"Guess she's pretty raw, huh?" He started to say more, then grew quiet.

I stopped moving, impaled on a sharpened stake of guilt and humiliation.

"I thought you might need some help." He nodded at the group of equine heads studying us from the shedrow. "You've got that race later and all. I could ride some for you."

I refrained from throwing my arms around him. "That's really nice, Will. Thanks."

His gaze fell away. "I'm doing it for Lorna."

* * * *

At eleven o'clock, cars jammed the parking lots outside the grandstand. I nosed my car into the lot reserved for jockeys. There weren't enough riders in the entire mid-Atlantic region to account for all the cars crammed into this area.

I sardined my battered Toyota between a Dumpster and a shiny new Mercedes. What a surprise, the luxury vehicle didn't have a jockey sticker. Whoever drove it, they had no business being in this lot. With glee that might have been evil, I left enough room next to the Dumpster to squeak out of my car, but only four inches between me and the Mercedes. The owner would have to crawl over from the passenger side, except that big console and stick shift I could see through the window might be a problem.

I headed for the jockeys' entrance at the back of the building, pulled my cell out, and rang Cormack. I'd tried all morning, reaching his voice mail every time. Surely he would have called if he'd found Lorna? Could they get a search warrant for the bottling plant if her trail led there?

Part of me wanted to chuck the race and search for her, but I had an obligation to Jim, to Daffodil, and to myself. I didn't feel especially obligated to Amarilla, but she'd be pissed as hell if I put in a no-show.

I hesitated, then pushed the numbers to reach Bobby.

His voice snapped. "What?"

"Don't bite my head off. It's Nikki."

"Oh. Sorry. I thought it was...listen, I'm really busy. Can I call you back?"

He sounded tense and preoccupied. "Just tell me if you've heard from Lorna," I said.

"Uh, no. Gotta go." He disconnected.

I stared at the phone. Screw him. I shoved the cell back into my purse and pushed through the door leading to the jocks' room.

I set my bag on one of the counters in the blue ladies' area and hung my dress clothes on the rod next to it. I headed for the kitchen, hoping they'd have something to tempt a nervous stomach.

Tables and chairs were scattered about the room, and a plate glass window made up one wall. Some out-of-town riders I didn't know sat near the window. Outside, I could see part of the paddock and the track, with the backstretch barns in the distance.

Two jockeys stood in front of the counter, probably waiting on the sizzling burgers and fries bubbling in a deep fryer. You'd think they wouldn't eat the stuff, but some lacked willpower and paid for it in the hot box.

Delberto Belgado stopped talking to his buddy, Enrique, when he saw me approaching. They both stared at me. Jeez, had everyone heard about last night?

"Hey, Nikki," said Enrique. "That's cool you're in the big filly race. Good luck!"

"Thanks." Maybe I was just paranoid.

I got a turkey on wheat, and joined Kim Kravel where she sat reading *The Daily Racing Form*. I remembered her anger at Susan Stark when Stark's erratic riding had almost cost Kim her win.

She glanced up from the *Form*, breaking into a wide smile. "I see you're in the Princess. You like your horse?"

"She's got a shot."

"Saw that work she put in," Kim nodded. "You might get up there today, if you can get past Fletcher's New York shipper."

Fletcher's Belmont stable held an awesome arsenal of top runners. His entry was the favorite. Though she'd won lucrative stakes in New York, she was still a Virginia-bred and thus qualified for the Princess.

"Fletcher's horse is Sea Change, right?" I asked.

Kim ran her finger down the page. "Yeah, the three horse. You won't like her speed figures. They rock! And Cornelio Valentinas is riding her."

I was riding against a champion jockey? We stared at each other.

"Let me see." I reached for the page. "Damn." Sea Change had multiple speed figures over 100. How could Daffodil beat that?

"Don't look so bummed," Kim said. "Your filly doesn't read the *Form*."

I was more worried about Daffodil reading the other filly's eye if they went head to head. I studied the remaining entries. The big purses had attracted some of the nation's top riders.

"Damn," I said. "Eduardo Carmanos is in my race."

"That's trouble, right there," Kim rapped her finger on the table in time to her words. "They don't call him 'The Intimidator' for nothing, and he's riding the nine horse, Jamestown Jessie. Awesome animal, that one." She glanced at me more closely. "Are you all right? You look kind of tired."

"Rough night." I bit into my sandwich.

38

The noise of the crowd brought me up short as I stepped into the paddock. The mob made me uneasy, as if I were on-stage. Wasn't every day Colonial had races like the Princess and the Virginia's King. Not every day top horses and jockeys showed up, either.

I glanced at the other riders strutting into the paddock. I'd never met any of them, only watched them on television. I felt two feet tall, way out of my league. Look at it this way, I told myself, these guys don't know anything about you and the Cobra hood. Vastly reassured, I marched past Carmanos and Valentinas without blushing or gawking.

Amarilla waved at me from the grassy center-oval where she stood with the baron. She wore her big rhinestone sunglasses and a yellow-dyed fur coat with brown trim. She shifted her weight from one boot to the other. The baron patted her arm and sucked on his curlicue pipe, sending puffs of smoke into the air like a little factory. His massive belly appeared to have let itself out a notch. Probably all that sugar in his illicit bourbon. Did he know the cops were on to him?

Jim waited for me in stall eight with Daffodil. His jaw tight as a steel trap, he tapped his pursed lips with one forefinger, a sure sign of nerves with Jim. Ramon held the filly, his eyes cutting anxiously left and right, checking out the competition. I heard him mutter, "*Madre de Dios.*"

Daffodil, statuesque and calm, wore her innate elegance like a princess's crown. She radiated a much needed confidence the rest of us seemed to lack. Could we win this thing?

The paddock judge called, "Riders up!"

Jim boosted me into the saddle, saying, "You know what to do, Nik."

My senses sharpened as my world shrank down to Daffodil, me, and the competition. The warmup of twelve horses, the load into the gate, played in slow motion.

Daffodil strode into the metal cage, her ears pricked forward, her entire focus on the green path stretching away to the first turn. The horse to her left scrabbled its legs and fought with an assistant starter. Daffodil ignored the ruckus. *Good Girl.*

I sensed a stare from the right and glanced over. Carmanos, on Jamestown Jessie, gave us the once-over, his lips curled in an arrogant smile, his eyes predatory over a sharp, hawklike nose. Had he seen Daffodil's speed work in the *Form*? I hoped he didn't give it too much credit.

They were still loading the eleven and the twelve, so I glanced at the tote board. We lay under the radar at ten-to-one. Hopefully these hotshot riders would dismiss our chances, too.

The last filly loaded. A few riders with scrambling horses cried, "No, no, no!" Finally, silence.

The bell shrilled, metal clashed, the announcer screamed, "They're off!"

Daffodil broke mid-pack. Horses walled us in from all sides where we lay five lanes off the rail going past the grandstand the first time. Didn't want to get hung wide going into that first turn, but for the moment I sat almost motionless, reins long, letting my horse relax.

Two fillies between us and the rail engaged in a speed duel and spurted ahead. I steered Daffodil into the empty spot, saving precious ground as we swept through the first turn.

Unlike the flap-like-a-chicken locals I usually rode with, these pros were cool, their whips motionless. The few asking for early speed used their hands and legs with an admirable economy of motion as the field churned out of the turn and raced into the backstretch. Around me, the thunder of hooves under half-tons of live weight rocked the air.

Immediately ahead, a horse broke down, crashed forward, and spun her jockey into the rail. I reined Daffodil right, flashed around the fallen horse, sucked in the horror, and sailed on.

Maybe five horses lay ahead, one of them gray, probably the favorite, Sea Change. I glanced under my arm, looking back. Jamestown Jessie closed in on Daffodil's right flank. Carmanos had us in his sights. No room up front unless I went wide. I waited. Carmanos waited, too.

Nearing the last turn panic broke loose inside me, and I almost asked for speed. No. Remember Hall-of-Fame jockey, Pat Day. There was a reason they'd nicknamed him Wait-All-Day.

Inside the last turn two of the lead horses slowed, drifting away from the rail as their strides shortened. *Now.* Daffodil sped for the gap, but Jamestown, with Carmanos whipping and driving, got there first. Carmanos pulled his filly sharply into our path, making me stand in the stirrups to avoid clipping Jamestown's heels. Son-of-a-bitch!

Daffodil took a few strides to get back in gear. Damn that Carmanos, he'd pegged my filly as a threat, made her stop and start over. Cost us almost five lengths.

Ahead, Sea Change had only one horse left to pass. Jamestown stalked the gray favorite, only half a length off her flank.

The speed horse in front labored in exhaustion. The two favorites' movements springy and effortless by comparison. A bay filly ran hard just behind them. Daffodil's long legs floated down the track, rapidly closing the distance.

Out of the turn now, top of the stretch. I reined right, showing my filly daylight. She opened up, her lungs pumping oxygen in rapid mini-explosions as she flew past the bay and took aim at the favorites.

The front runner was finished, legs rubbery, speed diminishing, she appeared to roll backwards as the favorites and Daffodil passed by. Only Jamestown and Sea Change ahead of us now.

Daffodil opened a gear I didn't know she had, stunning me, bearing down on the favorites. Sea Change on the rail, Jamestown a neck behind on the outside, with Carmanos glancing back to see who was coming.

We were outside Jamestown, about to draw even. Carmanos pulled his filly into our path again, leaving us no option but to shorten stride. *Bastard!* I used the reins and my legs to steady Daffodil, hoping to keep her together, praying she'd regain her stride quickly.

Jamestown had a tendency to lug right. She'd take me over to the grandstand before she'd let me by on that side. If I tried to go between the two, they could squeeze me out. But would they expect a local female rider to have the balls to do it?

I pointed Daffodil for the narrow space between the favorites, drove with my legs, pumped with my body, flashed the whip on her right flank twice. All heart, she dug in, grinding it out, gaining an inch at a time.

Valentinas glanced back, saw me coming, and urged Sea Change on. The gray filly shot forward, opening up a length. I drew even with Jamestown, determined to slug it out with Carmanos. Racing stewards tend to watch the stretch drive with sharp eyes. I didn't think the jockey would dare try anything else.

Carmanos flipped his whip to his left hand, and reaching back to strike his filly on the flank, he almost smashed Daffodil in the face. Instead of backing off, she pinned her ears. Carmanos had lit her fuse.

Ahead, Sea Change opened up by three. Almost to the wire. No catching that filly today, but damn if I'd let Carmanos take second place from me! I pushed Daffodil down that stretch, my movements a nanosecond faster than hers, asking her to match me. She did, digging deep into her heart like she dug into that turf, shoving first a nostril, then her eye, and finally her neck past Jamestown's head.

We flashed under the wire. I couldn't resist a little fist pump in the air. I'd run second in a $500,000 stake. *My God.* I'd just earned $10,000!

39

Ramon waved me in like I was taxiing off a runway after a rough flight. The minute he grabbed Daffodil's bridle, I dropped the reins, dragged in more air, and slid from the saddle. Then I leaned forward and planted a kiss on Daffodil's neck.

Jim stood nearby, a smile transforming his face, his eyes glowing with pleasure.

"You worked hard for that."

Ramon removed Daffodil's tongue tie, patted her neck, then glanced over as I loosened the girth.

"That Carmanos, he piece of shit, no?"

"I'd like to kill him."

Jim's smile got even bigger. "You just did."

A good moment, but my eyes searched for Lorna, wanting to see the excitement on her face, hear her rude and rowdy comments about Carmanos. Of course, she wasn't there. My high sagged.

What had I done? I pulled my saddle from Daffodil and headed for the scales to weigh out. Amarilla, with the baron in tow, pounced on me as soon as I stepped from the scale's metal plate.

"Nikki, you give my Daffodil such a wonderful ride!"

The baron pulled his pipe from his mouth to speak. Now I'd hit the big time, I must be worth his attention.

"That fellow, Carmanos, gave you a run for your money. Handled him brilliantly, my dear." He shoved his pipe back in, puffing emphatic clouds of smoke.

"Thank you." I panned the area, hoping to see Cormack, Will, or even Bobby.

"I am so excited!" Amarilla clapped her hands in that childlike way she had. "You come to the suite. We have champagne!"

"I'm sorry, Amarilla. I have to be somewhere else." Like looking for Lorna.

"I insist, my dear," the baron said.

"Yes," Amarilla's voice grew petulant. "You must."

"I can't." Yet I didn't want to alienate these people. Hadn't I burned enough bridges? "Maybe I could come by later?"

"Of course." Her eyes narrowed as she spat the words. She took the baron's arm, and they moved away.

Grabbing my purse and dress clothes, I headed for my Toyota. Where should I look for Lorna?

I rushed through the parked cars heading for the landmark of the Dumpster. The shiny Mercedes had left, and my car appeared lopsided. I stared. Both tires on the Toyota's right side were flat as pancakes.

"Shit!" I felt like throwing myself down, pounding my heels into the ground in a temper tantrum. *"God damn it!"*

I marched back into the jock's room and ran straight into Will.

"Nikki, you got steam coming out of your ears. Carmanos really pissed you off, huh?"

"It's not that." I explained about the flat tires.

He appeared to be fighting a smile.

"If you laugh, I'll kill you."

"Just call track maintenance. They'll have an air pump."

They did, but said it would be about an hour before they could get to my car. I stomped into the ladies area with my dress clothes and changed. A familiar guilt stabbed me as I pulled on Lorna's boots.

* * * *

A uniformed security guard opened the black metal gate leading to the concrete apron crowded with racing fans. I moved past the mob pressed against the paddock's rail where they watched the horses behind me being saddled for the next race. The Virginia's King Stake was the race after next and the hum of anticipation grew along with the pile of discarded beer cups overflowing nearby trash cans and filling the air with the yeasty scent of brew.

Lines of handicappers snaked from the betting windows beneath the large portico sheltering the side entrance to the grandstand. Ahead of me, a group of men stood in a circle, holding Racing Forms, trading war stories, and halting my forward momentum.

"You could always bet that son-of-a-gun if he drew the one hole," one of them was saying.

I started to skirt around them, when a soft voice said, "Nikki? Is that you?"

I turned, surprised to see Bunny. In her shapeless ankle-length beige dress and lumpy brown wool sweater she resembled a sack of Idaho potatoes. She held some kind of notebook in both hands, her grip strong enough to whiten her knuckles. A strong emotion flared in her eyes. Anger?

"Can we talk over there?" She nodded her head toward the black wrought-iron fence separating the apron from the parking lot beyond.

"Sure." I'd never seen her so alert.

"Have you seen Chuck?" Her eyes panned the area as she spoke.

"No." Why look for the husband she always avoided?

"I hate him! *He* should be dead."

"Easy, Bunny." I glanced around, saw no one within earshot. "What happened?"

"This," she hissed, jabbing the notebook at me. She squeezed her eyes shut and when they opened, her rage made me flinch.

"Found it two days ago," she said, "where Timmy hid it in the attic."

"Your son?" The younger one.

"Yes, my baby. It's been there all along. He had a fort up there when he was little. Always hid things. But I was in that damn fog, wasn't I? I never thought to look up there. Until I stopped those pills."

She must mean those pills Chuck forced on her. It that why she looked so angry?

"I pretended to swallow. He doesn't know I've been waking up." She paused, her eyes losing focus, as if caught in a memory. "You've been so kind to me. You can help me."

What was she talking about?

"Tell them what he did. I…I can't. But he has to pay for what he's done!" The last few words rose in an anguished cry. She began to rock back and forth from one foot to the other.

"Bunny, who has to pay for what?" But I'd lost her. She'd closed up, weaving side to side. One hand pressed against her stomach, the other pushed the small, vinyl-covered book into my hands.

"Tell them!" With a small cry, she turned, and moved quickly away through the crowd. I started after her, but curiosity stopped me.

I opened the book. Hand written block letters marked the first page:

Property of Tim Cheswick.
PRIVATE!

My fingers trembled as I turned the pages, searching for the last entry. I found it and started reading.

40

Todd and I will deliver the preemo stuff to that op-
eration near the airport today.

This crank will make Richmond ROCK! But Todd's
such a WUSS. All nervous and shit. Says these guys
are tough, but I'm cool with it. Old man even provided
firepower! GLOCKS! Those motherfuckers give us
any trouble, they're DEAD!

The ink on those last two words was so heavily marked, the pen had
torn the paper. He'd been stupid enough to write this down? Then I remembered a Maryland detective telling me half the time he didn't have
to solve his own cases.

"Crooks are so stupid," he'd said. "They give it all away in notes, on
FaceBook, emails to friends, when they've had too much to drink. Or
just because they have to brag about it!"

Apparently Tim was no different. I stared at the handwriting. *The old
man?* Had Cheswick sent his sons to their death?

I had to find Bunny. I spotted her going through the glass door into
the grandstand. I ran after her, but the growing line of bettors blocked
me. I dodged it, bolted inside, and stopped, my eyes searching for Bunny's lumpy figure. People jostled past me where I stood near the doors.
The throng inside swirled as race fans formed lines for fast food, to lay
bets, or headed to and from the escalator and elevators. The cavernous
cement-floored room smelled of salty popcorn, scorched cheese dogs,
and greasy french fries.

I didn't see Bunny anywhere, and she'd left me holding the damn
book!

Had to tell someone. I rang Cormack, reached his voice mail, again.
The security office was upstairs. Maybe Cormack was there, or they
could page him.

I slid the diary into my shoulder bag, checked to make sure my cell
was on, then rushed to the elevators. Worming my way to the front of
the line, I ignored the dirty looks, and rode to the administrative offices
on the second floor.

I found security and hurried in. Behind a glass partition, a woman with big hair, purple lipstick and too much rose perfume, worked at a desk. She looked up from her computer.

"I'm looking for Investigator Cormack." I stared at the teased and sprayed nest on her head. Maybe Lorna and Cormack had disappeared in there.

"He's not here," she said. "What's this in reference to?"

If I said, "an unsolved double homicide," she'd probably call for backup. The kind to subdue crazy people.

"Uh, he's been searching for a missing exercise rider. I have new info for him."

The woman studied her lilac-colored nails. "I can pass the information along for you. Or Assistant Investigator Dudley's here. Perhaps he can help you." Without waiting for a response, she reached for the big multiline phone on her desk.

I'd never heard of Dudley and felt a bureaucratic bog sucking at my feet. "Isn't there some way to reach Cormack? Can't you *page* him?"

She shot me a superior look, her penciled eyebrows rising in disdain. "We don't page the Chief Investigator for every person that walks in here. Who are you, anyway?"

Deep breath, happy thoughts. When I knew I wouldn't jump the partition and strangle her, I said, "Nikki Latrelle. La…trelle. This is urgent. The missing girl could be in serious trouble!"

Ms. Big-Hair rolled her eyes.

"Page him!" I took another breath. "Cormack knows my cell number. Please, have him call me."

"I'll see what I can do," she said, but made no move to do anything.

"I'll be on the fourth floor, in suite three." I glared at the woman, stomped from the office in the rhinestone boots, and caught an elevator.

Might as well put in an appearance and make nice with Amarilla while I waited for Cormack and my car tires to be fixed.

I found the usual social climbers lounging in the baron's suite. I recognized Katherine Crosby's handsome profile and dark glossy bob where she sat at a table with an older couple I'd seen at the castle. Katherine held a cigarette and smoke trailed from her hand.

Amarilla stood farther inside, her back to me as she spoke with two women in wool dresses gleaming with gold buttons, epaulets and decorative zippers. The diminutive Pemberton chatted with them in his little black suit.

At the bar just inside the doorway, I found the guy with the waxed moustache who'd served me George Dickel at the baron's bash. I could use a drink, but house wines, cheap brands of scotch, vodka and gin lined the counter. And, of course, the dreaded Gilded Baron.

I felt my lip curl. "What else have you got?"

He gave me a wink and glanced toward the far end of the room where the baron stood with some men, smoke rising from pipes and cigars. The beefy figure of John Duvayne, flattered by a well-cut gray suit, blocked a portion of light coming through the sliding-glass door to the balcony behind.

"How about this?" the bartender said, ducking behind the bar and straightening with a bottle of Wild Turkey 101 in his hand.

"You're the best." Remembering the last time, I said, "But make it a single with plenty of water, okay?"

"Your loss." He poured my drink, wrapped a little napkin around it and handed it over.

Tasted so good. Damn, a traitor *and* an incipient alcoholic. Virginia had done a lot for me.

"Nikki." Katherine gestured me to join her. "A pleasure to see you outride that Carmanos scumbag."

I pulled out a chair, sat, and set down my shoulder bag, oddly burdensome with the addition of Tim's notebook.

"*Nikki?*" Katherine stared at me.

"What?" I'd been lost in Tim's journal. "Sorry. Guess I'm still riding the race."

She leaned toward me, making enthusiastic comments, providing clever little asides of what other people had said about my race. I only heard bits and pieces as my brain whirled with thoughts of Tim and Todd being gunned down in that parking lot. The newspaper stories had never mentioned the Glocks. No doubt they'd been snatched along with the drugs.

I stared at the baron. He gestured with his pipe, Duvayne and the other men chuckling at some joke. Could the baron be the mastermind behind a meth ring? Did Amarilla know?

The last time I'd been in this suite, Susan Stark's death had left Amarilla shell-shocked, admitting she blamed herself for Paco's death. Then she'd clammed up.

"Excuse me," I said to Katherine, leaving her table and heading for Amarilla, who still faced away from me. Pemberton spotted me, and rushed over, his hands fluttering.

"Nikki, sweetheart! Such courage. I simply *had* to close my eyes. I was afraid you'd be *killed!*"

Amarilla spun around, her face lighting up like a child handed a birthday surprise.

"Nikki!" She turned to her companions. "This is the jockey! She is wonderful, no?"

The women enthused. One, with a flashy diamond choker, said, "And are you riding in the Virginia's King, as well?"

I always ride in high-heeled boots with rhinestones. "No." I edged closer to Amarilla. "May I talk to you? In private?"

Uncertainty crossed her face.

"Ladies, shall we refresh our drinks?" Pemberton, ever my confederate, herded Amarilla's companions to the bar, reminding me of a Bantam rooster with large, gaudy hens.

"Amarilla," I said, grasping her arm. "What did you mean when you said you felt responsible for Paco's death?"

She tried to back away, but I held on. "Do you want someone else to die? How did you know Paco?"

She sighed as resignation shadowed her face. Her excellent posture deflated to the stoop of an older woman.

"Some of his family, they come to my country from Panama, as servants in house where I stay." Her words rushed out now, bubbling from some dark place inside. "I know him since little boy. He learn to ride on my horses, then become jockey in Panama." She faltered, glanced toward the baron.

I needed to keep her going. "And he came here…?" I had to lean in to hear her response.

"He want to ride in America. I…arrange it. I bring him here, and he die."

"Where did you bring him, I mean when he first came?"

"He stay with me at baron's farm, then he go to Laurel."

The baron? "Did he meet anyone else when he was here? Bobby Duvayne? Another man, maybe one that was at the party the baron had for you? *Someone* gave him diet drugs."

"Maybe that Bobby. I don't know. If I did, I tell you. Someone should pay!" *Bunny's words.*

I stared at the baron. "Is it him?"

She shook her head. "I not know. But I no think so. He not that kind of man. I get drink."

She pulled her arm from my grasp and moved toward the bar. I took a swig of Wild Turkey and headed for the baron.

41

"Excuse me, Baron von Waechter?"

His gaze flicked across me and back to his guests. I hoped he didn't plan to show me off.

"May I speak to you, privately?" I asked.

"Certainly, my dear." He ushered me away from the group of men. "What can I do for you?"

"Amarilla told me Paco Martinez stayed at your home when he first came here."

"Who?" But his flinch and involuntary back-step gave him away.

"The young jockey from Panama who died from a methamphetamine cocktail?"

"Is *that* what killed him?" His eyes widened.

He was either a good liar, or he really hadn't known. "But you knew him? He stayed with you, right?"

The baron glanced back at his guests as if making sure they couldn't hear. "I knew him. But I'd just as soon it didn't get around he spent time at Vindenberg Hall. And what's this about methamphetamine? Was he a *drug* addict?"

His teeth clenched the pipe so hard, I expected something to snap. Nearby, Duvayne stared with open curiosity as the baron jerked a gold lighter from a pocket, flicked up a flame, and stoked his tobacco.

"Amarilla should never have brought him to my home."

My hand waved at the heavy smoke. "I'm trying to find out how he got the drugs. Did you see who he hung out with?"

"My dear, I saw nothing. He was Amarilla's toy. Excuse me. The Virginia's King is about to go off. I have guests."

Self-involved, phony prick.

Where was Cormack? I dug out my cell to make sure it hadn't spontaneously switched to vibrate, then glanced at my watch. The baron was right. The big race would run in minutes. I could watch from outside, then check with maintenance about my car.

When I slid the cell back into my shoulder bag, my fingers brushed against the journal. I wanted to read more about Tim, too.

Near the window, away from the cluster of people, Duvayne had moved close to the baron, the body language of both men tense. The baron shot a glance at me, then shook his head.

"The horses are on the track!" someone cried.

People drifted to the suite's window, surrounding the baron and Duvayne. Someone slid the glass door open, and several people stepped onto the balcony, as the group watched the colts warm up for the big stake.

I hurried toward the hall, but a man blocked my exit. Chuck Cheswick.

I stared at Bunny's husband, my rage building. What better place to confront this man than a room crowded with people?

"I *know* what you did."

Cheswick's mouth tensed. A red flush colored his cheeks. "What are you talking about?"

"Bunny found Tim's diary. You sent your sons to sell those drugs."

"You don't know shit!" Cheswick jabbed a finger against my collarbone.

"Thought you had your wife under control, Chuck."

I whirled. John Duvayne, big and heavy limbed, stood right behind me.

I stared at him. "*You* knew about this?" Suddenly I didn't feel safe. I might be in a room full of people, but their attention was out on the track.

"Von Waechter said she was asking a bunch of questions." Duvayne shifted so his muscular body blocked me from the group at the window.

"Shit, she didn't tell him about that stupid diary — "

"No," Duvayne said.

"This bitch is about to find out everything. We have to get her out of here!" Cheswick grabbed my arm.

"I'm not going anywhere with you!"

Cheswick's grasp tightened. Duvayne closed in on my side, one hand grasping my shoulder, the other reaching for my neck.

I grabbed a breath and screamed. In that instant the track announcer cried, "They're off!" The P.A. system and a great roar erupting in the grandstand drowned out my cry as the Virginia's King thundered toward the history books.

Duvayne's big fingers pressed hard against the side of my neck. "We've got two minutes to get her out of here," he said, and the room went black.

42

I fluttered to the surface inside an elevator. Cheswick's long arm propped me up. My head spun. A throbbing pain burned the side of my neck. How long had I been out?

Next to Cheswick, Duvayne stared up at the indicator lights. The elevator was headed down, passing the second floor.

"What are you doing?" I asked, my voice a thin rasp.

Cheswick tightened his hold. "Shut up."

Duvayne remained silent.

The doors opened at the first floor. The area near the elevators was deserted. The main entrance to the grandstand lay directly ahead without a ticket taker or program seller in sight. A babble of voices and excited cries came from behind the elevator banks. The race must be in full swing.

I shifted my weight, kicked Cheswick's shin, tried to break loose. He grabbed my shoulder, pulling me tight against him. My weak scream would never be heard over the noise. I could probably run naked through the grandstand and not be noticed.

But we weren't going through the grandstand. They manhandled me to the right, through a door labeled, TRACK STAFF ONLY.

No. I smashed a heel onto Cheswick's foot. He laughed and gripped me harder. "Cut that shit out." Duvayne grabbed my hair, yanking viciously.

"John, hold her a minute." Cheswick shoved me at Duvayne, then ripped off my shoulder bag. Dumping the contents, he found Tim's notebook and slid it into his waistband. He snatched up my phone, turned it off, then loaded my stuff back, and thrust the bag at Duvayne.

"Let me have her." Cheswick grabbed my arms with both his hands. He held me so high my feet bounced along the floor as he rushed down an empty hallway.

Duvayne slammed a door open, and Cheswick whisked me through a cold, musty storeroom filled with supplies. No people, no voices. Ahead, a loading dock. We passed a Dumpster, and Duvayne tossed my purse inside.

Then I saw the liquor truck and screamed, struggling harder.

"I'll knock you out." Duvayne threatened with a meaty fist.

They half carried, half-dragged me to the vehicle. In the distance hoof beats pounded, and the roar from the grandstand crescendoed.

I wasn't going in that truck! I kicked and twisted like a wild thing, bit Cheswick's arm. Cursing, they wrestled me to the rear doors, threw me inside.

I hit the metal floor hard, my head slamming against the edge of a wooden pallet. The doors crashed shut and what sounded like a chain rattled on the handles outside. Then a metallic click, like a padlock. I fingered my head, wincing with pain. Blood leaked from my scalp behind my right ear.

An overhead bulb dimly lit the interior. Aside from the pallet, only the remnants of a cardboard carton lay in the truck. The words, "Pseudoephedrine - Product of India" were visible on a torn strip.

The engine turned over. The truck rammed forward and threw me against the rear doors. I grabbed a metal handle and twisted it down. *Locked.*

At least they hadn't tied me up. I crawled to the pallet. Long nails held its solid, one-by-four inch boards together. If I could pry one loose, it would make a weapon. I kicked and wrenched frantically until my fingers were bloody and stuck with splinters. The damn pallet was built like a house.

Think!

I slid a boot between two boards and turned my foot, trying to lever the wood apart. One of the nails began to give. I alternated pulling with my hands and prying with my foot. Two nails finally gave way at one end. I started on the other. I got the board loose, tried holding it with both hands — like a baseball bat.

I shuffled back to the doors on my knees, and sagged against a side wall. I breathed slowly as dark thoughts filled my head. I'd known Cheswick was a creep from the get go. Why had I been so blind about Duvayne?

These two must be behind the deaths of Paco and Susan. Why else would they be so desperate? I'd found out Cheswick had used his sons to deal drugs, sent them to their deaths. *Then I'd told him!* Could I have done anything more stupid?

My senses sharpened as the truck jerked to a halt. I gripped the board. Voices sounded outside. Something clicked, rattled, and the doors creaked open. Cheswick leaned in to pull me out. I slammed the wood at his head. He jerked to the side and the blow hit his shoulder. Scooting past him before he could grab me, I jumped from the truck, ready to run.

A metal click to my left.

"Forget it, honey. I'll do you right here." The large barrel of a hand-gun pointed at me. Duvayne held its rubber grips with both hands.

As Cheswick climbed from the truck, my head dropped in defeat. I let the board clatter to the pavement.

Tight-faced with anger, Cheswick backhanded me across the mouth. The blow left me reeling. Tasting blood. Duvayne hurried toward a building, leaving Cheswick to drag me in his wake.

Movement flickered beyond the fence. Half hidden among the branches of a pine — a *face?* I blinked, saw nothing.

Cheswick pushed me into a concrete-floored bay. A spray gun lay on the floor. *I'd seen this before — the body shop at the bottling plant.* Cheswick shoved me through a door into some kind of storage room, where John Duvayne threw folders into a box. Next to him a paper shredder whirred and a flurry of confetti shot from a side spout into a trash can.

I stared about as Cheswick dragged me through this room. Looked like it had been recently picked clean. A few tatters of cardboard and shreds of bubble wrap littered the floor. Except for a soda and snack machine on the back wall, the room was empty.

Next to the snack dispenser, a metal door opened, and two men stepped into the room. They pulled elaborate safety masks off their faces as they moved toward the soda machine.

"Help me!" I shouted.

One man spun, stared at us, then quickly dropped his gaze to the floor. He shoved trembling hands into his pants pockets. The other man never turned around, just stuffed change into the machine and pressed buttons.

"Jake, you blow out the lab like I said?" Duvayne asked.

"Yes, sir," The man at the soda machine turned to face Duvayne.

One of the stretch-Hummer guys. The one with the wide shoulders and carefully groomed Fu Manchu beard.

"What about that last batch? You finish it?"

"Yes, Mr. Duvayne," said Jake.

Such careful deference to Bobby's father. Cheswick wasn't in charge here, Duvayne was.

"Then load it up. Trucks outside. And Jake," Duvayne said as the two men headed for the rear door. "Is everyone else gone?"

"The workers, yeah. I sent them home, just like you asked."

"You," Duvayne said, pointing at the man who'd been unable to meet my gaze.

"Y-yes, sir," he stuttered.

"Take the rest of the day off."

"Chicken shit," Cheswick muttered, as he watched the guy scurry from the room. Laughing, he shifted his grip on me.

Duvayne turned to Cheswick. "Get her in there, Chuck. You know what to do."

43

I slumped and dragged my feet as Cheswick wrestled me toward the back wall. Behind us, Duvayne ignored my struggles and continued boxing his files.

"Damn it, Jake, give me a hand," Cheswick shouted. "Should have knocked the bitch out."

Jake grabbed my arm. I searched his face for some sign of kindness or remorse, but his eyes were flat and empty. The two men propelled me to the door, where a red eye glowed from a key pad mounted on the wall. Jake worked a combination of numbers and the lock released with a hollow click.

A noxious odor like ammonia and nail-polish remover curled around us when Jake opened the door. Fumes stung my eyes, made them water and squeeze shut. The roar of the exhaust fans filled my ears, but I could still hear Cheswick.

"Thought you blew this place out."

"Man, you shoulda been here earlier," said Jake. "The levels are safe now."

"Not for long." Cheswick's chuckle as he shoved me through the doorframe raised hairs on the back of my neck.

I blinked, trying to focus. The rectangular room wasn't that large, maybe 15 by 20 feet. Against a nearby wall, tools, beakers, cans and jars were strewn on a wooden workbench. Ahead, a long metal table held cartons of clear plastic vials filled with crystals.

A meth lab.

At the room's far end a device resembling a giant crab pot squatted on dark, iron legs. It looked large enough to boil a human. Gauges and wires sprouted from its pockmarked, grimy surface. Large buckets and metal canisters with nozzles littered the floor beneath it. A blue pipe suspended from the ceiling, one end curving down, opening over the cooker like a single nostril sniffing for dinner.

As they pulled me toward this monstrosity, a man bent over buckets, hosing them out. A stream of water flowed across the cement floor before disappearing into a rusted grate. The man wore a mask. A plastic hood covered his hair. He started violently when our movements caught his attention.

The eyes behind the mask fixed on mine, and my heart hammered with recognition.

Jake released his hold on me and glanced at the guy. "You can take that crap off, if you want. It's safe now."

The man shook his head no.

"I *know* it's you." My voice rose into a pleading cry. "Bobby, help me!"

He remained silent, staring at me through the white mask as the door clicked open and John Duvayne entered the room.

"Don't bother cleaning those." Duvayne waved at the buckets. "There won't be anything left after this place blows, anyway."

Bobby turned a lever on the nozzle, shutting off the water. He dropped the hose, pulled off his mask and the plastic hood. His hands shook as he removed a leather smock. Beneath it, the ruby-studded cross glimmered on his chest.

"You had to bring her, too?"

"They've been nothing but trouble since they got here." Cheswick's hold on me tightened. "This one was working for that investigator before she even came to Virginia."

"That's not true," I cried, then remembered. *Amarilla*. She'd seen Cormack with me at Paco's funeral.

Cheswick glanced at Jake. "Tie her up."

"No," said Bobby.

On the far side of the squat cooker, Nike shoes and the lower half of a pair of jeans protruded from behind a bunch of multi-gallon plastic jugs. Bound ankles were tied to one of the iron legs.

"Lorna," I screamed, pulling from Cheswick's grasp and stumbling forward.

I thought the jeans moved, then Cheswick and Jake overwhelmed me, shoving me to the floor, binding my hands behind my back with nylon rope, dragging and tying me to one of the black metal legs.

Cheswick's lips curved in an unpleasant grin. "Bobby, get the duct tape."

"*No*," Bobby said, again.

"Do it," said Duvayne. "Stop acting like a baby."

Cheswick smirked, enjoying the younger man's discomfort.

"Lorna," I called through the metal legs, turning toward her as much as the tight ropes allowed.

A jug wobbled and matted red hair appeared over the plastic containers as Lorna managed to sit up. Her eyes were huge, her mouth covered with gray tape, her face bruised and filthy.

"Don't let them do this!" I yelled at Bobby.

"Shut her up." Duvayne's voice bellowed across the room. He was like a bull, inflated with rage, ready to smash any obstacle blocking his path.

"*Listen* to me, boy." He raised a huge fist at his son.

Bobby shrank back, cowering. I knew Lorna and I were lost.

44

Bobby turned from his father and stared straight ahead as he moved toward the workbench, his body stiff, feet dragging.

Jake pushed a rolling cart to the long table and loaded boxes of crystal meth. He lifted the second carton, revealing a roll of gray tape. He snagged the tape and held it out to Bobby, who stopped moving altogether.

I waited for Duvayne to shout at his son, but he was measuring ammonia into a beaker. Next to him Cheswick drained a large can into a bucket. Jake shrugged and dropped the tape on the table. He rolled the cart out of the lab, leaving the door open behind him.

"Lorna," I called, just loud enough that she could hear me over the fans. "Are you all right?"

She nodded, her face pinched and white. Tears left streaks in the grime on her cheeks. Her gaze slid to Bobby, who walked toward me now, gripping the tape, refusing to look at us. As he got closer, Lorna moaned behind her gag, her eyes beseeching, locked on Bobby. He ignored her. Pretended not to see my frantic struggle with the nylon rope.

A dull clunk, followed by a loud thud, came from outside the lab. The rolling cart burst into the room, barreling across the floor, heading straight toward John Duvayne and Cheswick. The two men attempted to grab it before it crashed and spilled vials of meth.

The cart smashed into Cheswick. He staggered and tried to catch a carton of vials sliding over the edge. He grabbed the box, holding it aloft as he fell to the floor on his back.

A figure appeared in the doorway. I stared, astonished to see Mike Talbot, his face flushed, his eyes blazing, almost triumphant. He still gripped that damn shovel and held it up almost like a sword. Dirt crumbled off the blade onto the floor. Red Virginia clay and grass stains smeared the legs of his pants.

"I found her!" he shouted. "I *knew* it, but no one would listen."

The most coherent words I'd heard from this guy. But what was he talking about? Duvayne knew. His face paled.

"Shut up, Talbot. You're nuts!"

"No. Catherine loved *me*." Talbot turned to Bobby. "I loved her. We were going to go away, take you with us. Be a family."

"What the hell are you talking about?" Bobby asked, his voice shaking.

Talbot pointed at Duvayne. "He murdered your mother. Buried her in the woods. I *saw* him do it! But I…" His voice faltered. "I…I got lost out there, couldn't find her. No one would help me! They put me in that *place*."

He stared at his hands. "I'm sorry I took so long, Catherine."

He was obviously crazy, talking to a dead woman. *If* she was dead.

"You're wrong!" Bobby yelled. "My mother walked out on me."

"No," said Talbot. "She would never have left you."

"Liar," Duvayne shouted. "I'm gonna shut you up!"

He lunged at Talbot, but dodged at the last second to avoid the shovel blade swinging toward his head. Talbot's shovel missed, and Duvayne rammed a solid right punch into Talbot's jaw. The skeletal man crumpled to the floor. Duvayne snatched the shovel, raised it high, and slammed it at Talbot's head.

I closed my eyes, heard a muffled scream from Lorna. Bobby yelled, and my eyes flew open as the younger man diverted the path of the metal blade with his shoulder. He grunted in pain as the shovel clattered to the floor.

Panting, sweat dripping from his forehead, Bobby faced his father. "Is this true?"

"Of course not. You can't believe his crap." Duvayne's eyes smoldered.

Behind them, Cheswick regained his footing and carefully set the box of meth crystals on the cart. "Look, Talbot's just one more asshole to add to the party. Get on with it."

"No," said Bobby. "You can't."

Duvayne put a hand on his son's shoulder. "We have to. You know that." But Bobby jerked away.

On the floor, Talbot moaned and rolled onto one side. He propped himself up on a bony elbow, holding out a dirt-stained hand to Bobby, the palm facing down.

"Do you remember this?" A ruby glimmered from a gold ring circling the man's little finger. The large stone glowed blood red, just like the one on Bobby's cross.

Duvayne shrank back, as if frightened.

Bobby reached a trembling finger to the ring. "Where did you get this?"

"From Catherine. I've been trying to tell you. I *found* her!" That triumphant flush bloomed on Talbot's face again.

Bobby backed away. Uncertainty clouded his eyes. He stared at his father.

"You didn't…"

"Bobby." My voice came out as a dry croak, barely audible. I took a breath and forced volume into the words. "You *know* it's true! Look how he beats you. He probably beat your mother. For God's sake, he's going to kill us!"

"That's it," said Duvayne. He grabbed the tape from the table and thrust it at his son. "Either you shut her up, or I'll do her now and make you watch! You wouldn't like that, would you?"

Bobby snatched the tape, hurried toward me.

Duvayne's derisive voice chased behind. "You're a sensitive pansy, just like your mother."

Bobby squatted on the floor before me. As he ripped off a strip of tape, the blade of a small knife winked at me from his right hand. He pressed the duct tape over my mouth, then ran his arms behind me, quickly sawing the nylon rope into pieces.

"Get Lorna out," he whispered and pressed the knife's handle into my palm.

He stood abruptly, darted to the shovel, and hefted it in both hands. Spinning toward Duvayne, he slammed the blade into his father's head.

I tore off my gag, scuttled beneath the cooker and grabbed Lorna's ankles. Adrenaline pumping wildly, I sliced the rope like butter, freed her hands, and pulled the tape from her mouth. She tried to speak, but couldn't get the words out.

I heard another thud and glanced up as Bobby smashed John again.

"Let's get the hell out of here," I said.

But Cheswick rushed us.

Lorna, who was closer, scrambled awkwardly to her feet and watched him come. She let him grab her, then shoved her knee into his crotch, before tottering to the floor. But she found her voice.

"You piece of shit," she said, scooting backwards.

The guy was resilient. He fought the pain, seemed to put it aside, and lunged at me. I raised the knife, thrusting it at him. Cheswick's momentum drove the blade into his abdomen.

Shock whitened his face. His hands clutched at the knife's handle, and he began to sink to the floor.

I stared, horrified, dizziness buzzing my head.

Lorna struggled to her feet and grabbed my arm. "Fuck him, let's get out of here!"

We ran past Bobby where he knelt on the floor next to his father. Past

Talbot who'd managed to stand, but weaved drunkenly. Through the lab door, past the inert form of Jake on the cement floor of the storage room. Out the bay door, into the sunlight and straight into a SWAT team, bristling with weapons and bulletproof vests.

Behind them, I saw Cormack sag with relief. His buddy, Andy, put an arm around the investigator's shoulder. The long-haired black-and-white dog sat on the ground next to them.

I'd swear that mutt was grinning.

45

As I shoved the last bag in the Toyota, clouds blocked the morning sun and turned the cottage's white stucco to a drab gray. After the cops sorted out the mess at the plant, Lorna had moved in with Sable. I'd only stayed at the cottage because Cheswick was locked up in the county jail, without bail, for the attempted murder of the Virginia ABC agent, Atkins. I'd been glad to hear the guy had come out of his coma okay.

Still, it was creepy, staying in that cottage without Lorna, but checking into a motel with a cat and a rooster wasn't an option.

I glanced at my watch. Cormack was late, and I wanted to hit the road. But he'd said something about giving me an update, answering my questions. Since the arrests at the plant, the police had kept a tight lid on what the papers called the "Crystal Lab Murders."

A low yowl came from the Toyota's back seat — no doubt Slippers warming up for the long ride home in his hated cat carrier. Beside him, Mr. Chicken's metal cage rattled as the rooster pecked at a dish of corn.

Frost from the night before hardened the ground beneath my feet. I hugged my coat closer, the sharp tang of pine drifting across the grass as I heard gravel spinning beneath approaching tires.

Cormack stopped his black SUV, climbed out, and walked over. His breath, a visible white vapor, hung in the crisp air.

"All packed?" he asked.

"Just about. Can you tell me about the case yet?"

"Now, I can. That Investigator Anderson seems to think they got everything wrapped up. Long as y'all are available for those trials next spring, you're free to go."

I'd no intention of staying, but nodded agreeably. Cormack had always been straight with me.

"You think they'll do much time?" I asked.

"Who, Cheswick and Duvayne?"

I nodded.

"Oh yeah," he said, "they'll do time. Lock 'em up just like your buddies in the back seat there. Those boys didn't stop at selling meth pills to the local ladies. They distributed crystal meth up and down the eastern seaboard, and Anderson intends to nail 'em for the deaths of Paco Martinez and Susan Stark. Seems they had a special cocktail for jockeys. Used meth, diuretics and who knows what all."

"And Catherine Duvayne?" *Buried in the woods all those years.* I shivered. "They'll get Duvayne for her murder, won't they?"

"They will." His expression was almost smug.

"What about von Waechter? He *had* to know about the meth lab."

"Maybe not. The baron isn't the hands-on type. He let Duvayne run the place, claims he thought the lab was a body shop. But he's got some charges comin' to him. State of Virginia and the IRS aren't too pleased with him skippin' those liquor taxes."

Cormack glanced down the hill toward the big Victorian. "How's Miss Bunny doing?"

"Great!" I smiled. "She's so different without those drugs. She's selling the place. Has a sister in North Carolina. Gonna move down there."

"Good." He paused, his eyes settling momentarily on the cottage. "You and your friend patch things up?"

"Lorna, you mean?" When I'd tried to apologize, she hadn't wanted to hear it. Even if she forgave me for Bobby, our relationship would never be the same. "Not really."

"Sorry to hear that."

"What will happen to Bobby?" *How had that slipped out?*

"You women still can't resist that boy?" Cormack shook his head. "After what he did?"

"He saved my life." Maybe my words came out too sharp, but the miracle of Bobby slicing that rope would stay with me forever.

"That may be, but he knew what those two men planned to do to you two. Hadn't been for Talbot showing him Catherine's ring..."

A breeze rustled a withered leaf across the cold ground, lodging it against my foot. I glanced back at Cormack.

"I know."

We stayed silent a few beats, then Cormack grinned. "Don't worry about young Duvayne. He's testifying for the Commonwealth's attorney. They'll have him paroled out in no time. As for Talbot, he's got that cousin lookin' after him. Word is, findin' Catherine put him on the road to recovery."

Remembering that triumphant flush on Talbot's face, I didn't doubt it. Maybe Bobby would be all right, too. He was out from under his father and he knew his mother hadn't abandoned him. Had loved him. *But Bunny's boys...*

"What happened to the Cheswick sons? Was Bobby involved?"

Cormack pursed his lips, blew that soft whistle through his teeth. "Bobby left with a woman just before 11:30. Left those two boys alone to sell a load of crystal meth. It was Cheswick's connection, two men he knew from North Carolina."

"So, what, those guys just gunned down the boys, took the drugs, and kept the money?"

Cormack nodded. "Except those fellows from North Carolina vanished. Anderson thinks Cheswick and Duvayne might have hunted them down."

"*Jesus.*" I pulled my jacket tight again. Shifted closer to my Toyota. Overhead, the sun broke through the clouds, highlighting a trace of bright crimson and emerald green on the dead leaf near my feet.

Cormack stared at me a moment, then sighed and took a half-step back. "All right, then, Nikki. Y'all have a good trip."

"Thanks, Cormack. I wouldn't have made it without you." I stepped forward, shook his hand. His eyes seemed to glisten as I climbed in my Toyota.

* * * *

I pulled up next to our barn as Mello and Ramon finished loading supplies into the smaller trailer for our trip home. The meet had ended the day before. The departure of horses, grooms, and exercise riders left an empty feeling — like children might get at the end of summer camp.

Next to the shedrow, Jim's trailer, hooked to the Ford 350, waited for the horses to load. In the distance, Lorna and Sable walked back from the kitchen with Cokes and bags of chips. At least Lorna and I were on speaking terms. She'd agreed to drive back with Sable in my Toyota while I drove Jim's rig with the horses.

I wrestled the animal cages into the back seat of the Ford's stretch cab and went to help Mello and Ramon load up. I hadn't spoken to Amarilla. A commercial Sallee van had arrived to take her horses. Daffodil was already gone.

"I declare," Mello said, leading Hellish from her stall, "it be mighty fine to get back to Maryland. Yes, sir. Mighty fine, indeed."

"*Amen,*" I said.

With Lorna's help, we got the six horses loaded, and I climbed into the Ford's cab.

"Hey, wait up." Will hurried toward me. "You weren't going to leave without saying goodbye?"

As little as he'd spoken to me the last two weeks, I'd been uncertain about approaching him. I shrugged. "You leaving soon?"

"Yeah." He put one foot on the running board, grabbed the open window frame, and swung up to my level. His eyes were green, intense, and hard to read.

"So you're going back to Maryland?"

"Yeah. You heading that way?"

"No. Allbright's got first call on me for the Gulfstream Park meet."

"Oh." The disappointment, knowing he'd be so far away, took me by surprise.

"You ever thought of riding down there? It's fabulous. Warm. The ocean. Takes you right through January and February."

"Sounds great. But I can't leave Jim. He'd never send me to Florida, anyway."

"Yeah, I guess not."

Did he sound disappointed?

"Take care of yourself, Nikki." He hopped down, walked away without looking back.

I turned the key and cranked the big engine. Shoved the shift into first gear.

"Nikki, wait!" Lorna ran around to the passenger side and opened the door. "I thought…I thought I'd better ride with you. That McNugget might get loose, cause a wreck or something."

"He *could*. You better get in."

She did, and I released the brake.

We rolled out of Colonial Downs and headed for the highway.

Acknowledgments

My thanks to Virginia Commonwealth Attorney, C. Linwood Gregory, for his time and advice on my questions about prosecution in the State of Virginia, and to Maryland veterinarian, Dr. Forrest Peacock, for endless patience and equine medical advice. Additional thanks for technical advice and support go to both Joseph M. Roney, Director of Security & Enforcement for the Virginia Racing Commission, and racehorse trainer Barry G. Wiseman.

CPSIA information can be obtained at www.ICGtesting.com
Printed in the USA
LVOW061545040412

276154LV00005B/79/P